SLAY ONE

RIVALRY

LAURELIN PAIGE

Hot Alphas. Smart Women. Sexy Stories.

ISBN: 978-1-942835-74-5

Editing: Erica Russikoff at Erica Edits

Formatting: Alyssa Garcia @ Uplifting Author Services

Proofing: Michele Ficht

Cover: Laurelin Paige

Beta Team: Candi Kane, Melissa Gaston, Amy "Vox" Libris, Roxie Madar, Liz Berry

SLAY ONE

RIVALRY

Written with Sierra Simone

Porn Star | Hot Cop

Written with Kayti McGee under the name Laurelin McGee

Miss Match | Love Struck | MisTaken | Holiday for Hire

For Candi and Melissa,
who champion with soothing words
and kindly, but surely,
lured this beast out from inside me.

INTRO

Long ago, I learned how to be made of nothing.

Trained my body to convert every experience, every encounter, every observation into emptiness before metabolizing and processing them inside of me. I run on nothingness. I feast on void. My fuel is black and cold and nothing, nothing.

Every breath I take in, the oxygen transforms into wisps of oblivion. Feel it as I exhale (feel nothing). Hear the sound of nothing as it exits from my lungs and circles like a fog around me.

Flesh and bone and blood no longer are my makeup. I'm stacks of naught, packed into my being at the molecular level. My skin, my muscles, my organs, my cunt—cells of non-existence, masquerading as bits of human. Touch me, I'll feel nothing. Bruise me, fuck me, love me—nothing, nothing, nothing.

Everything within me has been altered and adapted.

There's nothing real anymore. Nothing solid. Nothing

worthy.

Only pieces of limbo. Only nihilism. Only nothing.

Nothing wrapped securely around my core, an impenetrable seal.

Nothing jammed in all my spaces, crammed in tight, protecting the last embers of a once-blazing heart. I'm barely aware of its beat anymore through the layers of vacuity, barely feel the steadiness of its pulse.

I hear it sometimes, muffled by the padding of nothing squeezed around it, tick-tick-ticking like a metronome. Like a faraway clock. Like the click of a turn signal. Like my uncle's pocket watch.

Like a bomb counting down to detonation.

Like a bomb, waiting to explode.

1

"You really screwed this one up, Celia. Hudson is officially out of reach. You let him slip away, and now everything you dreamed of is over."

I rolled my eyes, even though my mother couldn't see my face through the phone. I was tired of this speech. I'd heard a variation of it at least three times a week since my childhood friend had gotten married over two years ago.

As for my dreams being over...well, it had been a long time since I'd imagined myself ending up with Hudson Pierce. That was my mother's aspiration, not mine. Not anymore.

There wasn't any use in arguing with her. She found some sort of comfort in lamenting over her daughter's failures, and this particular lament was one of her favorites.

"From what Sophia says, he's even more devoted now to this marriage than he ever was, and I'm not at all surprised. A man will leave a wife easily enough, but when she gets pregnant, forget it. He's sticking around."

I leaned my head against the window of my Lyft car and sighed. "How is Sophia these days?" It was a manipulative redirection on my part. It disgusted me that she pretended otherwise, but Hudson's mother wasn't exactly on friendly terms with Madge Werner like she once was.

Pity.

That was also my fault. Hudson's fault too, not that either of our mothers would ever concede that fact.

I knew my tactic worked when my mother huffed loudly in my ear.

Just as I'd thought. My mother hadn't directly spoken to Hudson's mother about any of this. Likely, she'd picked it up through the grapevine. A friend of a friend or overheard it at a charity luncheon. What else did the rich bitches do these days to keep themselves entertained?

My own methods of amusement certainly weren't of the popular variety. But they were definitely more fun.

Or they once were, anyway. Even The Game had lost its spark in recent years.

"I don't even know why I bother talking to you about this," my mother droned on. "It's your own fault you're not with Hudson."

There was his name again. *Hudson.* There had been a time when it hurt to hear it. A time when immense agony had wracked through my body at the two simple syllables. That was a lifetime ago now. The bruise he'd left was permanent and yellowed with age, and I pressed at it sometimes, saying his name, recalling everything that had transpired between us, just to see if I could provoke any of those emotions again.

Every time I came up empty.

I owed that to him, I supposed. He'd been the one to teach me The Game. He'd been the one to teach me how to feel nothing. How to *be* nothing. How ironic that his life today was happy and complete and *full*.

Good for you, Hudson. Good for fucking you.

My mother was still yammering when the car pulled up at my destination. "You don't even realize how much you gave up when you let him get away, do you? Don't expect to do better than him. We both know you can't."

Indignation pierced through my hollow cocoon; anger in its varied forms was the one emotion that seemed to slip in now and again. My mother didn't know shit about me, no matter how close she perceived our relationship. Couldn't *do better* than Hudson? God, how I longed to prove her wrong.

But I didn't have any ammunition. I had nothing. I wasn't dating anyone, not really. I had my own interior design company that barely made enough to pay expenses, and I didn't even take a salary for myself. I was a trust fund baby for all intents and purposes, living off my father's business, Werner Media. And while all of my choices were purposeful, I couldn't exactly explain to my mother that the majority of my time and energy was spent on playing The Game. There was no one who would understand that, not even Hudson anymore.

With no comeback, my best bet was to end the call.

"I'm at my meeting. I have to go now, Mom." My tone was clipped, and I brusquely hung up before she could respond.

I gave my driver a digital tip, threw my cell phone in my bag then climbed out of the car. It was hot for early June. Humidity hung like thick cologne, and it clung to me even after I entered the lobby of the St. Regis Hotel. I was running late, but I knew this building from a lifetime of living among the upper crust of New York, and I didn't have to stop to ask for directions. The meeting rooms were a quick elevator ride up one floor to the level that had originally been John Jacob Astor's living quarters. The hotel had been kept in the elegant chic design of his time, and, while pompous in its style, I found the luxurious decor both timeless and elegant.

Since I was in too much of a hurry to admire the scenery, I headed straight to my destination. Inside the foyer for the Fontainebleau Room, I paused. The doors were shut. Was I supposed to knock or walk right in?

I was already digging out my phone to text my assistant, Renee, when I noticed a man in a business suit sitting behind a small table at the opposite end of the foyer. He seemed to be deeply focused on the book he was reading and hadn't yet seen me. I didn't know what the man I was meeting with looked like so I couldn't say if this was him or not.

Cursing myself for not being more prepared, I approached him. "Excuse me, I'm Celia Werner, and I'm supposed to—"

The man barely looked up from his reading when he cut me off. "I'll let him know you're here. Have a seat." He propped his book open by placing it face down on the table and then stood and circled around it to the door of the Fontainebleau. He knocked once then opened it, disappearing inside.

Somewhat baffled at the curt greeting, I scanned the foyer and found a bench to sit on. I took out my phone and shot a text to Renee.

Why isn't this guy meeting me at the office again?

I rarely took initial client meetings anywhere else. When Renee had first told me about the appointment, I'd assumed I was being hired by a committee or a board of directors and that they'd requested to interview me as part of a general meeting of some sort. It made sense in that case to go to them rather than the other way around. But something about the vibe of the situation made me start to doubt my first assessment. If there was an entire committee behind the closed doors, why had the man who greeted me said "him"? And wouldn't I have heard voices or people noises when the door had briefly been open?

While I waited for Renee's response, I pulled the client file from my bag and looked over the papers inside. The usual client questionnaire was on top, but, unlike usual, it was completely blank. I flipped to the next page, a background report. I ordered these on any client I considered taking on, not so much as a safety precaution, but more out of flagrant curiosity. My best games had been inspired by skeletons of the past, and I never passed up an opportunity to play.

I had no intention of taking on this particular client, however. In fact, I was only meeting with him so I could turn him down. The reason was laid out in bold in the first line of his information sheet: *Edward M. Fasbender, Owner and CEO of Accelecom.*

I didn't know much about Accelecom and even less about Edward Fasbender, but what I did know was that the hardball strategies of his London-based company were the primary reason Werner Media had never been able to penetrate the UK market. My father would be livid if I ever worked for his competitor, but he might be delighted to hear me tell him I'd rejected their offer. Proud, even.

At least, I hoped he would be. God only knew why I cared so deeply to please the man, but I did. It was ingrained in me at an early age to cater to the men who held dominion over me. My father was the lord of our household. If I could make him happy, I was sure my mother would stop her eternal lamenting. If I could make him happy, maybe I could *be* happy.

It was a ridiculous notion, but it had deep roots inside me.

I scanned through the rest of the report on Fasbender. Married very young. Divorced for several years. Hadn't remarried. Two nearly grown children. His father had also owned a media company that had been sold when Edward was a teen, just before both his parents had died. He'd built Accelecom from practically nothing, turning it into a multibillion-dollar company before he'd even turned forty-two, which would be in September. It was all pretty standard information, but, with years of experience, it was enough to help me create a solid picture of what kind of man Edward M. Fasbender was. Driven, calculating, strategic, monomaniacal. His dating history was too sparse for him to be attractive. He likely had to pay for his sex and didn't mind doing so. Egocentric and misogynistic probably as well, if I knew this kind of man, and I did. It would be fun rejecting his offer of employment, as shallow as the move might be.

My cell buzzed.

RENEE: He insisted on meeting at the hotel. You approved that before. Is that still okay?

I'd been eager to be amenable, I remembered now. The

more congenial I was in the outset, the more surprising the rejection.

`It's fine. Did he say what the proj-`
`ect was going to be?` Something office related, I suspected, since there was a committee involved. Oh, that was going to be even more fun, turning him down in front of people.

`RENEE: He said he'd only discuss it`
`in person.`

I added *controlling* to the list of character traits. And he definitely had a small dick. There was no way this asshole was packing.

Before I could ask Renee anything else, the door to the meeting room opened and the man from before stepped out. "He's ready for you now," he said, again making it sound like Mr. Fasbender was alone.

I shut the file folder, but didn't put it back in my bag, too eager and intrigued to bother with the hassle. I stood up and walked to the door of the Fontainebleau. As soon as I crossed over the threshold, I paused and frowned. Every time I'd been here in the past, the room had been set up with several round tables, banquet style. This time there was only one long boardroom type table, and though there were several chairs lined up around it, no one was sitting at them. My gaze swept the space and knocked into the one other person in the room—a man who appeared to be the same age the report had given for Fasbender.

But if this really was Edward Fasbender, I had grossly fucked up on my assessment of him. Because this man was not just attractive, he was overwhelmingly so. He was tall, just over six feet by my guesstimation. His expensive midnight-blue tailored suit showcased his svelte build, and from the way his jacket sleeves hugged his arms, it was obvious he worked out. He was fair-skinned, as his German name suggested, but his hair was dark and long at the top. While it had been tamed and sculpted in place, I imagined it floppy in its natural state. His brows were thick, but flat and expressionless, his eyes deep-set and piercing, lighter than my own baby blues, though maybe it was his periwinkle tie that brought them out so vibrantly. Whatever the reason, they were mesmeric. They made my knees feel weak. They made me catch my breath.

And his face!

His face was long with prominent cheekbones, his features rugged without being worn. He was clean shaven at the moment, but I was sure he could pull off scruff without looking gritty if he tried. His lips were full and plump with a well-defined v at the top. Two faint creases ran between his eyebrows making him appear intensely focused, and the slight lines that bookended his mouth gave him a permanent smirk, even when his mouth was just at rest.

Though, he might have meant the smirk in the moment. Considering the way I was standing frozen gawking at him, it was highly likely.

I shook my head out of my stupid daze, put on an overly bright smile, and started toward him, my hand outstretched. "Hi, I'm Celia Wern—" Before I could finish my introduction, the heel of my shoe caught on the carpet, and I tripped, spilling the contents of his file all over the floor.

Blood rushed up my neck and into my face as I crouched down to pick up the mess. It was awkward kneeling down in my pencil skirt, but I was more concerned about gathering the papers before he saw them. It only took five seconds before I realized the concern was unnecessary, because, even though I'd dropped the pages at his feet, he was not bending down to help me. I was right about his character, it seemed. Arrogant, egocentric. Asshole.

I shoved the papers back in the file and shot a glare up at him, which turned out to be a mistake, because there he was, peering down at me with that perma-smirk, and something about the position I was in and his exuding dominance sent a shiver through my body. My skin felt like it was on fire, and goosebumps paraded down my arms. His presence was overpowering. Overwhelming. Unsettling.

My mouth dropped open in surprise. Men didn't make me feel this way. *I* made men feel this way. *I* overpowered the men around me. *I* overwhelmed them. *I* unsettled them.

I didn't like it. And yet, I also kind of did. It wasn't only an unusual feeling, but it was a *feeling*. It had been a long time since I'd felt anything, let alone something so startling.

I swallowed and prepared to rise when he surprised me again, finally stooping down to my level.

"Edward Fasbender," he said, holding out his hand.

With a scowl, I took it. My hand felt warm in his tight grip, and I let him hold on past the length of a standard handshake, let him help lift me back to a standing position before I withdrew it sharply.

He smirked at this too—that mouth smirked at everything, but I could feel the smirk in his eyes as well. "I've been looking forward to meeting you, Celia," he said in his distinguished British dialect. "Have a seat, will you?"

If there had been any logic to not taking a seat, I would have continued to stand, simply because I hated conceding any more control to him than I already felt I had. But there wasn't anything practical about standing, so I threw my bag and the file on the table, pulled out a chair and angled it toward the head where, if the laptop and phone sitting there were any indication, I surmised he was going to sit.

"I hadn't realized I'd only be meeting with you, Mr. Fasbender." I purposefully didn't scoot the chair back into the table so he could have a prime view while I crossed one long leg over the other. I had nice legs. They were two of my best weapons.

The bastard didn't even glance down. With his eyes pinned on mine, he unbuttoned his jacket and sat in the seat I'd assumed he'd take. "Edward, please," he said sternly. He'd already made it clear he meant to call me Celia, even without my invitation to do so.

"As I was saying, *Edward*, I would have insisted we met in my office if I'd known you were reserving a meeting room simply for my benefit."

He tilted his head, his stone expression showing nothing. "It wasn't simply for your benefit. I've been using this room as my office while I'm in the States meeting with potential investors. It's unconventional, perhaps, but I'm already staying in the hotel, and so the location has proved convenient. Plus, I rather like the setting, don't you?"

I ignored how much I liked the low timbre of his voice and surveyed my surroundings once more. The Fontainebleau was one of the more lavish meeting rooms in the hotel. With the numerous crystal chandeliers, gold leaf plating, and ornate molding, the decor seemed to have been directly inspired by Versailles. I appreciated the luxurious look, but this was a bit on the abundant side, particularly when being used as an office. The fact that he liked it said more about his character. I added pompous and extravagant to my earlier assessment. He was probably even going to use the room as an example of whatever it was he wanted me to design for him.

No. Just no. Even if I were accepting his job offer, which I wasn't.

Refraining from commenting on the decor, I turned back to my subtle admonishment. "I'm sure this is convenient for you, but our discussion will be limited because of it. I've brought my computer and a portfolio, which will show you some of my work, but this would be much easier if you could see the models in my office. Maybe we can reschedule and meet there at a later time?" It would be even more delightful to reject him after stringing him along.

"That won't be necessary. I'm not interested in your design work."

The hairs on the back of my neck pricked up in warning, and I was suddenly glad for the man outside the door. Not that I couldn't handle myself. I'd been in much more precarious situations than this and survived.

"I'm sorry," I said, my voice cool and steady from practice. "I don't believe I understand." Though, I was beginning to have my suspicions. If I wasn't here about a design project, this meeting could only have to do with my father.

"Of course you don't. I didn't have any intention for you to understand until I was ready to explain."

He was such an arrogant piece of work. If I wasn't completely aroused with curiosity, I would have been out the door at this point.

"Since I'm here now, I'd appreciate it if you'd go ahead and fill me in. What is it you want from me?"

He leaned back in his seat, somehow seeming just as upright with his posture even in the reclined position. "What I want, Celia, is quite simple—I want you to marry me."

2

I felt my jaw go slack, but I refused to let it gape. Refused to let him see the extent of my shock. "Excuse me, what did you say?"

"You heard me." His expression remained unreadable except for the slight twitch of his left eye, which I guessed to be amusement.

Oh. It was a joke, then.

"Ha ha," I said, hating how uncertainty coursed through my body. It was an unfamiliar feeling. It made my breaths come shallow and my ribs feel tight. "Very funny. Do you use this opening a lot with potential new associates?" At least my voice stayed steady. Surprising considering how shaken my nerves were.

"I assure you, Celia, I'm quite serious."

Heat flushed through me. Embarrassment, as the situation became clear. I'd planned to fuck with my father's rival, and here, he'd beaten me to the punch.

I gathered the file and threw it into my bag. "I hope

you enjoyed making a spectacle out of me, Mr. Fasbender." Like hell was I calling him by his Christian name now. "I'm sure it's quite the life you lead where playing around with other human beings is merely a means of entertainment."

The words were out of my mouth before I realized the hypocrisy in them. I knew about such games. I knew about such forms of entertainment.

But he didn't know that, and I wasn't about to clue him in. I could be an exceptionally good actress when I wanted to be. "Most of us have to take our jobs seriously. Most of us don't have ample free time to satisfy such juvenile whims."

I rose to my feet, slung my bag over my shoulder, and spun toward the door.

"Sit back down, Celia."

He hadn't raised his voice, but it was sharp, and the authority in his command was indisputable. It stopped me immediately.

Slowly, I turned back toward him. I didn't even think of the action consciously. In fact, I could hear myself arguing with my body as I pivoted in his direction. *Don't do it, don't do it, don't do it.*

But it was as though I were a mechanical doll he was controlling by remote. I couldn't not turn around. I couldn't not give him more of my attention.

I was able to find enough restraint to not immediately sit down, at least. With my heart hammering in my chest, I stared at him with bold determination.

He raised his brows, as though it wasn't often that his demands were questioned. It might have given me a thread of satisfaction if I didn't sense the current of fury underneath the surprise. It was strong and swift and *there,* as clear as any word he'd spoken.

It scared me.

Thrilled me, too. How often did I meet someone as dauntless as I was? I'd never encountered someone who was more so.

I swallowed, and when his eyes flicked from me to the chair, an unspoken order, I sank primly back into the seat.

The edges of his lips curled into a faint smile, and, as enraged as I was at his gloating victory, the small gesture also sparked something warm and strange along my sternum.

"You'll find I hate to repeat myself," he said after a beat. "But let me say again, I am quite serious about my proposition."

In an attempt to get my bearings, I studied him. I had absolutely no read on him whatsoever. His motives, his mood—all incomprehensible, no matter how hard I tried to stare into him. I did notice he was even more attractive than I'd first thought, despite his stony expression. Maybe even *because* of it. He was completely composed and poised. Still, and that was unbelievably sexy.

But there was something beyond the steadiness of his gaze that said his mind was busy. Calculating. He had the air of a secret agent—cool and collected but constantly scheming. Always five steps ahead. Able to intercept anyone that got in the way of his mission. I could almost imagine a gun holstered on his hip underneath his suit jacket. He felt dangerous. Sinister.

Strangely, that just made him hotter.

Finding no answers in my inspection, I had to ask outright. "Why marriage?"

"You're a smart woman. Surely you can figure it out." He lifted one arm and adjusted his cuff, though it seemed entirely unneeding of adjustment. A show of boredom. As though this conversation and what I demanded from it were tedious.

I was rarely so disregarded. Especially in the midst of a proposal.

I'd have to work on that.

Sitting up a little straighter, I ran my tongue along my lower lip. "I don't suppose it's an attempt to get me to go to bed with you."

Edward chuckled, a demeaning chuckle that could only be meant to belittle me. "Come on now—such a juvenile attempt to discover if I find you attractive is beneath you." He abandoned the pretense of fiddling with his clothing and set his hands in his lap. "If you wanted to know, you could just ask."

Such a conceited asshole. Arrogant. Haughty.

It didn't help that he was also right.

Well, he could be *right*, but I wasn't letting him *win*. He thought he was pulling my strings, but there was no fucking way I was asking him what he so obviously wanted me to ask, likely so he could degrade me in some other dickish way.

I turned my head toward the mirrored French doors and considered the question more seriously—*why me*? It wasn't unheard of for a man like him to arrange his marriages, and I was the kind of match society found ideal. A typical blonde bombshell with good breeding and lineage, I made a perfect trophy wife, but there had to be hundreds of women that fit the profile. Women he already knew. Women who would be more likely to accept such a ridiculous offer.

So why me?

The answer was obvious.

I shifted my focus back to him. "It's because of my father."

"There you go. I knew you were more than just a pretty face." He rewarded me with his first real smile, revealing two crater-like dimples that were so disarming I barely registered his backhanded compliment.

It was with a great deal of concentration that I was able to return to the conversation. "I'm not sure what you think you could achieve by marrying me. My father would insist on a prenup ensuring my spouse would never touch Werner Media, and if he didn't have that assurance, he'd change his will. He might change his will anyway. My father is not as stupid as you seem to think he is."

His expression resumed its natural stoicism. "I don't think Warren Werner is stupid, not by a long shot. He doesn't trust me or my company, which is rather smart on his part. But I am what you'd call an ambitious man. I want to enter the U.S. market and there's no way that your father will allow that to happen, not the way things currently stand between us.

"However, there will be a day when Warren retires. Sooner rather than later, if I were to guess seeing how he seems to spend more time on the golf course these days than in the office. I'd like to take his place as the head of the company."

It was my turn to laugh. "There's no way he'd appoint you as his successor."

"Not right now, he wouldn't. Give the position over to his rival? Of course not. But, in a few years' time, pass the title on to the husband of his one and only beloved daughter? That's an entirely different story."

"You overestimate how much my father thinks of me."

"I doubt that. I have a daughter myself. I may seem detached and disinterested in her, but I assure you, there's not much a man like me wouldn't do for his flesh and blood. And I'm pretty certain your father is a *man like me*."

The insane thing was that I could practically hear my father saying something equally as patronizing.

It wouldn't work. There was a myriad of flaws with the scheme, not the least of which being that my father didn't actually have the authority to name his successor.

But that was neither here nor there. I wasn't accepting the offer. It was appalling that Edward thought I'd even consider it.

"Why would I do this for you? You seem to have a lot to gain in this deal, but what would *I* get out of the arrangement?" I only asked out of curiosity.

He leaned in and braced his elbows on the table. "Let's not play games, shall we? We can be honest here, you and I. What exactly do you have going for you at the moment? Your flat is owned in your father's name. You have one degree, in an art field. Your business barely runs in the black, a business that is neither innovative nor necessary. The lack of customers knocking at your door confirms that. You're almost thirty-two years old, unmarried, childless, living off your trust fund. You're not involved in any foundations or clubs, not on any boards. Your good looks might have gotten you through most of your life so far, but how much longer is that going to last? Not forever, I'll tell you that. Surely your parents aren't ecstatic about your current prospects for the future. Bringing home a husband of my caliber would change everything in their eyes, wouldn't it? Even though I come with a competing business, I would imagine they would consider me a major coup, especially when they hear how generous *my* prenup will be. I think when you really look at it, you're really the one getting the better end of the deal."

I felt the color drain from my face.

It wasn't the first time I'd had deprecating words thrown at me. This wasn't even the worst that I'd heard said, not on the surface, anyway. Heaven knew, I'd deserved most of the insults that had been hurled in my direction. They always slid off my back, never touching any part of me that might care. Call me mean or manipulative or a bitch, I could take it. I knew who I was, and I accepted it.

But there was something about Edward's delivery, his stark manner. Usually people said hurtful things out of emotion, and there was none of that here. Conniving as his tactic was, his assessment came only from a place of raw truth. These were truths that faced me every day in the mirror, and yet I found them the hardest to look at. They were the truths I worked the hardest to hide. Truths that, once acknowledged so frankly by someone else, stirred things. Shifted the icebergs drifting inside me.

I couldn't even try to refute it when I still had my mother's voice echoing with our earlier conversation in my head. *Don't expect to do better. We both know you can't.*

"You're an asshole." This time I said it out loud, and with venom.

Edward ticked his head to the side, a barely perceptible nod. "Perhaps."

I stood up and pulled my bag to my shoulder. "I'm leaving now, Mr. Fasbender." My glare dared him to argue.

He didn't even blink. "Without giving me an answer?"

God, he was bold.

"You should be smart enough to figure out my answer is no," I said, whirling away from him.

"Think about it."

"I won't."

I could feel him following as I stormed out of the room. I was midway across the Fontainebleau foyer when he called after me. "Oh, Celia, in case you're still wondering…"

I kept walking, determined not to give him the satisfaction of turning back.

It didn't stop him from saying more. "My answer is yes—I do find you attractive."

"Go to hell," I muttered under my breath. It was certainly where he belonged.

Eager to be out of the building as fast as possible, I took the stairs. I didn't stop walking when I'd made it across the foyer. I kept going until I was two blocks away, where I slipped into a coffee shop and sank down at a table. My heart didn't settle down to a reasonable pace for long minutes, and only when it did was I able to realize how severely I was overreacting.

Edward Fasbender was an arrogant piece of shit. His assessment of me didn't matter. I was still the woman I was when I'd walked in to his stupid meeting, and I'd been comfortable with myself then. There was no reason to feel any different now.

Really, all in all, it had been a mission accomplished. I'd gone in there expecting a different offer, but I'd rejected the man all the same. It was a victory. Truly.

So why did it feel like I'd walked out with the losing hand?

3

Of course I called my father.

After I'd bought a nonfat latte and a spinach salad from the counter, I pulled out my phone and called his cell. It was Tuesday, and, as Edward had accurately asserted, my father was more likely to be at the golf club than the office.

"What's up, Ceeley doll?" he answered in his typical manner. The endearment didn't have much commitment behind it. It was how he always addressed me, more a habit than anything else.

Not that I doubted his love for me. I was one of the things he'd created, and he loved all his creations. Some more enthusiastically than others, but that was to be expected, wasn't it? His business—his *empire*—had produced much more notably than I had, and it naturally deserved the accolades and attention he gave it.

"Are you busy, Daddy?" I could hear the distinct call of *fore* in the background.

"Nope. Just getting in the cart to drive to the next hole. Is everything all right? You don't usually call out of the blue like this."

"Everything's fine. I just had a question for you." I propped the phone on my shoulder with my chin so I could open up the wrapper on my plastic fork. "What can you tell me about Edward Fasbender?"

"Edward Fasbender?" He was understandably surprised. I'd never shown much interest in Werner Media and it was unlike me to ask about people associated with the business. "Why, he's the owner of Accelecom. That's a company in—"

"Yes, I know what Accelecom is. I wanted to know specifically about Fasbender." With my father mid-game, I knew his attention was limited. I didn't want to waste the time he was willing to give me to get information I already had.

"Well, he's a scoundrel, that one. A real devil. Ruthless, unethical, shady. Corrupt."

Devil. That was a description I could get behind.

That wasn't what stood out the most in my father's answer. Perhaps it was because I'd played my own game so long, but I had a habit of zeroing in on the dirty laundry in a person's background. "What do you mean by corrupt? I get that he's a rival, but does he actually engage in unscrupulous behavior?"

He chortled. "I'd say. Wouldn't trust that man as far as I could throw him. Zero credibility."

My father said the same thing about half the business associates he talked about and every politician. "Like, has he done anything illegal? Has he broken the law?"

"I wouldn't doubt it if he had."

Helpful, Dad. Real helpful.

"Does that mean you don't know of anything specific that he's done or gotten away with?" I needed details. I needed cold hard facts. I needed a lead.

"Of course I know specifics." He was starting to bristle, the way he did anytime someone pushed him in a direction he wasn't interested in going. "He did that...well, for one, he was involved in that... You know what, Ceeley, it's all complicated business stuff. Hard to explain, and you wouldn't understand all the jargon anyway. Leave these sorts of things for the big boys. Just trust me when I say he's not a good guy."

It was strange how I could both feel and *not* feel the sting of his condescension. I knew it was there, sensed the lash of his words and what they meant, what they suggested he thought about me, but they didn't actually hurt me anymore. Not like they once did.

There were benefits to being nothing.

More strongly, I felt the disappointment of having learned absolutely nothing. Whether my father didn't know anything solid about Edward Fasbender or he wasn't willing to tell me, I wasn't sure. Either way, he wasn't useful.

"Why are you asking about this guy?" His tone was suddenly suspicious.

"No reason. Just curious."

"No, no. This guy's name doesn't come up out of nowhere. There has to be something that put him in your head."

I speared my fork in my salad then picked it up and jabbed again. "He wanted to meet with me, is all. To discuss a design project, I think."

"He, *what*?" I'd only had half his attention before, but now he was completely present. "That bastard! Have you met with him yet? Whatever he says, it's a ruse. He's probably trying to get intel about me from you."

"Actually, I don't even think he realized who I was when he called in. And, no. I haven't met with him." Lying was my thing, but I didn't necessarily enjoy lying to my parents. They were good enough people, and I'd already lied too much to them over the years. Lies of omission. Outright falsehoods.

So why was I doing it now?

I stabbed again at the spinach.

"Good! Don't. Whatever you do, don't meet with him. Do not have any further contact with him."

"Don't worry, I'm not planning on it." At least that was the truth.

"And I don't believe that crap that he doesn't know who you are. He knows."

"It probably wasn't even him who reached out. More like someone on his staff that had no idea about the connection between the Werner name and Lux Designs." I didn't know why I was defending the devil. He most definitely knew who I was.

"I wouldn't be so sure, honey." Again, his tone was subtly patronizing. "He's very clever. And a menace. I don't like him one bit."

That was why Edward's plan was flawed from the outset. My father considered him an enemy. If I tried to marry the guy, I'd likely be disowned.

Which was fine, because I wasn't considering it.

And I wasn't getting anything useful from my father,

which meant it was time to end the call. "I'm sure you're right, Daddy. That's why I called you as soon as I realized who he was. I wasn't about to get involved with one of your competitors. Like I said, I was just curious."

"Smart girl. I'm at the next hole now. If there's anything else you need, we can talk later."

We hung up, but instead of diving into my lunch, I stared at it, thinking. If I were really smart, I would have told my father the truth. I would have detailed my entire encounter with Edward Fasbender, would have told him about the outrageous scheme he'd concocted and how he desperately wanted control of my father's business.

But, for whatever reason—be it that it had ended so humiliatingly or that I didn't want to confess that I'd met with his rival in the first place or some other motive I wasn't ready to admit to—*whatever* the reason, I didn't want my father to know.

So the lengths Edward was willing to go to get what he wanted remained a secret.

4

Even though I didn't live for my work the way my father did, I loved my office. One thousand square feet on the third floor of a building in Chelsea, it was one of the few things I'd acquired with my own means, and by my own means, I didn't mean with money.

I'd found the place when I'd been hunting for a location to open my business almost seven years ago. The real estate agent had shown me another space, an awkward unit with an extra thousand feet that I had no need for, that backed up to the spot I eventually acquired. My office hadn't been for sale at the time, but we'd been fortunate enough to run into the owner while looking, and he'd been kind enough to show us around.

Kind enough wasn't really the correct term. *Interested* enough, was more like it. Scott Matthews had been a forty-something-year-old accountant who enjoyed flirting with the twenty-five-year-old darling he'd seen poking around on his floor. He'd explained how his own business had grown too big for the small space, but he wasn't yet ready to part with it, in case he needed to downsize one day.

He was married; his ring was firmly lodged on his finger, his skin puffing out around it like he'd gained a few pounds since he'd last taken it off. He gave no indication of wanting to engage in anything that would break his marriage vows. He was simply talking to a pretty lady. No harm in that.

Except I was more than a pretty lady—I was a dangerous lady, even at that young age.

It had been easy enough to dismiss my realtor and then it hadn't taken much persuasion to get Scott to take me out to dinner. I'd been playing The Game by then for a couple of years, and while most of the schemes I'd pulled at the time were with Hudson, I'd decided to conquer Scott all on my own.

The thing was, I'd really loved his unit. It was the perfect size, the perfect location. It had the perfect vibe and wouldn't require much construction to make it what I envisioned. But even more, I'd loved the idea of convincing him that the space should be mine.

It really hadn't been as hard to seduce him as it should have been. After dinner, he'd taken me back to the very unit, and I'd let him fuck me against the front door and again on the counter of the office kitchenette. It was the second time that I'd gotten him to let me take the pictures. Filthy, naughty pictures. Pictures that showed everything and left nothing to the imagination.

If I was to believe him, and, in this case, I actually did, this was the first time he'd ever cheated on his wife. That should have been considered a victory in itself, and in another situation, I would have let it go there.

But I'd been ambitious, and I'd wanted that space.

All it took was threatening to show his wife the proof of his infidelity and the place was mine. Oh, he'd cried first, and begged. Even offered large sums of money, which I didn't give a shit about. In the end, when I'd told him I just wanted the office, he'd almost seemed relieved. Especially when he assumed that meant we could keep screwing around. Which, it didn't. Once I was done with a mark, I was done, but he didn't learn that until long after the deal was made.

The surprising part of the whole thing was how long I'd been able to keep the lease. I'd figured I had a year or two before he'd get tired of the looming threat, but he'd been desperate to keep his dirty little secret, and I'd been happy to benefit from the indiscretion.

I couldn't say for sure if I would have actually told his wife or not if Scott hadn't agreed to my terms. The best threats are the ones that will be followed through, but I hadn't planned on really telling her, in the beginning. I'd only set out to see if I *could* do it, if I could get what I wanted with just my body and a few hours of my time. Since I'd only wanted the space, there would have been no use in actually ruining his life, but, if it came down to it, I might have. Just for fun. Just to see what would happen next.

I should have felt bad about that. If I still felt things, maybe I would have.

In the meantime, I didn't have to worry about what I would or wouldn't do because the space belonged to me.

It was a simple layout with a reception area, an office for me, the kitchenette, and a consultation room. While the consultation room was intended for clients, I also used it when meeting with Renee. I'd designed it to feel casual with cushy couches and an oversized coffee table that could hold models for presentation.

Then, at the window, I'd installed a seat with plump pillows. I liked to sit here while Renee ran down production schedules and product information for our current projects. I'd lean my back against the curve of the alcove, my body lengthwise along the glass, my knees bent, my feet flat on the seat cushion. Three floors up was high enough to not be particularly noticeable to pedestrians and still be the perfect height for people-watching. I could lose long hours to surveying the passersby below, studying how they moved, how they interacted. Wondering what they thought, what their motives were. Wondering if they saw all the nuances of human behavior that I did.

That man there, does he realize his companion is irritated by him?

Does that young girl notice the businessman leering at her from across the street?

Is the smile on that woman's face genuine? Or is she empty and hollow inside?

Today, though, while Renee gave me a detailed rundown of the quality inspection procedure for a client residence—our only client at the moment—I wasn't watching the people below the window. Instead, as I had so often in the week and a half since I'd met with him, I was thinking about Edward Fasbender. Thinking about the things he'd said to me.

Your flat is owned in your father's name. You have one degree, in an art field. Your business barely runs in the black... The lack of customers knocking at your door confirms that. You're almost thirty-two years old, unmarried, childless, living off your trust fund... Your good looks might have gotten you through most of your life so far, but how much longer is that going to last?

They were words that carried bite, but the more time that passed, the easier it was to repeat them in my head. I'd said them to myself enough now that it felt like recovering from a sunburn. After the initial sting, the dead skin peeled away, exposing new skin underneath.

It was startling to discover that beneath this particular sting was arousal.

It took awhile to figure out what it was, the feeling was so foreign. That wasn't exactly true—my body got aroused all the time. I actually found sex enjoyable on a very base level. My skin reacted to human touch. My pulse quickened. My pussy got wet. I had orgasms.

But arousal was always confined to physical reactions. My mind and heart remained separate and unaffected. Disinterested. Nonconcordant.

This time, though, after I got past the harshness of Edward's words, I was turned on. Completely. With every part of me, and I couldn't help but want to examine that more closely. Maybe I had some humiliation fetish I hadn't discovered before, a very real possibility that I should possibly explore more thoroughly, but there was more to it than that.

I reacted to him, I realized, because he'd *seen* me.

I couldn't remember the last time someone had truly seen me, the last time anyone had even tried to look behind the pretty face, the well-cared-for physique, the expensive clothes, the prominent name. Those superficial aspects were more than enough for most. That was why it was so easy to play people the way I did.

Edward, though, had looked past all the bullshit, and while it was embarrassing that he'd seen me for the failure that I was, it was also a relief to be acknowledged.

Relieving and arousing.

What would it be like to go to bed with a man like that? To relinquish control, be stripped down bare...

I sat up suddenly. *What about sex?*

Renee broke off her instructions mid-sentence. "Uh, what did you say?"

Shit. I'd said it aloud.

"Nothing. My mind wandered. Go on."

She gave me an inquisitive stare and then went on. We weren't close enough for her to probe further. I wasn't close to anyone.

Later, when I was alone in my office, I rang her desk. "Can you get me Edward Fasbender's contact information?"

"Certainly. Are you following up with him? Would you like me to get him on the line?"

I considered. "No. Just get me his number."

I wrote down the number she provided and hung up. Then I retrieved my cell phone from my purse and dialed from there. I didn't want the company name to show up on the caller ID, and, while I knew my cell didn't show my name when I called out, I wanted him to have my number, for some reason I couldn't quite identify.

"Celia," he said when he answered.

My breath caught. He'd saved my number in his phone. I hadn't expected that and it almost threw my train of thought.

But I recovered. "What about sex?" I asked.

"Hmm." The simple sound reverberated low in his chest. I could sense an air of amusement. "Are you asking about sex in our marriage?"

It was hard not to be distracted by his voice. How had I not noticed how bewitching his timbre was? His accent was absolutely panty melting.

I shifted in my seat, crossing one leg over the other to press against the ache that had crept up unexpectedly. "Yes. I wondered. That."

God, I sounded like a complete imbecile.

"A perfectly natural question. I'd planned on discussing it the other day, but you ran out so suddenly."

The reminder of our previous meeting's events was all I needed to snap out of it. "You've got me on the phone. Get to the discussing now, will you?"

"Awfully eager, aren't you?"

Jesus, I didn't need this. "I'm going to hang up…"

"No obligation." It took me a second to register that it was the answer to my question.

No obligation. Oddly, it made me disappointed.

"No obligation, but it might occur?" *Please let that not have sounded as desperate as it felt saying.*

"No obligation because it *won't* occur."

A beat passed.

"Interesting."

"Sounds like you're thinking about it?"

"I'm not," I said quickly. Too quickly, and I wasn't even sure if I meant I wasn't thinking about the silly marriage proposal or wasn't thinking about sex with him. One of those, at least, was a lie.

"I'm not," I said again, more certain.

"That makes one of us." Then we were talking about the marriage, because why would he be thinking about sex with me when he'd just said it wouldn't occur?

I hated this, hated how unbalanced he made me. It was a simple phone call and he still had the ability to shift my world off-kilter.

And that was stupid. I'd been in situations more uncertain than this and managed just fine. I stuck my chin up and channeled that confident persona. "I hope you're used to disappointment, then."

"Quite frankly, Celia, I'm not, and I don't see any reason to plan for it now. You should understand something fundamental about me—I don't accept no as an answer."

I was still stammering for a comeback when he went on. "Good day, Celia. We'll talk soon."

Then the line was dead. And I was, once again, reeling. Once again, rejected.

Once again, aroused.

5

Hudson hadn't called it a game—that was my term. He'd called it experiments. He'd been conducting them for years before I learned about them, before he used me as one of his subjects.

I didn't realize until much later that they actually *were* experiments for him. He wasn't out to play people, though that was the ultimate outcome. He was studying behavior, trying to discover what made them work, what made them feel. What made them love. He was attempting to understand fundamental human emotions that he was certain he lacked in himself.

He didn't lack them, of course. He was the Tin Man come to life, searching for a heart that he hadn't realized he'd possessed all along.

Back then, I was just as unaware of his capability to love as he was. I saw him as he'd appeared—callous, cold, and cruel.

I'd envied him.

I'd suffered pain after pain after pain, some of the more recent injuries at his hand, and I'd wanted nothing more than to be numb. I'd wanted to be empty and void. I'd wanted to stop feeling.

And he agreed to teach me how.

I never knew exactly why he chose to let me in on his experiments when he'd let no one in before. Maybe it was because we'd grown up together. Maybe he'd had a sense of responsibility. Maybe he'd thought he owed me—he did, by the way. He'd definitely owed me.

Whatever the reason, he'd taken me under his wing. He'd taught me how to manipulate, how to prey, how to influence and exploit. The first time had been easy. It had been my job to flirt, then to seduce. The affair I'd had with Tim Kerrigan had been free of attachment, but it had empowered me. I'd set my sights on a stranger, and I'd drawn him into my bed, exactly as I'd planned. That had done quite a thing for my self-confidence. It had been so effective, I'd nearly forgotten the goal of the scheme.

Then, when his wife discovered our indiscretion, as had always been the objective of the experiment, my feelings changed. She'd been devastated. Heartbroken. They'd been newlyweds, and I'd destroyed their happiness. At least that's what she'd said to me the one time I'd come face to face with her. It hadn't stopped her from staying with him.

That day, though, when she spewed words of hatred and venom in my direction, I had a moment of anguish. It didn't feel good to be the bitch. It didn't feel pretty to be cruel and destructive. The whole point of playing these games with Hudson had been to feel nothing, not to feel terrible.

But as I'd stood in the wake of her attack, as I turned

my focus from concentrating on what I was feeling to observing her, the calmer I'd become. My reality altered. Instead of pain being a thing that lived only inside of me, I discovered it could exist elsewhere. Outside of me. Detached from me. Severed.

And that was why I'd played. Not because I'd wanted to see *what would happen if* but because when someone else cried and fell apart, when someone else's world was sabotaged, my pain diminished. The scars left by Hudson and Charles and all the others would lighten. The deeper wounds, the ones inflicted by the person I should have been able to trust more than almost anyone, wouldn't throb with intensity, wouldn't cripple me with their ache. Every bit of my pain grew smaller and smaller until I'd become numb.

Numb didn't mean gone, though. It was still there, somewhere, invisible and buried inside, waiting for me. I knew that as soon as I stopped playing it would return and take me over. That was how it had become a game in my mind. The objective was them or me. Someone had to hurt, and as long as it wasn't me, I won. As long as I was the one still standing, I won.

It was the only way I knew to survive.

Once upon a time I'd hoped that one day I'd overcome it. That I'd hurt enough people and break enough hearts, and I'd be empty for real. That the scars and the wounds would be magically healed, and I'd be new and pure and whole. I could quit The Game, then, and learn to feel again.

But I'd hurt enough people now. I'd hurt people who'd actually meant something to me. I'd turned The Game on Hudson. I'd hurt him. I'd hurt his wife. Pain very much lived outside of me. I'd seen it close up on the faces of the people I should have cared most for.

And still I felt it waiting for me, lingering in the shadows. A ghost that would always haunt me. A cancer that yearned to spread.

6

I was antsy after my phone call with Edward. The collar of my shirt felt too tight. I was roasting in my slacks. It was a scorching summer day, but the air conditioning was on in the office, and Renee, who usually complained I liked to run the place like a sweatbox, had her sweater on.

I was hot and bothered and rejected, and that pissed me off.

Too restless to concentrate on work, I opened my laptop and entered Edward's name into my Google search bar. I meant to scour the information that popped up, find his weakness, perhaps, or discover a skeleton in his closet. He had to have one. Everyone I'd ever met who'd held a position of power had something they were ashamed of. Something they were afraid the world would discover.

But instead of looking at the news items, I found myself clicking the images tab.

My screen quickly filled with a grid full of Edward Fasbender. Edward Fasbender at a media summit. Edward Fasbender on *Forbes Magazine*. Edward Fasbender at Accelecom. Edward Fasbender at LinkedIn. Business Insider had him listed as one of the Top Fifty Sexiest CEOs, because duh. *Fortune* called him one of the most innovative corporate leaders of the twenty-first century. There were pictures of him at charity banquets, at tech conventions, at the gym. Half of the images were for publicity only. Most of the rest were candid shots at different events, nearly always he was dressed in a designer bespoke suit. In every one he looked as hard and handsome as he had in person.

And, Jesus, could that man wear a tuxedo. As though it were a second skin. His head usually tilted with the perfect arrogant slant. As though he practiced looking good in a mirror. As though he knew how arrestingly good-looking he was. How uncomfortably attractive he was.

I had to shift several times in my office chair to ease the discomfort of staring at him so intensely.

Why the hell wasn't he interested in sex?

Was he gay? He'd been married, had kids. That didn't mean anything these days. Neither did the several occasions where he sported a beautiful woman on his arm. Were they beards? Was that the real reason he wanted an arranged marriage? Was that his deep dark secret?

For some reason, I didn't think so. There'd been too much heat in his gaze when we'd met in person. And he'd said he was attracted to me.

Hadn't he? Or had I made that up?

He baffled me. He annoyed me. He stirred something inside of me that I didn't recognize or remember noticing before. He was completely maddening.

I clicked an item that looked recent, a group picture of him with several other important-looking people in important-looking clothes. A new tab opened with a headline that said it was an industry awards showcase that had been held at the Hilton in Midtown a couple of weeks before. I skimmed the article and then scanned through the gallery, pausing to examine every image he was featured in. He rarely smiled, I noticed. Not really. Even at what was likely a jovial event. And he knew people that ran in the same circles my father ran in. I could identify several individuals, if not always by name, at least by face.

Then I got to the image that made me momentarily freeze. It wasn't of Edward, but of Hudson and his wife. I hadn't seen any pictures of him in ages, not since I'd curiously sifted through reports on his wedding a couple of years ago. It was startling to see him now, see how he'd changed. How he'd stayed the same. He looked older, but as distinguished as he'd always looked. He looked happy, the glow on his face matching the radiance of his bride. She looked happy too, with a hand resting on the small swell of her belly.

I took a long breath in and blew it out slowly.

I really hadn't been in love with Hudson, not in the end. Hadn't been for a long, long time. I'd been mad at him, yes. Mad that he'd left me. That he'd moved on. But I hadn't been in love with him.

And yet, faced with the image of his happy life, I felt a pang of something, a stray lightning bolt of envy in an otherwise black, emotionless sky. *That was supposed to be me.*

Everything would be different if that had been me.

I closed out of the tab and the brief flash of jealousy vanished with the disappearance of the image.

Voices in the lobby pulled my attention. Renee was talking to someone, another woman. A voice I couldn't quite identify. We weren't expecting anyone that I knew of. God, I hoped I didn't have to see anyone today. I wasn't in the mood.

Leaving my laptop open, I pushed up from my desk and headed to the door to investigate.

"I'm sorry, I don't see you on her appointment book." Renee was studying her computer screen as though she didn't have my schedule memorized.

I peeked cautiously out my door. Fortunately, my viewpoint allowed me to look out on Renee's desk, which meant the woman in front of her couldn't see me.

It also meant I only saw her back. Her hair was shoulder-length auburn, her dress a whimsical style that wouldn't be worn by most of the clients I worked with. Over her shoulder was an oversized portfolio bag, the kind an artist used to carry around small works of art.

"I don't have an appointment," the woman said patiently. "But if I could just have a second of her time…" She gestured toward my office, turning her body enough that I was able to better see her.

Fuck.

I withdrew quickly into my office, pressing my back against the metal frame of the door. I knew the unannounced visitor. Blanche Martin, an artist I'd met at a gallery exhibition a few months back. She'd had an underwhelming showing, as far as I could tell. Not one of her pieces had been purchased, and judging from the dreary amount of interest there was around her, she wasn't going to be selling any in the near future either.

Still, she'd been excited and eager to talk about her work.

It made for a perfect opportunity to pull her into one of

my favorite games.

It was an easy setup, which was why I played it so often, even though the payoff wasn't as exhilarating as some of my other games. It was a scenario I could easily walk into. One I could manage while balancing other elements of life.

"I really don't mean to intrude, but I swear she said I could stop by anytime." Blanche was incredibly determined, which was more than could be said for her unremarkable art.

I *had* told her she could stop by anytime. I'd also told her that I was an interior designer, and that a very wealthy, very well-known client of mine was interested in decorating his entire penthouse flat with the work of just one artist. And her work would be perfect for his vibe! But could she please work up some new pieces so that I could show him before we made the deal?

It was all bullshit, of course.

Obviously she was here to show me what she'd come up with. This was where The Game was supposed to get good. This was the part I lived for.

For some reason, I wasn't motivated today.

But I'd put in the work. And she was here…

With a sigh, I put on a smile and emerged from my hiding place. "Blanche! I was just thinking about you! What perfect timing!" I nodded to my assistant. "It's okay, Renee. I have a few minutes for Ms. Martin."

Renee was used to these types of encounters. While she wasn't involved in these conversations, she believed I was always on the lookout for the latest art trends. She didn't know any more than that, and didn't need to.

I ushered Blanche into my office and closed the door so Renee wouldn't hear anything that might be off-putting. She was a good assistant. I would have hated losing her.

"Thank you so much for seeing me, Ms. Werner. I should have made an appointment, but I've been so busy working on these pieces you asked for, and as soon as I was convinced they were ready, I didn't even think! I just came straight down here!"

I could practically hear the exclamation points in her speech. Blanche was even more enthusiastic than she'd been when I'd first met her. Even more optimistic.

The easiest kind of person to destroy.

"Now, Blanche, I know I told you to call me Celia. And no worries about stopping in. It's perfectly fine. Want to show me what you have?" The lines came automatically now, having performed them so many times.

"Yes!" She unzipped her bag, babbling on as she pulled out first one canvas then a second.

I moved my laptop to the side to make more room on my desk then pretended to scrutinize the paintings as she laid them out in front of me.

Except, I didn't really pretend. I actually looked at them, something I hadn't done while pulling this scam in, well, maybe ever. There had never been a point. I wasn't ever going to buy any of it, no matter how good the work was.

This time, though, there was something about them that pulled me in. Something that made me have to catch my breath. The first one was of a country garden. A green field of grass sprawled across the canvas, the edges punctuated with flowered bushes. A stone path meandered over the grass and through a white arbor covered with purple blooms.

The next canvas displayed a similar theme, another part of the same garden, maybe, but this time there was an open field of wildflowers in the background, and instead of an arbor, this one featured a large fruit tree, apples buried in its leaves and scattered on the ground around it. The centerpiece of the painting was a wooden swing, tied with thick rope to a sturdy branch. Both the swing and the ropes were worn, and it was impossible not to imagine the child who had spent her time here. A cheerful, naive girl who'd loved nothing more than to fly through the air and try to touch the clouds with her toes.

My eyes suddenly pricked.

I didn't want to look at her paintings anymore. I didn't want to give her a speech about her work—the art she'd obviously labored over for the last several months—not being a good fit for my client after all. I didn't even want to see her break down and cry.

I just wanted her to go.

"Oh, I know him! That's Edward Fasbender. My, he's such a looker, and even more attractive in person. Those pictures just don't do him justice."

I followed Blanche's gaze to my laptop sitting at the edge of my desk, the screen still displaying the image search from earlier.

My thoughts slid easily away from the uncomfortable place her paintings had taken me to what she'd just said. "Yes, that's him. He's a potential client. You've met him before?"

"I worked for him, actually. I lived in London for a while and had a job in the graphic design department of Accelecom. He was very hands-on with his staff. And quite particular. Hard to please. I hope he's easier to work with as a client than a boss."

My head swirled with intrigue. "Well, I don't know yet, since I haven't agreed to take him on. Your comment definitely gives me pause."

She blushed. "I shouldn't have said anything. It's been a few years now since I worked with him. He may have changed. Or it might have been me! I'm not a graphic designer anymore for a reason."

"Oh, please. You're very talented." It wasn't even that big of a lie. She'd gotten better since I'd seen her in the spring.

I glanced again at her paintings and felt that same stirring of unease. I still didn't want to look at them, but now I was interested in talking with her more about Edward.

I stacked the canvases on top of each other and held them out to her. "How about we do this...I need to speak to my client and see where his current thoughts are on this project. Then maybe we can meet again sometime this weekend and discuss this further."

Blanche's brows momentarily drew close together. She'd had yet to take the paintings from me. "Sure. Sure. I'm free Sunday, if that works for you. Do you want to just keep these to show him?"

I definitely did not. I wanted them as far away from me as possible. "That won't be necessary. I've seen enough to attest to the quality. Could you email me with digital photos of them and any other paintings you propose for this collection? I'll forward them on. And Sunday is perfect! How about a late lunch around two? I'll reply to your email with a restaurant."

Her earlier zeal returned and she finally took the paintings from me. "That sounds great! To be honest, I'm going to be sweating until then, but I can wait. It's only a couple of days."

"I totally understand. But, as you said, it's just a couple of days. I have an appointment soon, anyway, and I'd rather not be rushed when we talk." I was already escorting her to the door.

"Of course. Makes total sense."

"I'd love to quiz you some more about Edward Fasbender, too, if you don't mind." I could have kept her longer and drilled her right there, but I'd learned from experience that patience was a good friend. This way she'd have time to think of things she might not have thought of on the spot. Especially if she was as eager to please me as I believed she was.

"Whatever I can do to help! Thank you for all of this. You've really made my day!"

She walked out of my office with hope. The same kind of hope I'd once had about living a life like the one Hudson led with Alayna, a life filled with love and vows and swollen bellies. The kind of hope that was devastating when destroyed. It was the kind of hope I loved seeing in the people I played, and, normally, I'd cling onto it, fantasizing about how satisfying it would be to eventually deflate their aspirations.

But an hour later when she sent over an email with her art attached—images I didn't open—I wasn't thinking about the game I'd set up with Blanche Martin. As I replied with the address to a restaurant in Lenox Hill, I was thinking about what kind of game I'd play with Edward.

7

I didn't often dream, or, at least, I didn't remember if I did. Those had disappeared along with my emotions. Apparently there was no way to spin imaginings of the soul when a person no longer had a soul.

But I did have one recurring dream that visited me as regularly as the seasons. It was always vague, always a bit hazy, as though I were viewing it through a fog.

No, as though I were *in* the fog, because it was a dream about me, I was pretty sure. I could never actually *see* myself there, but I *felt* myself there. Felt myself there in that misty nowhere, a faceless man at my side and a baby in my arms. Every time, the infant was bundled so tightly that I couldn't see its face, couldn't tell if it was a boy or a girl, or how old it was, but I could feel the weight of it, could smell the very distinct baby scent when I lowered my nose toward its head. Could hear its gentle baby sounds as I tried to move the blanket to reveal the form underneath.

But I could never move the blanket. I couldn't move anything at all. My arms were missing, my body invisible, like I wasn't really there. Like I was nothing. Like the man and the baby were real, and I was a ghost clinging to their existence.

I dreamt it that night, and, as always when I dreamt it, I woke up sobbing.

Dumb, I thought, as my body shook with grief I couldn't actually feel.

I didn't even like babies.

8

I arrived early to the restaurant on Sunday. I hadn't planned to; it was just the way traffic worked out.

I'd made reservations, thankfully, but Orsay wasn't the type of establishment that seated guests without all members of their party present.

Usually, anyway. I had ways of making people change their minds about such stifling rules.

After a bit of flirting with the hostess—yes, my charms work as well on women as men—I found myself escorted to a table for two. I asked her not to send a waiter until my guest arrived, then I took the bench side of the arrangement, which allowed me to face the door. I liked having the advantage in these situations.

Unfortunately that meant I couldn't see anyone approaching from behind until they were well on me. Which was why I wasn't prepared when I glanced up at the two men passing by on their way out of the restaurant and locked eyes on none other than Edward Fasbender.

Startled, I felt my mouth fall open. What was *he* doing here? Lenox Hill wasn't exactly near St. Regis. Most importantly, what was he doing here *now*? Minutes before I was supposed to meet with someone to discuss him, no less.

His reaction was decidedly less severe than mine felt. His eyes widened in surprise then a smug smile uncurled across his lips.

"Vincent," he said to the man he was with. "I've just spotted someone I know. Thank you for meeting with me. I'll follow up with you sometime this coming week." He didn't wait for his companion's response before pulling out the chair across from me and taking the liberty of sitting in it.

Vincent nodded in acknowledgment and went on his way while I blinked in astonishment.

"Oh, hell no," I said, when I managed to get my wits about me, a difficult task in the shadow of Edward's presence. It was overpowering. *He* was overpowering. It was hard to think around someone so incredibly assured. So completely captivating. "That seat is not for you. I did not invite you to sit."

He gave me a bored sigh. "Come on, now. You don't want to make a scene."

I hadn't realized how loud my voice had been, but his comment didn't help to calm me down. Who was he to tell me what I did and didn't want to do? I had half a mind to very much make a scene. Whatever it took to get him out of that chair and away from me.

Except, I really didn't want to make a scene. It would please him too much to see me riled. There was no way I was giving him that satisfaction.

I straightened my back and made a deliberate effort to lower my voice. "Five minutes. You get five minutes to say what you need to say and then be gone."

"Fine." He didn't look at his watch to check the time, but I did. It was a nice piece, actually. A Piaget with a steel band and a sapphire face that had to cost a fortune. Worth it for how well he wore it.

Oh, please. It's a luxury watch. It would look good on anyone.

I forced my gaze up to his face. Which wasn't any less stunning. His eyes were so blue, so translucent. Hypnotizing.

Jesus, what was wrong with me? I had to pull myself together.

The waiter chose that moment to come take our drink orders, giving me a thankful distraction. "Not yet, please. This isn't who I'm expecting to—"

Edward bulldozed over me. "She'll take a Juliet. Nothing for me. And put this ticket on the credit card I just used."

The waiter looked more closely at Edward and, apparently realizing he'd served him once before that afternoon, nodded. "Yes, Mr. Fasbender. I'll be right back with that Juliet." He disappeared into the kitchen.

I was fuming. "I do not need you to order my drinks for me, and I most certainly do not need you to pay for my meal."

"Of course you don't. But I have extremely good taste. It's vodka and limoncello and something floral. You'll see. You'll like it." His English dialect was so enchanting, even with the added air of haughtiness. It was almost a form of delicious torture. Like being tickled—an ear tickle. "As for paying for your meal...what sort of potential husband would I be if I didn't prove I meant to take care of my wife."

I'd been dead inside for nearly a decade, and yet his use of the word *wife* in relation to me set something blooming deep and hidden inside me.

No, no, no. Close it off. Let it die. Stay numb.

"I hope you don't plan to use your entire five minutes to discuss that ridiculous scheme of yours." The irritation in my tone was directed at myself, but I was fine with him thinking it was all for him.

"Not all my five minutes, no. I have other things to say."

"Well? Get on with it."

Casually, as though he had all the time in the world, he brought his elbows to the table and clasped his hands together, his eyes never leaving mine. "You're stalking me," he said finally.

"No, I'm not!" I was flabbergasted. "How would I even... Why would I ever think you'd be at this restaurant? When there's a million other restaurants in Manhattan."

"That's what I find remarkable about your skills. You found me here, of all places."

Fury rose in me like smoke from a wildfire. What an egotistical, self-centered shithead. I'd done more than my fair share of stalking in my life, but to assume that I'd bother to chase after *him*...!

Never mind that I'd spent several hours researching him on the internet the night before. Or that I'd ordered a deeper background check, and maybe took a route that went by his hotel on my run that morning.

"I am *not* stalking you," I said definitively.

He chuckled as he leaned back into his chair. "I understand. It's all right. You're embarrassed. Honestly. I'm flattered."

"You're so...so..." I couldn't find a word to describe how exasperated he made me.

"*So*...what?" He tilted his head in that conceited way he did in all his online pictures. "Assertive? Potent? Charming? Probably not that. Undeniable?"

"Vexing. I was going to say vexing." I dug my fingernails into my pant legs under the table, afraid I'd reach across the table and claw his beautiful bastard face if I didn't.

He gave a sidewise nod that had the same effect as a shrug. "Could be worse. I believe you called me an asshole the other day."

"I still mean it, too." I lifted my chin as though I'd somehow won, but of course I hadn't. I was nowhere close to winning.

Which meant I was losing, and I hated losing.

I gave him a bristling frown. "What do you want? Why are you bothering me?"

"I'd like to know what you've decided."

"...*what I've decided*?" I found that I was constantly repeating his words back to him in question form because so much of what he said was outright incredible.

"About my proposal. We were just discussing it. You obviously have a faulty memory. Perhaps you should get that checked out."

That pompous little... "You're obviously not a very good listener. I already told you no."

His expression grew serious, and before he even spoke, I had the distinct feeling this was a look he used a lot in the boardroom. When he was about to make a killer move. When he was about to crush his opponent with new terms.

It would have been hot if I weren't currently his opponent.

"Would it make a difference if sex were on the table?" he asked solemnly.

"No?" It sounded like I wasn't certain so I repeated it again, more emphatically. "No."

His brow rose skeptically. "Are you sure?"

"Positive." I *was* positive. Nothing would change my answer, even as his allure tugged on my libido, making the space between my legs ache in a way they hadn't in a long time. In years. In a lifetime.

Still, even with my mind made up, I couldn't help being curious. "But, why isn't it?"

"Why isn't it on the table?" He appeared surprised by the question.

That was a point in my favor. It seemed that very little threw him. What a nice change of pace to be on the other side of the teeter-totter.

"Yes, why wouldn't you expect sex in a marriage?" More specifically, why wouldn't he expect sex *with me*? I was attractive. More than a few men had done really stupid things to get me in their bed. Throw away marriages and change long-term goals sort of stupid things.

Why wouldn't Edward want me as well? Why wouldn't he demand it?

The damn waiter came back then, setting my drink—correction, the drink Edward had ordered—in front of me.

Miffed at his timing, I shooed him away, telling him I'd flag him down when I was ready to order rather than explaining that the man sitting with me wasn't even the person I planned to eat with.

With the server dealt with, I pushed the drink aside dismissively, and reminded Edward where we were in the conversation. "I asked you a question."

He narrowed his eyes as though thinking it over.

My breath stuttered as I waited for his answer. I was nervous, for some insane reason. His lingering hesitation to respond wasn't helping matters. Each second that passed drew the tension between us tauter and tauter.

He knew exactly what he was doing. He had nothing to think over. He was the kind of man who knew every one of his motives before he said or did anything. It was almost impressive.

God, I hated him.

Just when I thought I couldn't stand it anymore, he spoke. "It's rather simple, actually. I have kids already. I don't need an heir. I don't want a baby with you."

I ignored the sting of his last comment. "Children are hardly the reason most men want sex."

"Yes. I'm well aware, my dear." So patronizing. So impossible.

"I am not your dear," I seethed.

"Not yet."

"Not ever!"

He grinned slowly. That self-satisfied smile of his was a nuclear weapon.

It was going to be my undoing, if I wasn't careful.

I refused to look at him any longer. I couldn't if I wanted to leave this encounter still a whole person, as whole of a person as I was these days, anyway. "You're avoiding the question. If you don't want to answer, then you can just go ahead and leave now. Besides, your time is up, and I have no interest—"

He leaned toward me and cut me off with a low rumble. "If you must know, *Celia*," he used my name pointedly, making sure I was aware he hadn't called me dear again. "I'm not an easy man to please in the bedroom."

"And that's different than any other room...how?"

He laughed, his eyes brightening with sincere amusement. "You learn quickly. I like that in a woman."

How could such a condescending comment make me feel so...*warm*? Heat spread through me like the early sun's rays spread across a new day. With extreme alarm, I realized I liked the thought of trying to please this intolerable man.

Because I liked challenges. That had to be why. No other reason.

Suddenly, it dawned on me what he'd really been saying. "Then you'd be going for sex elsewhere." I hadn't meant to sound disappointed.

"Would it matter?" he challenged.

"It wouldn't." I shook my head and amended. "It doesn't. Because I'm not considering any of this." Here I was again saying no, and still I was sure I was the one who'd been rejected.

I hated it. I hated him. I hated everything about him.

I especially hated the way he regarded me now, his gaze piercing and penetrating, as though he could see beyond the carefully coiffed woman in front of him to my very core, to the ice fields and dark caverns that lay at the heart of me.

Long silent seconds passed, seconds that stretched as tight as the pressure between us. Seconds where I formed a million things to say, and just as quickly dismissed each comment as immature or quaint or lame or just plain desperate.

Eventually, he took the burden off me. "This buttoned-up working girl look is a bit much." He gestured to the pearl buttons that ran below the collar of the peach-colored shell I wore. "It's the weekend. You should wear something more casual. Let your hair down."

"How dare you!" The harsh reaction came out before I could stop myself. "And who are you to talk? You're wearing a suit on Sunday. I'm guessing you didn't just come from church."

"I had a business meeting."

As if there couldn't be any other reasonable answer. As if I couldn't possibly work on the weekend.

It had the same tone of superiority that my father frequently used. I'd never been good at talking to him, either.

This conversation exhausted me. I was bored with it. Which was a gentler way of saying I was defeated by it.

I scanned over his shoulder, hoping to see my lunch date, and responded to him halfheartedly. "I doubt your meeting had anything to do with your choice of attire. All you ever wear is suits. I've never seen you in any sort of casual wear. If I hadn't seen proof otherwise, you could have told me you worked out in an Armani three-piece, and I would have believed it."

I knew I'd slipped up as soon as the words were out of

my mouth.

"You've been looking, have you? Of course you have. You wouldn't be a very good stalker if you hadn't."

Under the table, my leg bounced furiously with indignation. There wasn't anything I could say that wouldn't make the situation worse.

I attempted to redirect. "You know what *you* should do? You should grow a beard."

"A beard. Really."

I'd made the remark defensively, to criticize his look after he'd criticized mine, but I genuinely meant it. "Not a full beard. Something tamer. A Van Dyke, with your cheeks clean shaven." I could see it clearly. Could picture how it would add to his potency. Could practically feel how the rough stubble would feel under my fingers. Between my thighs.

"That's very specific. As though you've been thinking about me. Fantasizing about me."

My cheeks heated with his acute perception. "Uh, no. Not even a little. I was simply offering you a suggestion that anyone who has met you in person has likely thought but was too scared to tell you."

"I do believe people are afraid of me. Are you?"

"Hardly. I'm annoyed." And aroused. And maybe a little afraid. Or a lot afraid.

He stared at me with that same persistent stare, seeing more than I wanted him to see, I was sure.

I couldn't take it anymore, couldn't stand him looking. Couldn't stand him seeing. I put my elbows on the table and covered my face with my hands. "Your time has been up for…" I peered around my palms to note his watch before hiding again. "For four minutes. Do you think you could leave now?"

"If I grew a beard, would that change your mind about my proposal?"

I dropped my hands and glared at him with incredulity. His perseverance was remarkable.

"Well?"

"No. I'm not changing my mind if you grew a beard. It would just make you look better. Sexier." Oh my God, why did I keep talking?

He never missed an opportunity to humiliate me. "Sexier? Then you already think I'm sexy."

Sexy was an understatement. I thought he was irresistibly attractive and extraordinarily provocative, and if I had to sit across from him one more minute, I wasn't sure I could restrain myself from crawling over the table and demanding he kissed the fuck out of me right then and there.

Not that Edward Fasbender was a man who would ever take demands. He was the kind of man who had to be in charge. The kind of man who would slay me in every way if I let him.

I couldn't give him that opportunity. "It doesn't matter what I think about you, remember?"

For a minute I thought he might argue with me, might change his entire game and say *forget this marriage bullshit, come back to my hotel with me*. Instead, he said, "You're right. It doesn't."

But his eyes...they said something else. I was sure of it. As sure as I'd ever been of anything.

"Celia! Sorry I'm late, I got on the wrong train and then I went the wrong direction when I got on the street and then—" Blanche broke off when she noticed the man sitting in the seat that was supposed to be hers. "Oh."

She blushed, and I felt for sure she was about to spit out an awkward apology of sorts to him as well, but before she could, Edward stood. "Excuse me. I was just leaving." He pushed away from the table. It was then he truly looked at her. "You work for me."

She shook her head, her cheeks growing even redder. "Not anymore, sir."

"That's right." He stepped out of her way, letting her take the seat. "I look forward to hearing from you, Celia. Or you'll be hearing from me. Good day, Ms. Martin."

Like hell, he'd be hearing from me. But I knew it would be ten times worse if he had to come to me.

Fuck, I needed a drink.

As soon as he turned to leave, I grabbed the blasted Juliet and took a long gulp. Fuck him, it was actually a really good cocktail.

I'd drunk too soon, as it was, because not three seconds later he pivoted back toward me. "Oh, and, Celia...I recommend the oysters. They're delicious and slippery. Just like you."

I definitely hated him. I definitely wasn't going to marry him.

And I most definitely wasn't ordering the oysters.

9

I stared after Edward for longer than I meant to, my eyes trained on the front doors for thick seconds after his tight backside disappeared into the summer sun.

Blanche looked over her shoulder, following the line of my gaze. "I'm sorry I was late," she said again, "but maybe I should have been even later?"

With a frown, I brought my attention to her. It took another beat before I realized she was insinuating I might have liked to have been alone with the devil longer.

No. Absolutely not. No, no, no.

"No," I said, a much tamer dismissal than the one going on inside my head. "I hadn't meant to... I didn't know he'd be here. He sat himself down. After I'd told him I was expecting someone, even. Then he harassed me. Basically that's what he did, he *harassed* me, and I didn't—" I cut myself off when I noticed the hand holding my glass was shaking.

This wasn't the woman I was. Not the person I'd want-

ed to meet with Blanche Martin. I was flustered and babbling and off-kilter. I was a million miles from being Celia
Werner.

Tossing my napkin on the table, I began to slide across
the bench. "Could you excuse me for just a moment? I
need to use the restroom." I was on my feet before she
could respond.

Quick, anxious steps carried me to the bathroom where
I braced myself with both hands over the sink and sucked
in air like I'd been on an oxygen-restricted diet. I confront-
ed my reflection, a hot mess version of my usual self. Stray
blonde strands of hair had escaped from the bun that had
been perfectly coiffed earlier. My makeup was near perfect, but my skin was pale, my eyes wild. I looked frazzled.
Like I was open and on display. Like all of my insides were
scattered around me for everyone to see.

"Get yourself together," I scolded the unrecognizable
woman in the mirror.

I turned the faucet on cold and wet my palm, then wiped
the cool water along the back of my neck. The shock of
temperature settled my thoughts. My breaths were coming
easier now. My shoulders were less slumped. My expression less agitated. I felt myself come together bit by bit,
like a reverse clown car. All the ugly pieces of my nothing-
colored interior collected and tucked away neatly where
they belonged.

There. Much better.

And now that I was no longer ruffled, a new determination rose up in my sternum. A single-minded resolution to
find something on Edward Fasbender. Something small, if
that's all there was. *Anything.* Anything I could use to fuck
with him the way he fucked with me.

Resolve was empowering.

Resolve was fuel.

Resolve was motivation to go back to the table and endure a tedious lunch with Blanche.

Five minutes later, with my hair fixed and my lipstick reapplied, I returned to the table. I gave my companion my most winning smile. "So. Have you decided what you'd like to order?"

Blanche, it turned out, was a Belgian waffles kind of woman. The kind of woman that wore a bright purple and orange checkered sundress to a fancy French restaurant. The kind of woman that worried not about appearances or waistlines or fitting into a specific box. The kind of woman who chattered like a schoolgirl, her points of conversation spiraling around in circles like a butterfly flitting from one aromatic blossom to the next. The kind of woman who painted gardens and springtime.

She was the kind of woman who felt passionately and wasn't afraid to let everyone around her know.

I was a La Salade de Poulet sort of woman, myself. The sort of woman who ran a wearisome three miles on a treadmill daily and wore her hair up, even on the weekends. The sort of woman who knew what she wanted and was direct about it, and if I ever had the inclination to emote about every colorful object in sight, I was sure that I would keep it to myself.

The contrast in our characters made for a laborious afternoon as Blanche shared whimsical bits of her life from her recent breakup with her girlfriend to the ups and downs of her art career to the promising interest from an art gallery that had landed her in London for a brief spell. If I'd been interested in playing her, I would have hung on every word she shared, collecting details to spin into a game.

As it was, I was only interested in Edward Fasbender, and it was taking a lifetime to arrive at the information I hoped to glean from her.

But I was patient. I'd learned long ago that extricating knowledge from an unsuspecting individual came easiest if the individual felt comfortable and relaxed. Listened to.

So I listened as we dined, calmly waiting for my opportunity.

"Then when the Camden exhibition fell through," Blanche said eventually, dropping her fork and pushing her mostly clean waffle plate away, "I had to decide if I wanted to stay in the UK or come back home, and coming back home seemed like such a dreadful fail, and I couldn't bear for Darcy to say I told you so, even though we'd been broken up for months by then, so I applied for any job posting I was even close to qualified for. Accelecom was the first place that offered something with a decent salary." She propped one elbow on the table, rested her chin on her palm, and wrinkled her brow. "I have to say, I'm surprised that Fasbender remembered me, let alone my last name. I didn't interact with him all that often."

I wasn't surprised. Edward seemed like the kind of man who cataloged everything, a fact I'd do well to remember.

Right now, I wasn't remembering much of anything because here was the opening I'd been waiting for. "What else can you tell me about him?"

"About Fasbender? Hmm. I don't know what's relevant."

"Anything. Everything," I encouraged.

She considered for a moment. "He's a brilliant businessman. Built the whole company on his own, really. I think he excelled because he was a visionary. He's good at determining trends, and he successfully predicted the scope media would take clear back in the early days of the internet."

"Yes, yes." This was all stuff I'd already discovered on my own. "But what kind of *man* is he?"

Blanche fretted, as though she were afraid to be unhelpful. "Dedicated. Innovative. Ambitious. Hot—obviously." She gave a crooked grin.

Very hot. Disturbingly hot.

I fidgeted in my seat, as though movement alone could jostle out thoughts of how wickedly attractive the man was.

"He's extremely wealthy, as I'm sure you know," Blanche went on. "Brilliant. Methodical. A perfectionist."

I tried not to groan. She'd babbled on all afternoon, and now I got little more than one-word answers. Not very helpful in building a character case against him.

I was going to have to spoon-feed her. "What's his personal life like?"

"Well. He doesn't have much of one, I don't think. He's married to his work. I have a hard time picturing him with any sort of family, though he does have one. Or *had* one. He's divorced and his two kids, a son and a daughter, are both grown. Oh, he has a sister too—Camilla. They seem to be really close. She works for the company as well."

I sat forward eagerly. "*Close...*how? *Close* like there's something funny going on?"

"Close like he took care of her after their parents died. After he was out of foster care himself, that is."

"I didn't realize he was orphaned." It was a lie, obviously, because I had known, but I didn't want to seem like

I'd been studying him. Or stalking him.

"Yep, an orphan," Blanche said, grimly.

I paused, as though I was letting it sink in, and in that pause, it *did* sink in. Before it had been words on a paper. Now, it pressed heavy on my insides. There was something especially tragic about being left alone in the world, I supposed, and to be so alone that society was the only willing caretaker...

Not that I cared about people's tragedies in the way most others did. For me, these details were useful rather than sad. A man who'd been orphaned would have certain characteristics that would be easy to manipulate. He would possibly be afraid of rejection, afraid of attachment. Afraid of ever being weak.

There was potential there.

But there was also that pressing inside me, pressing like too much bread in my stomach. Like I'd swallowed something too hard and thick and it wouldn't settle in me. This wasn't the kind of way I wanted to fuck with the man. It wasn't the right kind of pain.

Blanche recovered quickly from her morose. "That's what makes him so incredible, though. That's what I mean when I say he became successful all on his own. While raising his sister plus getting married and having children so young... He was only twenty when Hagan was born. He's just in his forties, and both those kids must be in their early twenties now. Genevieve was starting university when I was there. I met her once, at a company event right before the semester started. Real pretty girl. Serious. Smart too. Both she and her brother planned to follow in the family business, though I had the feeling that Edward would prefer his daughter just got married."

"Why's that?"

She paused. "I don't want to go so far as to say that he's a misogynist... Traditionalist is maybe a better term."

I perked at the new potential. "Do you think that his traditional values have hurt him in any way? Maybe they're what led to his divorce?"

"I don't think so. I mean, I wasn't around when he'd been married, but, from what people said, it was quite a shock when Marion left him for another man. Everyone thought they'd be together forever. Edward had apparently doted on her like she was the center of the universe. My ex-coworker, Kelly—she's worked for Accelecom since the beginning—she said he was completely devastated when she left."

"Doted? I can't imagine that man doting on anything." And why, when I tried, did that heavy feeling in my stomach dissolve into something sharper, more acute? Something akin to jealousy?

"Me either. But Kelly said he got even more serious and even more driven after that, and she swears it was because of heartbreak. Anyway, if Marion Fasbender thought her first husband was too traditionalist, she sure didn't choose anything different with her second husband. This new guy's a Catholic Spaniard who seems to think women should be kept barefoot and pregnant. Again, this is all from Kelly." She smiled guiltily. "And the internet. I've done my fair share of curious online snooping. I don't know much about any of that personally."

Information I could gather from a Google search wasn't helpful. I hadn't looked up his ex-wife yet but I certainly could, all on my own.

I groaned audibly. "This isn't enough. I need juicier

info."

"*Juicier* info?"

"More sensational. Has he had any scandals? Made any ethically harmful business decisions? Ever murdered anyone?"

The questions hung in the air unanswered for several seconds while Blanche's expression grew wary.

Perhaps I'd been a bit jarring. "Of course he hasn't murdered anyone. Just kidding. But, also, not really. If he has skeletons, I'd really like to know. Even if it's just water-cooler gossip."

She stared at me cautiously. "You really dig deep with potential clients, don't you?"

I sighed inwardly. She needed more from me, needed a clearer motivation, and I'd been lazy about giving it.

I had to up my game.

"All right, honesty here. This has to be just between you and me, though, okay? Edward isn't just a potential client." I leaned in like I was telling a secret. "He asked me to…to go out with him."

I could feel it was the correct angle the minute I turned into it. The air loosened around us as Blanche visibly relaxed. It was always best to play the truth, or as close to it as possible. I should have gone this route from the beginning.

"Oh!" Understanding dawned across her face. "Ohhhhhh."

Her renewed interest spurred me on, the words now flowing easily. "And since he's a rival of my father's, it becomes really tricky. I have to question his motives. Is he really interested? Or is he trying to get close to my father?

I can't just go out with him without truly considering who he is as a person. My dad would kill me if I said yes, which is why I should just say no, but…" I lifted my eyes to appear as though I was staring dreamily in the distance.

Blanche picked up where I'd left off. "But how can you say no to that man? He's got something about him."

"I'll say." My skin tingled thinking about him. Thinking about his penetrating gaze and his plump lips and how it would feel to have both his gaze and his lips doting on me.

I blinked away the insane notion. Doting wasn't what I wanted from Edward. I wanted to see him on his knees, yes, but not adoringly. I wanted to see him writhing.

And I was so close to finding out something useful. Something that might give me what I wanted.

I narrowed in on the prize. "So you can see why I need to know everything I can about him, right? If he has something to be ashamed of…like, if he's really a misogynistic asshole, then I should know and just say no now."

Blanche shook her head cautiously, as though she were afraid she'd give a wrong answer. "Like I said, I'm not sure he really is an asshole, not like that. I didn't exactly see evidence that he was anti-female. He had plenty of women in powerful positions in the company. And he gave Camilla a job, so that doesn't make sense, does it? And I don't know anything that might be considered scandalous. Except…" She bit at her lip hesitantly. "There is one thing I've heard… It's not gospel, but maybe it's a thing?"

"What? Tell me." I was greedy for whatever secrets lay on her tongue.

"Okay, um. Right. Okay, there were rumors he was into…" She glanced around, as if Edward might have returned and was eavesdropping on our conversation.

Satisfied w ith h er s urroundings, s he l eaned i n and whispered. "I heard he was into something kinky."

"What kind of kinky?" I wasn't as quiet as Blanche had been.

Her cheeks flushed red. "Something with sex."

I managed not to roll my eyes. "Yes, but what kind of sex kinky? Is he into bondage? Rape play? Golden showers? Cuckolding? Erotic humiliation? Is he a masochist? A crossdresser? A pedophile?"

Edward's own words replayed in my mind. *I'm not an easy man to please in the bedroom.*

Was he a dominant? A sadist?

I shivered at the possibility.

"I don't...I don't know." Blanche's eyes glossed over, overwhelmed. "That's a lot of options, and I don't know anything about most of what you said."

"What *do* you know, Blanche?"

"Well, I know what a pedophile is. And bondage. And cross-dressing."

"I mean about *Edward*." I'd lost my patience. "What do you know about sex and Edward?"

"Oh, right. Just this rumor I heard through the grapevine that someone had seen him at a sex club. On more than one occasion."

Now we were getting somewhere. "Any idea what the name of the club was?"

"I'm afraid not." Her shoulders sank dejectedly. "I'm sorry I'm not more helpful."

"No, you're good. This is good." It was *something,*

anyway. A lead. Something I could potentially work with. Something I could potentially hang over his head.

At least, that was the reason I was giving myself for the nature of my interest.

"Any idea how long he's going to be in the States?" I asked, suddenly worried about how much time I had to find out more.

"Not exactly. When you asked about him on Friday, I did email Kelly and ask why he was here, though. Out of my own curiosity. It appears he's been meeting with Visio-ware—have you heard of them?"

I nodded. Technically, they were another media competitor of my father's. Small potatoes. Probably not even on my father's radar. "What's he want with them?"

"I think he's trying to negotiate a merger. I'm not sure if you're aware, but Accelecom has been trying to enter the U.S. market for quite some time. I think Edward would do almost anything to make it happen."

Like try to marry his rival's daughter.

Something seemed to click in Blanche's head. "Oh, maybe that's why he wants to date you!" As soon as she'd said it, she realized what she said might have been offensive. "I mean, that's *not* why he wants to date you. Look at you! Who wouldn't want to date you? You're perfect." Her face went red again. "I mean, I'm sure he's really interested in you. But I see why you might be worried."

I smiled faintly. Edward had already laid out his real interest in me, of course, so there was no reason to be offended.

But I did like thinking he was attracted to me as well. He'd said as much, so it was easy to think.

But also confusing because then why didn't he want to sleep with me? Why didn't he think to even find out if I was interested in the same kink he was interested in? Was he not really attracted to me? Was he already so sure I couldn't be right for it? Right for *him?*

"Anyway," Blanche interrupted my thoughts. "I don't know how the negotiation is going, but I do know he'll be here for the rest of the month."

"Oh?"

"He's hosting this year's International Media Innovators' Banquet on July twelfth. Kelly mentioned that as well. Is that useful?"

"You know what, Blanche? I think it is." In more ways than one. At the very least, it meant I had three more weeks.

And with this settling in the conversation, I knew where we had to head next, the part that I usually relished most about these types of encounters. The part where I acknowledged the reason she'd met with me in the first place, to discuss her art.

After all the info she'd given, after all the time she'd invested in this afternoon, being let down would be particularly hard on her. Particularly delicious for me.

Delicious and slippery, just like you.

My eye twitched remembering Edward's parting remark.

It was because I hated him being right, because I hated him seeing me so clearly that I changed course. "I'm sure you're eager to hear about my client, if he wants to purchase your work, and, I'm sorry to say that he's going to pass." I paused just long enough to let the disappointment sink in before snagging it back away. "But! I'm so certain the pieces you've completed are right for the sorts of projects I work on that I'm willing to buy the two you brought into my office as well as the four others you sent via email. Just tell me the amount, and I'll write a check tomorrow."

I'd maybe even actually look for a place to display what I bought.

Not the painting with the garden swing, though. No, that one would be burned as soon as I had my hands on it.

I wouldn't tell her that. "So what do you think?"

If I weren't so distracted, I might have discovered something counter to my usual M.O. I might have discovered it was just as satisfying to put a smile on someone's face as it was to take it away. Might have discovered it was just as delicious to give as it was to take. To build dreams as it was to tear them apart.

But Blanche's tears of elation were background noise to the tune buzzing at the forefront of my mind—a driving melody of fascination. A hum of intrigue I hadn't felt in years that had nothing to do with her, and everything to do with the man we'd spent the last half hour talking about.

10

I didn't usually have to find the game that belonged with the person.

While I didn't experiment in the way Hudson did, his methods had informed the way I played. Schemes presented themselves by the nature of the characters we came across. Like science, the schemes began with a question, not a subject. Here's a pair of newlyweds—would they throw away love for the right distraction?

Here's a man who desperately wants recognition—what would he give to receive it?

Here's a woman recovering from an obsessive personality disorder—what would it take to make her relapse?

The experiments were never conducted out of spite. I'd never had to look for the question hidden in a subject's past.

Which was what made Edward Fasbender a different animal. There wasn't an obvious game about him. There was only my resentment. Only my malice. Only my complete dedication to throwing him off balance the way he'd thrown me.

And so I had to dig to find the question. I had to search to find the game.

While lunch with Blanche Martin hadn't been entirely productive, she had given me several leads, and I spent the next few weeks following them, splitting my attention along various paths, hoping that at least one would take me to a scenario that posed an evident ploy.

The easiest trail was the International Media Innovators' Banquet, but it was the one I hated using most for a number of reasons. First, it wasn't a promising lead. Edward was a host, and that meant he'd be present for the banquet, but what would be scandalous about that? What game was there to play there?

Second, it was a lead that would require my presence. I'd found no potential drama through my research of the event. The attendees to be honored were not remarkable beyond the works that had precipitated the invitation. There was a question of why Edward would choose to be involved in such a benevolent affair, but the answer seemed glaring—he was likely sincerely interested in innovations in a field he loved. For me to discover anything more about the event, I'd have to attend in person.

That led to the third reason I was reluctant to pursue this avenue—I'd have to find a way to get invited. It wasn't really a big dilemma, considering my father was also in the media world, and I was sure he could get me there if I wanted, or connect me with the person who could.

That meant that I'd have to involve my father, which was the fourth reason this was not a good plan.

It was the final reason that gave me the most pause—

attending the event would mean seeing Edward. It would mean being in his world, on his turf. He was always formidable, always a man who could knock me off my feet, always a man who stole the breath right from my lungs, and if I chose to walk into *his* event, I'd be going in more vulnerable than ever.

Strangely, the prospect of seeing Edward again was also the reason I didn't cross the banquet off my list entirely. There was no denying I was drawn to him. Or drawn to the power he held over me, anyway. I wanted to dissect it. I wanted to open it up and tear it apart and analyze the whys and hows of his control.

Maybe Hudson had made me into a scientist after all.

The other leads were more vague but also held the most potential. His relationship with women and his sister, Camilla. The death of his parents. His divorce. His sex habits.

All but the last required straightforward investigation. It took time, yes, lots of time, and I was thankful that I only had the one client and no current games in the works so I could devote my energy to the project. It was a task that I would normally find monotonous—there was a reason I'd stayed with Hudson's method of choosing subjects rather than employing this new tactic.

Surprisingly, though, I found researching Edward compelling. I realized fairly quickly that he was an onion. Every detail that I discovered, each layer that I peeled away from the story behind the man led to another equally complex and fascinated layer, none of them ever providing any answers, just more questions. One question in particular came up over and over, at each new finding—why? Why did he do what he did? Why, why, why?

It appeared he was indeed close to his sister, who he'd taken custody of after he'd aged out of the foster care system himself, but then he'd also taken care of her more recently, when her husband had died leaving her a pregnant widow. She'd moved in with her brother then, and, as far as I could tell, she and her toddler son still lived with him. Why? Why not set her up in her own place? He had enough money for that.

His marriage brought a similar question. His ex-wife Marion had indeed left him for another man, but despite the fact, even though the courts removed any obligation of alimony, he'd given her a settlement of an undisclosed amount as part of the divorce proceedings. Why? Did she have something over him? Was there more to the story? Was he just...nice? That certainly didn't lend credence to the idea that he might despise women.

His parents' deaths were also intriguing, his father's life having ended in suicide when Edward was only thirteen. Why? What would drive a man—a parent of two—to kill himself?

This particular why, however, was one I was able to dismiss after further digging. The same year, Edward's mother had a battle with cancer. His father sold his business, perhaps to focus on his wife's health, but ended up losing her. With his company and his childhood sweetheart gone, he must have seen little reason to keep on living.

That had to do damage to a kid—losing both parents in such a short timeframe, one of them having left by choice. There were definitely wounds there to exploit, but I couldn't see the best ways to use them.

Rather, I didn't want to see them. That begged its own question of why, one I hadn't tried to answer.

Discovering about his sexual proclivities was the trickiest lead to follow. I couldn't just use Google to find what I wanted to know, though I tried in every peripheral way I could imagine. I looked for sex clubs in London that were near his home and near his office. Looked for connections between him and the owners of more prestigious clubs. I found lots of names, lots of possibilities, but nothing definitive.

Once I discovered how long Edward had been in the States—three months already—I started searching for a club he might be visiting locally. Surely he'd be seeking out entertainment while in New York. But there were too many in the city and, short of hiring a detective to follow him, no way to tell if he'd visited any of them.

I put up feelers where I could, joined sex forums, and made several different profiles hoping to bait him out or attract someone who might tell me where to find a man who fit his description. Without knowing what he was into specifically, though, it was hard to actually describe him.

I looked very closely at Marion, his wife, inspected her pictures for bruises, searched for reports of domestic abuse, hunted for gossip about the reasons for her affair. Everything seemed to show they'd had a model marriage, even after an apparent shotgun wedding. If Edward had practiced kink with his wife, it hadn't been a destructive element to their relationship.

Although, she had left him in the end.

Lots of people got divorced. Lots of spouses cheated. Lots of people got left behind.

Still, I couldn't help asking why.

A week before the banquet, I had nothing, despite the numerous hooks I had out in the ocean. Defeated, I called my father.

"Why do you want to go to that dreary old thing?" he asked. I knew he would. I'd prepared for this.

"Daddy, I want to go for you, of course."

"For *me*?"

I took a deep breath and reminded myself that sticking to as much of the truth as I could was always the safest lie to tell. "Remember that Accelecom guy? The one you said was a devil? Ever since he tried to use me to get close to you, I've been wondering what I could do to turn the tables on him. Then I found out he was hosting this banquet. He's the keynote speaker, even! There's a good chance he's going to talk about some of his own innovative strategies, and, since there's no press allowed, and since Werner Media isn't a participating corporation, I thought, wouldn't it be a great idea to have someone on the inside to hear what he has to say?"

I bit my lip as I waited for his reply.

"Oh, honey, that's not something you need to be concerned about." But he was intrigued, and he proved it, entertaining the idea with his next question. "I do know someone who could probably arrange for you to help with the banquet setup. Maybe you could stick around in the background afterward…"

Within the hour I was officially on the committee overseeing the table decorations. I was still high with the victory when Renee walked in carrying a canvas wrapped in brown paper.

"Is that the art for the master bedroom?" We'd been waiting for a piece to show up for my client's penthouse design.

"Actually, it's another piece from Blanche Martin. She had one more in the collection, it appears."

"Huh." I'd already received the first paintings, and, while I hadn't yet bothered to destroy the garden swing piece, I hadn't opened it either. They were currently all stacked in the corner of my office.

Without prompting, Renee tore off the packaging of the latest canvas, revealing another landscape, still a garden of sorts, but this one was less traditional. The flowers pictured grew wild intermingled with long grass; the only sign of human touch was the carefully pruned cobblestone path that ran through it, disappearing into the distance.

"That's nice," Renee said, then, before I had time to really study it, she turned toward me, blocking my view of the painting behind her. "Also, I have something to tell you."

"All right." I closed my laptop and gave her my full attention, my curiosity piqued from her hesitant tone.

"I'm giving you notice. I'll work through the end of this project, through the end of the summer, but then I'm...I'm..." She stumbled over the next part. "Then I'm going to do something else," she said finally.

"What? Why? Are you unhappy here?" Granted, I wasn't the most generous employer, but I wasn't terrible.

"I'm not exactly unhappy," she said, seemingly careful about her choice of words. "But I'm not exactly happy, either. It's just not fun anymore. It used to be, back in the beginning. I don't know what's changed. Me, probably. Whatever it is, I need to do something different now."

I could tell her what had changed—me. I'd started my business when I still had passion, when I analyzed person-alities in order to design matching decor rather than to find weaknesses to exploit.

It *had* been fun, I remembered now. Where had all that joy gone?

"I'm sorry," Renee said, sincerely. Followed by other words, necessary words, niceties exchanged by both of us before she went back to her desk, leaving me alone.

In a daze, I stared at the painting long after she'd gone, studying the stones that meandered so prominently in the foreground of the wild garden before dissolving into nothing in the background. There weren't any people in the image, but it was clear to me it was a piece about leaving. Someone had walked that path, someone had followed to the only place it led—away.

I had something in common with Blanche Martin after all. She knew, like Edward Fasbender knew, like *I* knew, that eventually everyone leaves.

11

Though the Innovators' Banquet was on Edward's turf, I did have one advantage—I'd come prepared.

I'd planned the conversations I meant to have with him, practicing various reactions in the mirror. I'd dressed provocatively, choosing a red midi dress with cleavage, rather than my usual more conservative attire. I'd worn my hair down, instead of up-knotted.

I'd dressed *for* Edward.

It was counterintuitive, catering to his wishes in order to get the upper hand, but it was all that I had. It was enough to give me a confident air. I walked around the South Salon of the Mandarin Oriental, supervising the set-up, like I belonged there. Like I owned the place. With all the authority of a goddess. The fierceness of a dragon.

Bustling around in heels was always risky, however, no matter how well comported I was, and once again my shoes became my downfall. Literally.

It was my fault for being meticulous. I'd noticed the

water in one of the decorative bouquets was low, and, having no water can available, I'd carried the large glass vase to the restroom outside the salon. After filling it to the appropriate level, I'd set off toward the banquet room in such a hurry that I slipped on the marbled floor, dropping the floral arrangement to the floor with a loud crash.

It was there, with me on my hands and knees, cleaning up broken glass, surrounded by calla lilies and long-stem roses, that Edward found me.

"Shit," I mumbled when I realized he was the owner of the Italian leather shoes standing in front of me. Since it was also the same moment I sliced my palm with a sharp fragment of glass, I was easily able to pretend the cursing had been for the blood dripping from my fresh wound.

"You seem to have trouble with walking," he said, bending down to the ground, where I was firmly pressing two fingers over the bleeding cut. "Let me see it."

"I'm fine," I said with a scowl, pissed off that, after all my attempts at preparation, this was how our encounter would take place.

"Let me see it."

His tone was emphatic and forceful without his voice raising in the least, a tone that said *I do not like repeating myself and you'd best do as I say or else.*

I was more than mildly curious about what that *or else* would entail, but I was also so caught up in his command that I held out my hand immediately, without a second thought.

"This isn't too bad. Probably won't even need a bandage after a minute or two." He traced the cut with a single finger, collecting the droplets along the path.

Mesmerized, I watched as he brought the tip to his

mouth and sucked the blood clean. He seemed to suck the air from the room at the same time because all of a sudden I couldn't breathe.

I still hadn't caught my breath when another, thinner, trail of blood formed on my palm, and this time, without any warning, he brought my palm to his mouth and licked the wound clean.

I felt that lick down low, along the lips of my pussy. Felt it on my buzzing clit, as though his face was buried between my thighs instead of inches from my own.

I peered up, and his cerulean eyes trapped mine, and I wondered if a deer, frozen in a lion's sightline, was as sure that its hunter could hear its thudding heart as I was sure that my hunter could hear mine.

I opened my mouth to say something, I wasn't sure what, but whatever I'd planned, it wasn't what came out. "You grew a beard." I'd only just noticed the new facial hair that clung to his chin and above his lip, in exactly the pattern I'd suggested he adopt.

Had he done that for me? He had to have. There was no other option, and something about that knowledge, knowing that he'd changed something about himself *for me,* made me heady and weak. Manipulative, though the move might be, because surely it was meant to...to do *something* to me. Why else would he do it?

It was every bit as sexy as I'd imagined. Sexier. Before he'd been suave and sophisticated. Now, he was also rugged and dangerous.

He's always been dangerous, I reminded myself, just as he blew a fine mist of air across my cut.

"Ow!" I yanked my hand away, then, the spell now broken, raised up to my feet.

Edward stayed crouched, the lower position doing nothing to steal his power. "Did it sting?" he asked, the corner of his lip curling up in a cruel grin.

"Yes, it stung," I retorted, annoyed. And aroused.

Annoyed at being aroused.

With a huff, I spun back toward the bathroom I'd come from, intending to clean my hand before returning for the mess on the floor.

Also intending to get some space from the man who somehow always managed to steal my wits.

Except, before the door could shut all the way behind me, it swung open again, and Edward strode in after me.

"You're a predator," I said, meeting his eyes in the mirror above the sink. They were like magnets for my own, drawing my gaze toward them and locking them in place at every opportunity.

"Your hand was bleeding. I was being a conscientious host."

I'd meant he was a predator for following me into the women's restroom, but he'd obviously thought I was referring to what he'd done in the hall. With his tongue. On my skin.

Yes, he'd been a predator then too. And I'd been willing prey.

Stupid, willing prey.

I didn't know what to say. I had no words. All that planning, and I was dumbstruck.

So I didn't say anything. I simply turned my focus to my hand and let my hatred seethe silently in his direction.

If he was attuned to it, as he was attuned to everything,

he didn't let on.

Or he liked it. That was a possibility too.

With seemingly no intention to leave, he leaned his hip against the counter and watched as I ran the faucet over my palm, the water mixing with the blood, making it look like my cut was gushing when, in fact, it was nearly stopped, just as he'd suggested it would soon.

His accuracy about this was like salt on, well, on my fresh wound. Like the sting of his breath across my palm.

I shivered, unable to help myself.

And now I wasn't just annoyed, I was pissed. At myself. At him, too, but mostly myself.

I slammed the faucet off with my elbow and reached past him to tear a towel from the dispenser, which I crinkled up and dabbed at my palm. The rough paper scratched and irritated my sensitive skin, turning it an angry red. Turning *me* angry red.

I let out a frustrated groan, then whirled my exasperation on him. "What are you even doing here?"

One of my pre-planned talking points came rushing back at me in the beat that followed. "You're stalking me," I charged. It was supposed to have been an accusation with weight, meant to have been thrown at him when I innocently discovered he was at the same banquet I was attending, and *how dare he*! Much the way it had come across when he'd said it to me at Orsay.

Now, spat out so sourly, it sounded lame and desperate, probably because I was lame and desperate.

Grinning like a cat that had caught the canary, Edward gently took my hand in one of his and pulled the blue paisley square from his front pocket with the other.

"Am I?" he asked, the raw timbre of his voice oddly soothing. "Stalking you?"

"Yes, you are." Rapt, I stared as he patted my palm dry with the handkerchief. I was shaking. Could he see that? Could he see how his touch seared into me? How it boiled? How it burned?

"That's cute that you think that. I'm not, obviously, as this is my event, which, of course, you already know." He wrapped the printed material around my hand, fashioning it into a bandage. "And if your presence here is an attempt to hint that you expect me to court you, I shan't do that either, so get over yourself and accept my offer."

"You're the one who needs to get over yourself. I'm not interested." I jutted my chin out as if to dot the i of my disinterest.

Or to bring my lips closer to his.

He was already so near, his mouth only inches from mine and so tempting. As tempting as it was off limits, because I was certain it was. Even more tempting *because* it was off limits.

I wasn't conscious of leaning in, wasn't aware of the physical movement that brought my face to his. I only knew that there was this thing that I had to have, had to have badly, and that thing was his mouth pressed to mine. That thing was the taste of him on my tongue. That thing was the aching relief of his kiss.

My lips moved slowly against his with a cautious sort of eagerness, coaxing him open with a hint of my tongue. There wasn't a question—my mouth was there, taking whether he gave or not—and yet, it felt like begging. Felt like I was pleading with the very shell of my soul to let me in. To kiss me back. To kiss me well.

He let me work for it, allowing me to suck and rub and beg and plead for a space of several humiliating and tortured seconds.

Then, abruptly, he twisted one arm—my uninjured arm—behind my waist and spun me so my back was pushed into the tiled wall. Pressing his palm against me, just below my neck, he held me firmly in place while he kissed me hard. Kissed me rough. Devoured me, wrenching my arm to the point of pain as he sucked my tongue and swallowed my cries and bit at my lips until I could taste the faint metallic tang of blood under the distinct flavor of Edward Fasbender.

And, God, that flavor was *everything*. His *kiss* was everything.

Everything that I didn't own, didn't possess. Everything outside of me and unknown to me. Every single thing, and it threatened to fill me, threatened to erase the very nothing that I professed and practiced to be with its substance. With its wholeness. With its entirety.

With its everything.

I wanted it and didn't want it all at once. I wriggled my arm behind me, trying to break his hold, but I wasn't sure that, if I managed to get free, I wouldn't just use my hand to clutch him and bring him closer. It was awful and wonderful, I didn't want it to go on, and I hoped it never ended, and if either of those things happened and it destroyed me, then so be it.

The damage was already done. I was already destroyed.

Then, just as suddenly as the assaulting kiss had begun, he broke it off.

"You wouldn't be able to crawl when I was through with you," he said, his face still only an inch away, his palm still crushing against my sternum. "And that would be just one night. You couldn't take a marriage with my demands, and I'm more interested in being married to you than fucking you, so this is off the table." He released me with brutal abruptness, as though he were disgusted by me and my mouth and my body and what he'd done to me and my mouth and my body.

"And so is marriage," I snapped, as if I could have any impact in return.

He chortled. "We'll see."

He was gone before I could deliver any sort of comeback, leaving me mad and turned on and violated and unsatisfied.

And victorious. Because I'd gotten what I'd needed—the beginnings of an idea.

12

Y*ou wouldn't be able to crawl when I was through with you.*

From those words, from the way Edward had wrenched my arm around my back, from the way his eyes had glazed when his breath stung my fresh wound, it seemed safe to assume he was a sadist.

A dominant too, a fact that made my pulse race more than I wanted to admit. I'd never been the submissive in the bedroom. Even when I let a man spank me or rough me up, I always found a way to top from the bottom. The idea of letting someone—letting *Edward*—have true complete control was out of the question, but letting him believe that he had control was a different story all together.

I intended to make that happen.

But first, I had to be sure the plan was genuinely feasible, and to do that, I had to find out the extent he practiced his sadism. That required either seeing him in action or speaking with someone who had. Both options could be dismissed as too difficult to orchestrate, but I was up for the challenge.

And now I had enough information to put out more precise feelers, which gave me a good place to start. Using LadyPrey, one of the profiles I'd set up to do my fishing, I posted in each of the forums I'd joined.

Submissive seeking opportunity to play. Luxurious club environment preferred. No strings. Pain welcome.

Numerous responses arrived, most invitations to private hookups. I deleted all of these. I wanted the clubs. I wanted a place where I could easily talk to a variety of women about their sexual encounters without drawing any attention to myself.

It was a couple of days before I got a reply that was useful, from a profile going by the name FeelslikePAIN. `You want a one-on-one thing or a party situation?`

`LadyPrey: Party situation sounds good. As long as it's a big party.`

`FeelslikePAIN: I have something. But it's a hefty membership fee.`

Hefty membership fee was less a deterrent and more a bonus. Edward would likely attend clubs that employed exclusivity.

`LadyPrey: Money isn't an object.`

`FeelslikePAIN: I'll see what I can do. Watch your email.`

Over the next several days, I checked my LadyPrey Gmail account obsessively. I even set up the emails to forward to my regular account so I'd get the notification on my phone when it came in. For four days, there was nothing. Well, nothing beyond spam advertisements for sex toys and strip shows and reminders from Google to finish setting up my profile. Nothing that I didn't immediately delete.

On Sunday, though, the fifth day, there was something different. The subject line was simple and vague: **Invitation to Join.** A single, bold red word filled the inside of the email: **Open**. The word was underlined, indicating a hyperlink.

"Jesus, fuck," I muttered to myself, my pointer hovering over the link. Was this really what I hoped it was? Or was I going to click and quickly lose my laptop to a nasty virus or hackers?

I was too invested to ignore it. Too eager to even move to another computer, preferably one that wasn't mine. Holding my breath, I clicked.

Instantly, a web page opened up displaying a series of questions, each followed by a space to answer. At the bottom of the page was a button that read Submit for Approval.

1. Are you over the age of 21?
2. Are you a New York native or just visiting?
3. Describe your current relationship status.
4. Who referred you?

I was midway through entering in my answers, taking time to make up the details of my LadyPrey persona as I typed, when a notification from FeelslikePAIN showed up in the bottom corner of my screen.

FeelslikePAIN: Type the following as

```
your answers and nothing else: 1.
Red. 2. Yellow. 3. Green. 4. Black.
```

Ah, clever. If an invitation ended up in the wrong email inbox, someone who hadn't legitimately been referred to the club, the admins would know by how the respondent answered the questions. Good thing I'd been slow with my reply.

I erased everything I'd entered in already and replaced my answers with the answers FeelslikePAIN had provided then hit submit. Next came a screen asking for payment information with no indication of the membership fee. The only method of paying was through anonymous bitcoin, a method I'd used a time or two on the dark web for previous games, which was not reassuring. Sure, *I'd* be anonymous, but that made it just as hard to track *them* down, whoever *they* were, when the whole thing ended up being a scheme to get to my bank account.

```
I sent a message to FeelslikePAIN. This is
requiring a lot of trust on my
part.
```

```
FeelslikePAIN: Good sex always does.
```

There were so many reasons I shouldn't, so many reasonable objections playing through my head. How many times had I secretly mocked people for being so gullible? So naive? I'd always promised to stay vigilantly aware. This scenario asked me to set aside that promise, and that ate at my conscience on a very base level.

But obsession had a way of undermining wise intentions. It suppressed all reason with its monomaniacal agenda.

Stupidly, I authorized payment from my bitcoin account. Before I had time to regret my decision, a new window popped up on my screen loaded with terms and instructions and dates and locations. With a victorious smile, I trained my eyes on the bold red headline:

Welcome to The Open Door.

13

My triumph was quickly overshadowed by the dread of reality. The Open Door was, as FeelslikePAIN had suggested, not an actual club. There was a membership fee, yes, but the weekly Saturday night get-togethers weren't held in one location, but rather was hosted at various private locations, like rotating parties rather than events sponsored by an establishment.

The difference may have been slim in the eyes of most people, but, for me, it was distinct. In less than a week, I was attending a sex party.

I'd never been to a sex party.

That wasn't true, though. I had been to a sex party, for all intents and purposes. More than one. Years ago. I'd gone, but not willingly.

Except that wasn't true either. I'd never said no. I'd never tried to get out of it.

Still, I'd been powerless. I'd vowed never to be in that situation, or any even remotely like it, ever again.

That meant that if I was going to follow through with this ridiculous idea, I had to be extremely prepared. I had to find ways to keep the control in my hands. I had to go on my terms, and no one else's.

Six days was almost not enough time to get ready. The physical items I needed were easy enough to gather—underwear, a stunning but sexy dress that would be easy to move in, temporary hair dye and a mask to keep my anonymity.

It was the mental preparation that was more difficult to undertake. Having never been to these particular parties, how could I know what to expect? Would it be formal and structured? Would it be casual and laid back? Would it be a combination of both? Would there be performances or games or icebreakers? Would everyone already know each other? Would I be the only newbie? Would I be put in the spotlight?

Would it be like the sex parties I'd been at in the past?

God, I hoped not. I prayed not.

I thought about asking FeelslikePAIN for more detailed information, but I didn't want to risk the chance of her—him?—trying to take me under her or his wing. I needed autonomy for this. I needed freedom.

Since there was nothing to do with the unknowns, I had to concentrate on the knowns, the things I had complete control over. By Monday, I'd reread The Open Door's terms and bylines so many times I had them memorized, grateful that there were strict policies enforcing consent such as a restriction on liquor. On Tuesday, I scoped out the building for this week's party. Wednesday, I studied the floor plan and researched the listed owners, a couple who'd earned their wealth in dog food. Thursday I left the office early to purchase a new dress and heels, both of a style that Celia Werner would never wear. I fine-tuned my persona as I spent Friday night weaving temporary brunette highlights into my hair.

Early in the day on Saturday, I ventured out to explore local costume shops for a mask.

The website stated a good many members chose to attend the parties in disguise so, conveniently, I wouldn't have to worry about being the only person wearing one. The mask had to be just right, though. While I knew it was a stretch to worry that Edward would be there that night, if he were, I knew he'd be astute enough to recognize me if I didn't really cover my face. There were many designs that only hid the eyes. Masks meant more for fun than concealment. I wanted less Mardi Gras, more Venetian. Full-face masks weren't any better. While they did the job I wanted, they were uncomfortable and made it hard to breathe. I had a devil of a time finding something in between, and I had to leave several stores empty-handed.

It wasn't until the fourth shop that I found what I was looking for. The mask came down over the nose, but not all the way, leaving plenty of room to breathe comfortably. The eyepiece extended up over the forehead and each side dropped lace along the jowls, almost completely covering my cheeks.

My favorite part, though, was the red and yellow plumes that swept down one entire side of the mask.

"Feathered dragon," the shop owner said behind me as I tried it on in front of a mirror.

"Excuse me?"

"That's the name of the mask. Feathered Dragon."

"I thought dragons had scales, not feathers."

The man shrugged. "Apparently not all of them."

"Huh." It was the right mask, though, the one that felt most like *me*, or who I wanted to believe I was, anyway, and I handed over my money.

That night, I examined myself in the mirror before heading out. My hair was knotted low at my neck in a new style. The red dress I wore had a slit running high up each leg, more provocative than any outfit I'd ever worn. The bodice was pure lace that only barely managed to cover my braless nipples. With the brown highlights and the mask, I looked unrecognizable.

I looked fierce.

I looked formidable.

There was nothing to worry about, nothing that could bring me down. I was ready.

I was a dragon.

14

I took a cab to the party instead of a Lyft. I didn't want any record connecting me to The Open Door. It was bad enough that my IP address had likely been captured during the financial transactions. In hindsight, I should have been more patient and gone to a public computer somewhere, but what was done was done, and considering the type of clientele that was usually associated with these sorts of events, I had to believe my information was private.

Except for the doorman, the lobby was empty when I arrived. I'd waited to come, wanting the party to be in full swing instead of being one of the awkward first guests. As per the website's instructions, I approached the doorman and told him the evening's code word—*exosculation*. In exchange, I was given a key card for the penthouse that would work in any one of the four elevators.

Efficient. The whole process was simple yet organized, and I admired the system as I rode to the top floor, even as I wiped a bead of sweat from underneath my mask. The disguise wasn't necessarily hot or stifling, and I didn't want to say that I was nervous. On edge, perhaps was a more comfortable term. Wary.

Excited?

Yes, that too. But I always felt some level of exhilaration when initiating a new game, and, while I hadn't exactly decided I was playing one with Edward Fasbender, my current course felt close enough to arouse that thrill.

The elevator doors opened into a private foyer where I was immediately greeted by two masked women dressed in couture lingerie and high heels.

"Good evening and welcome," one said, a lanky bombshell with red tresses that could only have come from a bottle. She wrapped her arm through mine and I stiffened as she escorted me to a table manned by another scantily clad woman set up in front of the foyer closet. "Please check your phone and purse here."

"Oh." I hadn't been expecting that, and the idea of leaving my personal items with strangers was unnerving.

Seeming to sense my apprehension, the woman behind the table smiled reassuringly and handed me a polyethylene bag with a self-adhesive tape strip at the top and a black Sharpie. "Your privacy is respected here. Write whatever identifying information you'd like to on the label. I'll seal it in your presence and put it in the safe behind me."

Very efficient.

I let out a slow breath and, after drawing a quick sketch from memory of my mask, I dumped my clutch and my phone into the bag. The attendant sealed it and wrote the number two-hundred-nine in the corner, then, with the Sharpie still in hand, asked, "May I have your wrist?"

Cautiously, I held my hand out toward her. She turned

it over, and wrote the same number on the inside of my wrist.

"Your claim number," she explained before turning to the safe with my sealed items.

Ignoring my tense reaction, the redhead linked her arm through mine once again and led me out of the foyer and down a short hall. "The games are being played in the main room. There's a demonstration currently in the dining room. All other rooms that are unlocked are for play. Baskets with lube and condoms are located throughout the apartment. Please use them liberally."

We turned the corner and the apartment opened into a spacious great room with twenty-foot-high ceilings. *Spacious* was probably not the right word. The place was gigantic, covering what had to be about three thousand square feet, and it was filled with at least a hundred people.

I felt my eyes go wide to take it all in. Adults of all ages were gathered in bunches like any well-attended party. Most of the men were dressed in tuxedos or suits, though a few had begun to lose pieces of clothing to the floor while the furniture was littered with discarded jackets and bowties. The women were more plentiful and more often naked or stripped down to designer underwear, though enough wore cocktail dresses to make me not feel out of place. A sensual, pulsing beat pumped through the sound system, an undercurrent to the buzz of energized conversation and flirting laughter. Pillows were generously strewn across the space, *so many* pillows, and the air smelled of a combination of expensive perfume and sex. All around me, people were kissing and groping and grinding and fucking in groups of two, three, seven, ten, a libidinous carnival of depravity and debauchery.

It was shocking. And stunning.

Breathtaking in its horror and its beauty.

"Have fun."

I barely heard the redhead as she let go of my arm and disappeared somewhere behind me. I was too fascinated with everything in front of me. Having forgotten for the moment my reason for attending, I walked through the crowd, taking in the details of the scene. In the corner, a woman was erotically spanking an older woman draped across her lap. Next to her was a half-naked man sucking off another man dressed in high tails while he also gave a hand job to a man who had a sign around his neck that read "Touch Me." A woman wearing nothing but metallic pasties and a cat mask crawled across the floor toward a man holding a riding crop. A kissing orgy was taking place on a huge pile of pillows in the center of the room while a smaller orgy was all out fornicating on the couch next to them.

As the redhead had said, there were games being played. Nearest the front of the room, a very handsy game of suck and blow was taking place. One person passed a dollar to the person next to them using only his or her mouth. At closer look, it was a hundred. Of course. How could I expect anything less? Further in the room a group was playing naked Twister, and still further, a wicked game of Truth or Dare was underway.

Everywhere there was touching. Everywhere there was sex. It was intensely erotic, and maybe in another lifetime I would have found it arousing. And I *was* aroused, on one level. I felt flushed. My pulse had quickened. My pussy was wet and swollen.

But my head wasn't in it. My head was never in it. I enjoyed sex, for the most part, on a purely physical level. My body knew how to respond, how to give good orgasms.

My head, though, always remained detached and separate, safe behind the ice walls I'd built around me. Just like every other emotion, arousal was one I'd grown numb to, even in this environment, with shameless licentiousness surrounding me.

It was like that all those years ago, too. I'd disassociated then as well. I'd had to in order to survive. Was that where the nothing in me really began? Not with Hudson, but in the depravity of that first sex party way back then?

That night had been nothing like this one. This party was celebratory and empowering and consensual where the other had left menacing shadows over my existence. The difference gave me the last burst of confidence I'd needed, and any traces of my initial anxiety melted away.

Still, I clung to the wall as I made my way through the room. I hadn't seemed to attract much attention, as of yet, and I wanted to keep it that way. While many of the people were wearing masks as I was, others had lost the pretense of disguise. It was a surprise to realize how many faces I recognized, some because they were well-known entertainment, sports, and political figures, others because they ran in the same elite circles of the wealthy that I did. A nude woman bent over in the Twister game with a hand on red and a foot on yellow was a reporter for a major news show. The man fingering her was a Broadway director.

Another woman who called herself Miss T wore a mask, but I could swear she had the exact same jawline as Hudson's secretary. Though, to be fair, I saw traces of Hudson in all sorts of things that had nothing to do with him. Not as much these days, but at times.

It wasn't until I saw my father's CEO of children's programming going down on a man in drag that I had the jolting realization that I might *really* know some of the people here. Jesus, what if Hudson himself was in attendance? Or his *parents*? Or *my* parents?

That thought was a reminder of my purpose. I needed to get on with this and get out of here. I stopped gawking at the festivities and concentrated on my task, looking for someone who might have interacted with Edward at one of these things. The good thing was I was pretty sure I'd found exactly the kind of place he might attend. Another good thing was there were plenty of women who seemed to enjoy S&M play. Now to find one that wasn't currently occupied…

After making mental notes of all the possible candidates I'd already come across, I decided to leave the game room and scope out the more private areas of the unit. My parents lived in a more than decent size apartment, but this penthouse was one of the largest I'd seen in the city. More than eight thousand square feet total, if I had to guess. And no rooms were off limits to play. That left a lot still to explore.

I slipped through the chef's kitchen where a sextet was having fun with whipped cream and chocolate sauce and into the dining room. This was where the demonstration was supposed to be taking place, and indeed, something seemed to currently be happening on the table, but there were so many people gathered around, I couldn't see exactly what, at first.

But then, a couple in front of me broke away from the assembly, leaving a small window in the crowd for me to slip through and watch. The demonstrator was an older man with gray hair in a tux with a red jacket, his eyes directed at the woman dressed in a schoolgirl outfit who was on her hands and knees on top of the table next to him. Her skirt was flipped up to expose her cotton white panties.

"Who wants to pull them down?" he asked the onlookers. "Who wants to show us what our innocent girl is hiding underneath?"

The crowd roared enthusiastically, volunteers rushing to be the one he called on.

A memory shot through me, through all of me. Through my head, through my bones, through my veins, turning my blood to ice. *How much to touch her here? How much to be the first?*

A wave of tremors came over me, as though it weren't my body itself shuddering, but as if the ice walls around me were actually bars of a cage, and that cage was being rattled. I could feel a scream building inside me with no place to go. It was trapped, stuck in my throat. As much a prisoner as I was in the presence of those memories.

I couldn't be there anymore. I had to leave. If not the party, at least the demonstration.

Shoving through the bodies, I made my way out to the opposite side of the dining area than I'd come in. This fed me into the family room, a quieter space despite the abundance of guests. I looked around absentmindedly, my eyes scanning past the two men masturbating in the corner and the trio fucking on the sofa and stopped when they came to the woman in a black sparkly wrap dress kneeling at the foot of a man sitting in an armchair.

Then my heart really began to pound.

Not because of the scene I was witnessing—the man stroking the head of the woman at his feet—but because the man was Edward Fasbender.

15

My first instinct was to run. Dash from the room and get the hell out of there before he spotted me.

But my feet wouldn't move. I could barely even breathe, my entire body frozen like a deer in the sightline of a hunter.

The fear of being caught was real and overwhelming. It clouded my head, which was why it took a few seconds to remember I was in disguise. He wouldn't recognize me behind my mask. Relaxing in the realization, my pulse began to slow. Not completely, but to a more reasonable tempo, at least. I could think clearly again. This was what I'd come for, ultimately. Well, I'd come for someone who'd possibly been with Edward and here was a woman who was with him for sure.

Having Edward here too was actually a bonus. Wasn't it?

I decided to believe it was.

Pressing my back against the column of wall behind

me, I took on the role of voyeur, and trained my eyes on the scene. He hadn't noticed me, which gave me even more confidence. My breaths came easier as I studied him. Like most of the men in attendance, he was dressed, but not to the nines as some were. His black suit was tailored, fitting him like it was sewn on, just as the other suits I'd seen him in had been, but this time he wasn't wearing a tie. His white dress shirt was unbuttoned at the collar, and, even though he wore a vest over it, this subtle change in his usual attire gave him a casual look. His facial hair had grown in thicker but still looked impeccably groomed.

He was devastating.

Completely, utterly devastating.

So much for getting my breathing under control. My legs were so weak from looking at him, I wasn't even sure I could have stayed standing without the support of the wall. I was suddenly very aware of the slickness between my legs, of the tight beads of my nipples. The hair on my arms stood in the grove of goosebumps that had sprouted over my skin.

How long had it been since a man had affected me like this?

Years. More than a decade.

With seeming disinterest, he stared at the woman on the floor who was practically humping his leg at this point. His impassivity was a ruse, though, judging by the bulge in his pants. And with a bulge like that, there was no way he was wearing underwear.

Devastating.

"Your desperation is embarrassing, Sasha," he said callously. Or I thought he said, it was hard to tell for sure across the low buzz of the room.

I couldn't make out her response, but whatever it was must have pleased him because he yanked her up to straddle his lap, her back to his chest, and now a new sensation gathered inside me. A covetous heat pressing against my lungs, filling up the cavity between my ribs, restricting the beating of my heart. I wanted to be Sasha. I wanted to sit on his lap. I wanted to be the one who pleased him.

It was a sensation that both pissed me off and turned me on. I seethed underneath my mask, not wanting to watch anymore. Unable to look away.

Edward remained stone-faced as he tangled his fingers in her dark brown hair and tugged sharply, so sharply her head touched his shoulder, exposing the long column of her sepia-toned throat. His nose traced the curve or her neck while his free hand clawed across her decolletage, leaving a trail of scratches in its wake.

I remembered his hand on my throat when he'd kissed me, remembered it so vividly that it felt like it was me that his nails scratched now, and I shivered despite my rising body temperature.

I swore I could feel his fingers as they trailed down over her bosom to find the sash of her wrap. With one pull, the dress fell open, and after Edward rearranged the material to his liking, I could see she was completely bare underneath.

My breasts grew heavy, my nipples tighter mirroring the taut, brown tips on the woman before me. And when Edward brought his hand up again to roughly squeeze her tit, I had to bite my lip to stifle a gasp.

I could *feel* it. Could feel the shot of electricity from my own breast to my pussy as though he were fondling me. Could feel it because I wanted so desperately to be feeling it.

He moved to her other breast, handling it just as brutishly, and, then, when she moaned with pleasure, his eyes lifted and locked with mine.

The air hitched in my chest. Adrenaline coursed through my veins. He'd seen me, was *seeing* me, and still I couldn't look away. His lips curled up in a self-satisfied smile, and for one terrifying second, I was sure the jig was up, certain that he knew who I was.

But of course he didn't. He'd merely realized he had an audience, and the conceited bastard couldn't help gloating about it. He even appeared to gloat about it to Sasha, whispering in her ear before letting go of her hair and helping her tilt her head up to look at me as well. Her grin was almost as cocky as his, though warmer in its fullness. As though she were welcoming the guest of my gaze.

Again, I wanted to flee, but I was incapable, held in place by the weight of my curiosity. I had to know what happened next. I needed to *see* it. I wanted to *feel* it.

Now with an onlooker to entertain, the show progressed quickly. Edward once more said something in Sasha's ear, likely instructing her because immediately she spread her legs wider, proudly displaying bare mocha lips and a hint of pink skin.

Taking her hand with his, he brought her fingers up along her slit, gathering wetness before settling on her swollen clit. Continuing to guide her, they rubbed at her bud in small tight circles. His other hand came back to pull at a steepled nipple, twisting it so cruelly her torso involuntarily tried to buck away.

And mine arched forward.

And all the while, his eyes never left mine. As though I was the woman he was fucking with his fingers. As though it was me he wanted to take to the brink of pleasure. As though he weren't using my desire to destroy me.

I swallowed. My throat felt too moist. My chest rose and fell with rapid, shallow breaths. My hands felt heavy and useless at my sides. My fingers curled into the material of my dress, half needing an anchor and half wanting to pull up my skirt and relieve the ache of my pussy.

I wondered what my eyes showed. My stare was leashed to his and while his eyes showed almost nothing beyond pupils dilated with lust, I was sure mine gave away much more. Could he see the storms brewing inside me from this distance? Could he see I was on the edge, ready to combust with rage and heat and jealousy? Ready to explode with raw lust. I hadn't even actually been touched, and I could feel an orgasm brimming.

Edward lifted Sasha's hand from her clit and, after bending her pinky and thumb into her palm, moved it down to her gleaming wet entrance. He released his grip on her, letting her thrust her three fingers in and out on her own. She was close, as close as I felt, I could tell from the erratic shift of her hips back and forth, rubbing his erection underneath her.

I pressed my own thighs together, trying to temper the building fury between them.

All it took was Edward pinching her clit, and then she was convulsing with waves of pleasure.

His eyes left mine to glance at the woman writhing on his lap, and, with the tether between us cut, I bolted free, taking off in search of somewhere I could be alone, somewhere private. Somewhere away from those piercing, wretched eyes.

The first open door in the hallway led to an empty

bathroom. I slammed the door behind me, having enough sense to lock it before I pulled up my skirt and shoved my hand down my panties. My pussy was hot and drenched. My fingers slid easily against my coated clit.

Bracing myself on the sink counter, I rubbed furiously and didn't stop even after the first orgasm ripped through me. I had to get it all out, all of *him* out. Had to get rid of this poison he'd put inside me. My knees buckled as a second wave rolled over me, and still I kept on, rubbing until my skin felt chafed and on fire. Rubbing, rubbing, rubbing until I was shaking and tears were rolling down my cheeks, until I'd let out a loud guttural cry of relief.

Until I'd yanked the last of my pleasure from my cunt and was free of that devil and the dark, agonizing curse of desire.

16

I was sweating when I'd finished.

I removed my mask and tucked the strays of my hair back into my knot as best as I could. Without my purse, I couldn't fix my makeup. Luckily most of my face was covered by the disguise, but my mouth was still visible and my once-red lips were now pale and blotchy. I dabbed at them with a tissue then stared at my reflection.

I looked wrecked, and I was.

Some dragon.

After all that, I hadn't even gotten what I'd needed. I'd verifi ed that Edward liked things a little bit kinky, but I'd already guessed that. He was a bit of an exhibitionist, a bit of a dom. A bit brutal. So what? None of that was useful.

I'd learned more about me from the experience than I'd learned about him, and what I'd discovered wasn't something I wanted to know—the man had power over me. Real, ruinous power.

Fuck him for that. *Fuck him.*

The handle of the door jiggled next to me, followed by a knock when it didn't open. "There are bedrooms for what you're doing," a female voice called.

Ah, shit. She'd probably heard me.

Whatever. This was a sex party, after all. I couldn't possibly have been the only woman to get herself off in here tonight.

"Just a minute," I called out tersely. With a sigh, I donned my mask and opened the door.

"Oh, it's you," Sasha said when I walked out.

Of all the people who could have been waiting for the bathroom, it had to be her.

She'd put her dress back together, and she looked unfairly more put together than I felt, and she'd been the one who'd actually had an orgasm.

Well, I'd had one now too. Three, actually. Perhaps the unbalance was warranted.

"I bet you needed that," she said with a knowing smile. Friendly. As though we weren't strangers, as though we were close now that she'd come in front of me.

No. We were *not* friends. The only reason she wasn't the enemy was because that title was already taken by her lover.

Thinking of Edward again and the way he'd touched her made my stomach twist. It was definitely time to leave.

Without saying anything, I stepped out of her way so she could get past, but just as she was about to shut the door behind me, I reconsidered. "Sasha," I called to her. I waited until she turned around. "That is your name, isn't it?"

"Yeah." She didn't ask how I knew, possibly realizing

I'd overheard it earlier.

"That guy you were with..." I paused, glancing around to be sure he wasn't lurking nearby while trying to decide how to frame my question. "Do you know what he's into?"

"Trying to steal my ride home, are you?" But the smile remained, suggesting she was teasing. "Or are you warning me off? Because if you are, I already know what I'm getting into. I've gone home with him before."

My jaw clenched, and I had a strong urge to claw her eyes out.

At the same time, the back of my neck tingled with excitement. Maybe this night wasn't a waste after all.

I stepped toward her, closing the small gap between us. "What's he *like*? Is he...?"

"Is he *good*?"

That wasn't exactly the word I'd been looking for, but I nodded for her to go on, hoping she'd give me something worthwhile.

"He's real good, actually. If you can take a beating." She smirked. "Fortunately, I can."

Now as I looked at her I saw the signs I'd missed earlier—the fading bruises on her arms, the red marks at her wrists from some type of bondage.

"He *is* a sadist," I said, more to myself than to Sasha.

"You could say that. Roughest time I've ever had. Best time too. So thanks for the warning, if that's what you were about, but also no thanks because I'm good."

For the first time that evening, I gave my own smile. "Good for you. Enjoy yourself." I turned away before she could say anything else. I didn't need any more from her, and I was eager to get out of there in case Edward came looking after her.

With a satisfied buzz, I headed back to the main foyer. Checking out was as efficient as checking in had been. After producing my wrist for inspection, I was given my items, the bag they'd been contained in still sealed.

One of the hostesses that had greeted me called an elevator for me, and by the time I'd gotten my purse and my phone out, it had arrived. I stepped inside feeling smug. I'd gotten what I'd been after, and, even with the inconvenience of running into the devil himself, I was leaving undiscovered.

Except, before the doors could close, a familiar voice shouted to hold the elevator. A familiar *British* voice.

Fuck!

I did not want to share a ride down to the lobby with him. What if he talked to me? What if he expected *me* to talk to *him*? What if I did and he recognized my voice?

Panicked, I hit at the door-closed button, but the hostess stuck her arm in, blocking the doors from shutting, and a few seconds later Edward and Sasha joined me in the elevator.

I huddled in the corner, hoping I'd go unnoticed, even though there were only the three of us in the car. Hoping they'd be too wrapped up in each other to pay attention to me.

It was a hope I didn't send into the universe with much energy, though, since I simultaneously wanted him to never look at her again.

Unsurprisingly, his eyes fell on me. I could feel them even with my head turned away.

"Look, Sasha. It's our new friend. I wonder if she enjoyed your performance as much as you did." He was as patronizing with his tone as he ever was. I'd learned that tonight, too, I supposed. That he was this way with everyone. That it wasn't a demeanor he reserved explicitly for me.

I hugged my arms around myself. Maybe I could play shy. Or rude. I didn't care what his impression of me was as long as he didn't know it was indeed me.

Sasha draped her arm over his shoulder possessively. "Oh, she enjoyed it. I heard her in the bathroom rubbing one out."

My entire body flushed with equal measures embarrassment and anger. I had wanted that to belong only to me. It was bad enough that Sasha had witnessed it. I had definitely not wanted Edward to find out. Even with him not knowing who I was behind my mask, it gave him too much of a win. I hated that he had that power over me. It made me sick that he knew it too.

"That's a lovely shade of red your skin turns, little bird. That has quite an effect on me. It's going to be a miserable ride to my hotel, thanks to that."

My head shot in his direction, and I couldn't help but glance at the effect he referred to. He was visibly hard again. This close, I could see the outline of his cock through his slacks. It was big and brutal, just like he was.

My pussy throbbed in response, that traitor, and without thinking, I lashed out in response. "Your misery is *not* my problem, you asshole."

Fuck, I thought too late. *Fuck, fuck, fuck!*

Did he recognize my voice? Could he tell it was me? He stared at me, his eyes narrowing, and I held my breath, waiting for him to call me out.

"Of course it's not your problem," he said, eventual-ly. Harshly. "Considering the kind of party you just left, I thought you'd find the information stimulating. It was certainly stimulating for me to tell you. Pardon me for my erroneous assumption."

My heart thudded wildly against my rib cage, and it took almost all my restraint not to throw a punch. It took just as much strength not to fall down at his knees and beg for him to give me his kiss, his hands, his cock. To take out his misery on me.

How could every word out of his mouth make me hate him more while also turning every cell in my body into a blazing cell of want?

"Don't worry about this," Sasha said, palming his thick bulge. "I'll give you what you need."

I hated her for that, too. Perhaps she was my enemy as well.

He didn't say anything, didn't give Sasha any morsel of his attention, his stare staying planted on me. It should have been unnerving, and it was, but it was also something else. Something warm and electric. Something I couldn't identify.

The elevator doors opened in the lobby, and I rushed out ahead of them, dying to get away from them. Stupid, it turned out, since I had to wait while the doorman hailed a cab. Edward already had a car waiting outside.

I refused to look directly at either of them, but I also couldn't help watching them out of the corner of my eye. He opened the back door of the sedan and let Sasha slide in first. Then, before he got in himself, Edward called to me. "Do you need a ride, little bird?"

I scowled in response.

But just because I had no control where he was concerned, because he made me reckless and insane, I corrected him. "I'm a dragon, not a bird." At least I'd remembered to change my voice this time, making it lower than my usual pitch.

He paused, considering, those wicked eyes boring into me. "No. You might think you're a dragon, but you're definitely a bird."

I shot daggers after him long after his car had pulled away from the curb. He stirred so much inside me, feelings that had been dormant for so long.

They were the kind of emotions that could be burned as fuel, emotions with energy—hatred, vindictiveness, disgust. Spite.

Lust, too, but even that would be beneficial.

I intended to use them all, and now that I had what I needed, there was nothing he could do to stop me.

The game was on.

17

Most games didn't take much time to prepare. A few days. A week at the most.

This scheme with Edward was different, though. It was going to take a level of dedication I hadn't pursued before. I would need bandwidth to commit. My entire life had to be cleared.

Conveniently, I only had the one client, and his project would be wrapped up by the end of summer. Renee would be gone by then too. Her resignation, it seemed, had turned out to be fortuitous. All the dominoes were lining up, and I was motivated by the desire to get to the day I'd see them all knocked down.

The one concern I had was Edward's patience. There were five weeks still before August ended. Would he still be in the country then? Would his offer still stand?

Luck, however, continued to be on my side.

A handful of days after my visit to The Open Door, a Thursday on the last day of July, Renee walked into my office carrying a glass vase filled with the most stunning bouquet of flowers.

"These just arrived," she said as she set the arrangement on the corner of my desk. She handed me a small, sealed rectangular envelope with my name scribbled on the front. "Either you're seeing someone you haven't told me about or you have a secret admirer."

I often received flowers. It was the nature of the games I played. So many times the goal was to make them fall for me, and that led to a myriad of romantic declarations.

While I didn't ever tell Renee the entire truth about these liaisons, I usually fed her a story about whatever current relationship I was pursuing. It had made things easier in the beginning, prompted fewer questions. Over time, though, I'd come to enjoy these narratives as much as the reality. They were pretty stories, fairy tales with potential for beautiful happy endings, and I found something sweet in Renee's belief that they were happening to me, even while I was aware of the lie underneath the prose.

The satisfaction wasn't about that lie, though. As much as I loved playing strangers, I never found it gratifying to deceive the few people close to me, Renee being one of them.

No, it was about the hope. The brief glimpse of what was possible, seen through the eyes of my assistant. It was the closest I'd ever get to my own happy ending, and while I'd given up on that dream a long time ago, there was a nostalgic peace in letting the pretense exist, in letting it hang in the air before it again dropped into the bleak nothing that extended before me.

I didn't currently have a story for her, though, and the arrival of the flowers was as much of a surprise to me as it was to her.

I didn't like surprises. I hated being thrown off guard.

I studied the cursive on the envelope, the hasty scrawl of only my first name—Celia. It wasn't handwriting I'd seen before, and I made a mental list of possible senders. My current client had been in that morning, and his current frustration with a hiccup in his installation didn't lend to sending flowers. A former client seemed unlikely. Blanche, perhaps.

Edward?

Sentiment wasn't his style. On the other hand, the floral arrangement was familiar.

Renee read my hesitation as a sign. "I'll give you your privacy," she said politely, closing the door behind her as she left.

I barely looked up at her departure, and I was already smiling when I tore open the envelope to read the card inside.

I head back to London tomorrow. My offer stands.

– Edward

"What happened to not courting me?" I asked the air.

As if in answer to my question, I found a postscript on the back.

P.S. The flowers are for your secretary.

I laughed out loud. Bullshit they were for my secretary. The bouquet was a near duplicate of the arrangement I'd dropped at the International Media Innovators' Banquet. It was definitely meant for me. He'd picked it out *for me*.

And the message had been handwritten instead of

typed like when ordered online. If the handwriting was his, and I believed it was, it meant he'd seen to the transaction personally.

"London, huh?" Again I was talking to an empty room. "I can work with London."

As I sat back in my chair, I halfheartedly gazed at the beautiful display and began to think through altering my plans, all the while pretending that the flutter in my stomach had everything to do with excitement about my scheme and nothing to do with the man it centered around.

Exactly four weeks later, I walked through the empty rooms of my office, turning off lights as I went, looking for anything at all that might have been missed. The space seemed so much bigger now. I'd forgotten how spacious it had been that first night. How weird to realize how filled it had been with a life of nothing.

The nothing made it easy to pack. My apartment had been sorted through over the month. I owned my own condo—well, my father technically owned it, but it had been a gift from my parents when I'd graduated from college. He'd never gotten around to transferring the title, but the point was, there wasn't any need to move anything to storage since no one else would be living there in my place. I'd only had to crate what I couldn't live without. These I labeled and stacked in my living room so they were ready to be shipped when the details of my future life were arranged.

The categorizing of what was essential and what wasn't

had been so simple, I realized, because there was very little I was attached to. My extravagantly designed space was filled with high-end furniture and art, my closets overflowing with expensive clothes, and none of it mattered to me in the least. There had been only one item I'd deliberated over, or, one set of items, rather—the diaries I'd kept over the years documenting the details of the games. On the one hand, they represented everything I'd been living for, and I wanted them with me for that. They were comforting. Familiar.

On the other hand, I didn't want them to be found. By anyone, but especially Edward. That made them safer packed up as well, but instead of stacking them by the door for shipment, I hid the crate in the guest room closet.

The office had been even easier to deconstruct. Renee had taken the task on herself, hiring laborers when needed, and even when the client design was finished ahead of schedule, the office space was ready to be emptied the following day.

All that was left was to hand over the keys.

"Where the heck is everything?" Scott Matthews' voice boomed across the vacant rooms.

I retreated from the kitchen and walked out to greet him. "Gone, obviously." There had been snark in my comment, and I chided myself silently. I had meant for this to go peacefully, and this wasn't a good start.

Putting on a smile and a cheerier tone, I tried again. "I'm closing up shop for awhile. Leaving town."

He eyed me warily. "And I'm supposed to hold this until you return?"

"No." I stepped toward him, my hand held out toward his. "I'm giving you my key. The space is yours."

I had debated about keeping it, about holding on to it for whenever I came back, but not only did I have no idea when that would be, I also needed to look like I was truly shutting down my life in New York. I'd miss the place, of course I would. But it was greenery from a season that had passed, and there wasn't any good in clutching to the dead remains. If and when I returned, it would be a new season, and there would be a new space.

Scott was still skeptical, and, after everything I'd put him through, who could blame him? "What game are you playing now?" he asked, not taking the key.

I chuckled at his coincidental choice of terminology. I'd never referred to these schemes as games to any of the people I'd played. "No game. Well, not with you, anyway. I'm simply returning what I no longer need."

"Let me guess. You want something else from me. What is it? Money? Another space? Whatever it is, I'm not—"

"Scott, I don't want anything from you. Take the damn key."

He paused a moment longer before snatching the key from my hand. Once it was safely in his pocket, he visibly relaxed. "So," he said, strolling past me to stare out the windows. "You're leaving town? For good?"

I pivoted so I was addressing his back. "For good for now. Unless something changes."

"I guess I got used to you being in my life. I kind of thought I was stuck with you. Like, you'd be a permanent fixture." When he turned around, his eyes were filled with something I hadn't seen in them since the first night we'd met. He took a slow step toward me. "What do you say about visiting that kitchen again? For old times' sake."

I pressed my fingers at the inside of my nose, trying to contain the explosion threatening inside. "Jesus Christ, Scott. I've blackmailed you for seven years, and you still want to fuck me? What is wrong with you?" He deserved what I'd done to him. If I'd ever had any doubts, I didn't now.

He shrugged with one shoulder. "What can I say? You blackmailing me has always been kind of hot."

I rolled my eyes. "You're sick."

But I couldn't really judge him. The games that got me off were just as sick.

He grew serious, anger brewing in his eyes. "Okay, I'll take that as a no. If there's nothing else you need, I'd best be leaving."

His resentment toward me was earned, and it gave me an idea. "Wait. There is something else you could do for me."

"Aw, fuck. I knew it. I knew you'd never just walk away from this."

"No, no. Not like that. It's nothing that will cost you."

He raised a cautious brow and cocked his head, waiting for me to go on.

With my spine straight, I pushed my chin forward. "I want you to slap me."

He laughed. "You've got to be kidding me."

"I'm completely serious." And I was. I'd been punched once, by Hudson's wife when she was still his girlfriend. She'd broken my nose, and it had hurt like hell.

But that was the funny thing about pain—even though I could remember in my head that it had been an excruciating experience, I couldn't remember it in my body. Could I take it on command? Would it make a difference knowing it was coming?

Scott shook his head vehemently. "Nope. No way. I'm not falling for this, this...whatever this is. You're recording this, aren't you? I knew you were setting me up." He scanned the ceiling, searching for a hidden camera.

"I'm not setting you up, you asshole. I'm asking you for a favor." I was annoyed, but not so annoyed that I wanted to give up on my request. My annoyance actually cemented the idea in my head. "Here. Give me your phone." I held my hand out. "And unlock it."

He was reluctant, but he was also curious.

His curiosity won out, and a second later he was giving over his unlocked phone.

I quickly found his camera app and, after setting it to selfie mode, I hit the record button. "I, Celia Werner, am asking Scott Matthews to smack me across the face." I held my arm out to the side so the camera would capture my profile. "There. How could I possibly use this against you now? Just do it, will you? I know you want to. You've wanted to for years. I'll even record it, and you can replay it over and over, whenever you think about all the shit I put you through. How close I almost destroyed your—"

I was cut off by the sharp sting of his palm across my skin. My neck was thrown to the side with the impact, my breath caught by the surprise.

"Fuuuuucccck," I cursed, bringing my hand up to caress the burning skin. "That really hurt."

"You asked me to do it," Scott said defensively. Yet, his eyes were hooded and hungry, and I was sure if I'd asked him to do it again, he would have without hesitation.

"I did. I'm not denying that. It still hurt." With my

thumb, I stopped the recording and passed his phone back to him. "You can go now."

He nodded and turned to leave, then spun back toward me. "Actually, *you* can leave now. This isn't your space anymore. Remember?"

Now he had a backbone. Hitting me had given him confidence, that shithead.

There were a thousand ways I could bring him down. They ran through my head, tempting me with the ease of which they could be executed.

But Scott Matthews was small fish. I was angling in bigger waters now.

With a smirk that hurt my inflamed skin more than I wanted to admit, I walked up to him, until I was in his face. "Be careful about getting cocky. I still have that recording from that first night. I still could show your wife. You're right that this isn't my space anymore—that was *my* choice, not yours."

I stepped back. "But I'll leave now. I'm done here."

I was done, and I was leaving with a boost of confidence as well. I'd learned what I'd hoped to learn—pain sucked, but it was endurable. Especially when there was a reward attached, and the reward was worth it.

And, where Edward Fasbender was concerned, the reward would definitely be worth it.

18

"Was the flight good? Where are you going now? Have you checked into a hotel?"

I stifled a groan and tried to respond in a reasonable tone. "Mom, stop with all the questions, will you?"

Maybe I should have been happy she was so interested, but I'd hardly slept on the red-eye from New York to London, and I needed the little energy I had to calm the nerves that were growing increasingly frayed the closer my cab got to my destination.

"Celia, really, what do you expect? You tell us you've fallen for a client and you're moving to London immediately. You haven't even told us his name! We're your parents! It's our job to ask these questions."

Funny how she always talked in the plural, as if my father cared about the details of my existence.

With a sigh, I stared out the window. It was fall already in London while the New York I'd left had been clinging desperately to summer with its record heatwave and thick humidity index. It was fitting—new colors for a new life. I was ready.

I just wasn't ready to tell my mother.

"You're right," I said, an attempt to make peace. "I haven't been very forthcoming."

"You've been downright secretive," she said, unable to let go of her exasperation just yet. "This isn't like you!"

Well, that wasn't true. It was exactly like me. I was always secretive. I was just usually better about hiding the secrets from my parents.

I shouldn't have mentioned there was a guy. I should have told them I was leaving for a client and left it at that. This was one time where sticking close to the truth had backfired. Hindsight really was twenty-twenty.

I tried again to calm her. "I know, Mom. I said you were right. And I promise I'll tell you more, just not yet, okay? This guy—he's a client, and I'm not sure where any of this is going, and—"

"Oh, God, Ceeley," she cut me off, aghast. "Are you surprising this guy?"

Yes?

She lectured on. "You can't just pick up and move to another country without the guy inviting you!"

But I *had* been invited. Technically.

"Mom." I waited for her to take a breath to try to interject again. "Mom, stop. Please. It's not what you think."

"How can you know what I'm thinking when you *haven't told me anything?*"

I laughed quietly. It really was sort of funny how

worked up she was. Funny because, if she knew the whole truth, she'd have real cause to be worked up.

"What's so funny?"

"Nothing. I'm just tired. And, no, I'm not showing up uninvited. I'm designing his offices, after all. And I don't want to say anything more yet because I don't want to ruin it. You can understand that, can't you?"

There was a beat of silence where I could practically hear her wrestling with her need to *know* and her desire to see me happy.

It was her turn to sigh. "You have seemed to be in an awfully good mood ever since you announced this little adventure of yours."

I had been cheerier than usual, I realized now. All the past month, as I was planning and preparing, I'd had a steady buzz of low-key exhilaration. The thrill of this game was more emotion than I'd experienced in years.

It wasn't just The Game, if I was honest. The bursts of feeling had started even before. I could trace them back to that first meeting with Edward when I'd left pissed and indignant and humiliated, not to mention aroused. It was as though he'd awoken a beast that had been hibernating inside me, and now that beast's appetite drove me to take him down.

When I did, would that beast sleep again, returning me to the ice-cold safety of numbness?

I hoped so.

Though, this giddiness wasn't all that terrible of a feeling. When I didn't overthink it.

"So if you're happy, I won't worry so much," my mother said finally.

It was a chance to reassure her, tell her I was indeed happy. But, despite the excitement running through my veins, I couldn't bring myself to say I was *happy*. I didn't know what that felt like anymore. Maybe I never had, and telling her that I was now was too bold of a lie, even for me.

Thankfully, an outburst from my father in the background distracted her. "That's terrible, Warren, and you can tell me all about it as soon as I hang up from talking with our daughter." Her words came out muffled, as though she had pressed the receiver of the home phone into her shoulder. "Okay, I'm back," she said a second later.

"What's Daddy upset about?" I'd rather talk about him than resume our conversation.

"Something at work," she said dismissively, then decided to say more. "He was trying to set up a subsidiary in France, but there's some Fasfender guy who keeps blocking his attempts to expand in Europe."

A tingling ran down my spine. "Do you mean Fasbender?"

"That's it. That guy. He's complained to you, then, too?"

"He has." My stomach twisted into a knot. He was not going to be happy with what I had planned.

But he'd be happy with the final outcome. I knew he would. Maybe he'd even be proud of me. I just had to hope he wouldn't disown me before then.

"This is you, miss. Coming up," the cabbie said from the front seat.

"Mom, I have to go. I'll call you later, okay?" I wished I could leave her with something more reassuring, wished I could tell her I really was happy, wished I could tell my dad I was going to fix his Fasbender problems, but I knew better than to let my hand show early in a game. So, instead, I muttered a quick *I love you* and hung up.

Then I smiled, a real genuine, honest smile, because here I was in front of the Accelecom building. It was finally beginning.

I paid the driver and stepped out of the car onto the sidewalk. The building for the media headquarters was bigger than I'd expected. Even though it had the same population size as New York City, there were far fewer skyscrapers in London, and I'd assumed Accelecom would be housed in something with less vertical expanse. To my surprise, the building before me was one of the tallest I'd seen in the England capital.

I took a deep breath. There was no way security was going to just let me waltz in, and I wondered if I should break down and call Edward now.

I didn't want to. Not yet. It was important for me to walk into this with as much of the upper hand as possible, and that meant throwing him off his guard for once.

Deciding to scope out the situation before I made any rash decisions, I pulled out my props from my purse— a notebook, pen, and measuring tape—and headed in through the main doors. Thank God, I'd stopped at the hotel to drop off my bags before arriving, even though I'd been eager to head straight over. A suitcase would have been a real hindrance.

Inside, the lobby seemed less formidable. There was a cafe, a UPS shop, and an information desk next to a large directory. The elevators were divided into banks. The first two banks were open to the general public. The last was overseen by a security guard.

I was pretty sure the directory wouldn't list Edward's office—he was too important to be that prominently on display. That was fine. I'd already done my homework, so, not only did I know exactly where his office was located, but I also knew he would be in today. Without getting close enough to see what floors each bank of elevators went to, I was also sure I'd have to go past the guard to get to him.

But it was just the one security guard. That wasn't so bad. I'd feared there would be an entire screening like there was at the airport. My father had that kind of security at his office. It was overkill and ridiculous and completely unnecessary, but he liked the pomp and circumstance. Maybe Edward wasn't as narcissistic as my father after all.

The idea almost made me laugh out loud.

Well, I couldn't stand around gawking all day. If I was going to do this, I should just do it.

Throwing my shoulders back, I beelined toward the final elevators. I walked with purpose, not slowing down when I reached the security guard but strolling past him like I belonged.

It was surprising how many times that had worked for me over the years.

Unfortunately, this wasn't one of those times.

"Pardon, mum. Can I see your pass?"

I blinked at the guard, as though he spoke a foreign language. "A pass? I don't have a pass. I wasn't told I needed a pass."

"Everyone who wants to go to the upper floors requires a pass," he explained. "Who is it you're trying to see?"

"I wasn't told anything about a pass. Edward Fasbender personally hired me for a design job, and he's expecting

me in his office right now. If you want to keep him waiting, then you can go ahead and call up and let him know
I'm here." I glanced at the huge clock above the elevators
and shook my head. "I'm already late. He's not going to
be happy."

This was where I expected the guard would go back to
his desk, call Edward's secretary, and ask if I had clearance
to go up. There would be a bunch of fuss while his office tried to determine if I did indeed have an appointment.
That would take time and I planned to use it. As soon as the
guard walked away, in fact, I would dash into the nearest
elevator. Hopefully, I'd get to his floor before the situation
got sorted upstairs.

Only that didn't happen.

Instead, the guard pressed his finger against his ear
piece, as if to better hear a message coming through.
"You're good, mum. You can go on up."

I scanned the area looking for the cameras. They had to
be there. Edward had to have seen me. Why else would I
be cleared to go up so easily? I hadn't even given the guard
my name.

"Mum?" The guard had called the lift for me and was
holding the door open, waiting. "Wouldn't want to keep
him waiting. Like you said."

With a scowl, I stepped past him into the elevator. The
doors shut, and I cursed silently. *Damn him. Damn him for
being so smooth and damn him for always being a step
ahead.*

Except, he wasn't exactly a step ahead. So he might
know I was on my way up, but I could still create a little
chaos before we came face to face.

When the elevator arrived on his floor—the *top* floor—

I walked out with determination, headed down the main hall toward the back where I knew his office was located. Once there, I pushed through the glass door, and, ignoring his secretary, I went directly to the sitting area in front of her and began measuring the couch.

"Standard size," I muttered, as though disgusted. I nudged the piece of furniture from the wall and pretended to study the backside. "Could possibly be reupholstered."

"Excuse me, madam. You can't do that?" The secretary was on her feet, her hand braced on the phone.

She was curvy and pretty with big doe eyes and, so help me, if she was sleeping with Edward…

"Are these the original cushions?" I asked, forcing myself to maintain my character.

"I don't know," she answered, caught off guard. Immediately she frowned, annoyed that I'd gotten her flustered. "Could you please explain why you want this information?"

"No worries. I can find out." I moved on to measure the side table next to it.

"What is it you think you're doing?" This didn't come from the secretary.

No, it was a very manly, very familiar voice. A voice that sent a delicious shiver down my spine.

There he is. The secretary hadn't even managed to call him yet. He'd definitely known I was coming up. He'd been waiting.

I had to catch my breath before I turned to face him, then I had to catch it again when I saw him. He was leaning against the doorframe, looking as devastatingly handsome as always.

"There you are, Edward. Is that your office through there? I'm going to need to see that as well." It was a miracle that I hadn't stammered.

Before he could answer, I brushed past him and glided into the room beyond.

"This isn't horrible," I said honestly, surveying the dark wood walls, the oversized desk in the center of the room, the chocolate leather of his chair. "This paneling is going to have to go. It's nice, but it makes this space feel like a cave. The patterned ceiling is stunning, though. We're keeping that."

I crossed the room, circling his desk so I could open the curtains. With the light streaming in, the decor took on a whole new appearance. "That's better. This room was designed for the curtains to be open."

I could feel him close behind me, and when I turned again, he was leaning his fists on his desktop. His knuckles were white as though the furniture was the only thing keeping his hands from roughing someone up.

I'd liked that desk initially. Now I suddenly hated it.

"What. Is it. You're doing." He was so terse in his delivery, that it was no longer a question but a demand. A demand he was irritated to have to repeat.

Good. This was good. I liked seeing him this barely restrained. I liked it a whole lot more than I should.

"I'm taking notes so I can put together a design," I explained, as though it was obvious.

He let out an incredulous laugh. "I'm not hiring you to be my decorator."

"You are." I stalked toward him until I bumped up against the desk, the only barrier now between us. "My father already thinks that's how we met, and there's no way I'm telling him the truth. Besides, your office is badly in need of an update. And I'm a *designer.* Not a decorator. Don't make that mistake again."

His lips curled up into a smug smile. A ridiculously sexy smile. "This means you're accepting my offer then."

He still had the beard I'd asked for, and he was so attractive it was almost hard to look at him. It was even harder not to crawl over the bulky piece of furniture in front of me and give him my answer by pressing my mouth against his, but somehow I managed.

Instead, I held my left hand out and wiggled my bare finger. "It means, Edward, that I'm going to need a ring."

19

The driver opened the door of the Maybach, and I stepped out onto the carriage driveway and gasped. I'd come from wealth, and the home I'd grown up in had encompassed two penthouse floors in a Fifth Avenue highrise, which perhaps gave me a certain impression about what expensive homes were like in big cities.

Edward's home was nothing like what I'd expected.

Instead of an apartment or a townhouse, the building I stood in front of was a well-known, long string of consecutive mansions called Cornwall Terrace. The architecture was both historical and stunning, and the location was superb, at the edge of Regent's Park, no less. I quickly counted the rows of windows stacked before me. Four floors. Holy luxury! This residence had to cost a fortune. The view across the park alone had to be worth millions.

Once again, Edward had thrown me.

He did that a lot, it seemed. If I had to guess, I would have even said he thrived on it. At the very least, he enjoyed calling the shots. After I'd shown up at his office on

Wednesday, I'd hoped we'd sit down and talk about what happened next, made plans for our forthcoming marriage. But Edward had seemingly had enough of being the by-stander, and he'd quickly taken the reins in his hand, commanding I go to my hotel, settle in, and recuperate from my travels. He'd escorted me out of the building telling me he'd send a car for me on Saturday. We could "dine over discussions," he'd said, a term that made me bite back a smile.

Three days had been an awful lot of time to sit around. After all the planning I'd done over the last month, the wait had felt like an unnecessary delay, and I'd been more than a little eager and excited when the driver had pulled up in front of my hotel.

Excited because I was ready to get on with The Game, not for any other reason. Certainly not because I wanted to see Edward.

I'd found ways to occupy myself, but, standing now in front of his insane mansion, I'd wished I'd used some of that time to do more research on my fiancé. Exactly how rich and powerful was my husband-to-be? Did I really know who I was playing with? What level of game had I entered?

I was still standing in the driveway when the front door swung open and a liveried servant welcomed me with a nod of his head.

With a toss of my hair, I threw aside my self-doubt and walked in with my head held high. The entrance led immediately into a large reception area.

"Master Edward should be with you shortly," the butler said politely. "You may have a seat if you'd like. May I get you something to drink while you wait? Water? Wine? Tea?"

"No, thank you," I said, distracted as I surveyed my surroundings. The room was conventionally furnished, in the vein of a formal living space. There was a sitting area comprised of two black sofas, a white sofa, and two arm-chairs, all of which were tufted and ornate. The hardwood floors were stained dark chocolate, matching the color of the walls. Long white curtains with black valances draped each of the four windows. Two large filigree mirrors oc-cupied the opposite walls.

It all had a traditional, masculine flavor that was all well and good for a bachelor, but would need to be soft-ened if I were to be expected to live here. Even the very na-ture of the front room was old-fashioned. With no foyer or front hall, it was truly a receiving room, meant to receive guests, preventing them from needing to journey farther into the home. It was an outdated style of floor plan that I'd had little opportunity to encounter in my design work in New York City. It was fascinating and foreign all at once.

By the time I'd taken in enough to truly be aware of him, the butler had disappeared, leaving me alone. If he'd gone to inform my date that I'd arrived, Edward didn't rush to greet me. At least ten minutes went by with me sit-ting poised on the edge of an armchair, my nerves getting the better of me with every passing second. The tick-tick of the grandfather clock in the corner filled the quiet space, sounding louder than it actually was. The rhythmic beat magnified the passing time and heightened my anxiety.

He was doing this on purpose, I was sure of it. Making me wait. Like I'd said, he enjoyed unsettling me.

Too restless to sit any longer, I stood and ventured to-ward one of the mirrors to inspect my makeup for some-thing to do. I'd worn a floral jacquard A-line dress, and, though it had a severe plunging neckline, it was more romantic and casual than my usual attire. I'd left my hair down as well, remembering what he'd said earlier in the summer about appearing too uptight. It was a deliberate attempt to try to appeal to Edward, and while I'd frequently dressed for whatever role I was playing in the past, I'd had more of a struggle deciding to do it today, for some strange reason. Maybe because he'd asked specifically for me to be different, and I'd always hated letting anyone take authority over me. Or maybe it was because I wasn't entirely comfortable yet with the woman he wanted me to be.

Most likely it was because it wasn't about The Game at all. I'd dressed this way for him. Because I wanted to *please* him. And that wanting felt dangerous.

As I fluffed the curls I'd spent all afternoon applying to my shoulder-length hair, I caught movement low to the ground in my periphery.

My head shot toward the hall leading into the house. There was nobody there. I stared for long seconds, seeing nothing.

But I could *hear* something. Short, heavy breaths followed by a light giggle.

Curious, I tiptoed toward the doorway, hugging the walls of the room. I was just about to peer around the open door when a little face poked out and peeked at me. The laugh that erupted this time was still light even in its fullness. Light and adorable, making the insides of my chest feel liquid and warm.

"Well, who are you?" I crouched down to better see my new friend, a little boy wearing a dress shirt and vest paired with little boy blue jeans that were too cute for words. Having not spent much time around kids, I couldn't be sure of his age, but I guessed around two. He toddled the way I'd always imagined toddlers toddled, anyway, his steps unsteady as he came out from behind the door and into the room.

"Hi!" he said with another bewitching laugh, his face pinching up as his mouth opened wider with the sound.

And oh that face…

While his laugh was adorable, his face was ten times as precious. It was the cutest thing I'd ever seen in the flesh—brown hair, chubby cheeks, and blue eyes that were reminiscent of the shade belonging to the man I was betrothed to. There was no doubt they were related, a realization that should have set off alarms in my head, but instead had my gut twisting with inexplicable longing.

Was this what a baby Edward would look like?

Why did I suddenly want to find out more than anything I'd ever wanted in my life?

"Come away from there, Fred."

The stern voice drew my gaze down the hall to a woman I recognized from my online searches. I'd seemed to have forgotten Edward's sister lived with him, or at least hadn't expected to see her tonight. She was thin and pale and gorgeous, her dark brown hair and hazel eyes as captivating as her flawless skin. Even though she wore jeans and a simple long-sleeve black shirt, I felt plain in comparison.

She scooped up the toddler, and I stood to introduce myself. "You must be Camilla. I'm Celia."

"I know who you are," she said sourly, ignoring the hand I held out to her as she hugged the child—Fred—closer to her.

Stunned by the hostile greeting, I dropped my hand quickly and gaped.

"Good! You've had a chance to meet."

I glanced behind his sister and saw Edward coming down the stairs. He was arresting as always, but especially so with his laidback look. His hair lacked the usual slick styled appearance, and while he wore black slacks and a white button-down, he had the collar unbuttoned and the sleeves rolled up to his elbows. It was the first time I'd seen him without a jacket, and the tight fit of his shirt showcased an impressive set of pecs underneath.

Damn, Edward wore casual well. Too well for my good.

Camilla turned toward him. "Yes, we've met. Can you and I talk for a moment please?" She walked past the staircase and stopped to wait for him to join her.

He looked from me to her and then back again. "I'll be just a minute," he said to me, his gaze pointing at the receiving room behind me, a not-so-subtle hint that I should retreat there and give them their privacy.

I didn't like being ordered around, but I was on my best behavior, so I did as I was silently told.

Sort of.

I mean, I did go back into the room, but I hovered at the door, the way I had when I'd been looking for the child. Pressing my back to the wall, I listened in.

"You can't expect me to like her, Eddie. That's beyond reasonable." Camilla's voice was tight and filled with animosity.

I stiffened. I didn't need friends, and, in general, I wasn't bothered by enemies, but this woman's hatred felt intense without reason.

I strained to hear Edward's response, but his words

were hushed in comparison, so all I could hear was a low rumble.

Whatever he'd said, it didn't settle his sister. "Of all people, why does it have to be *her*?"

Apparently my father wasn't going to be the only one upset by the arrangement between me and Edward.

Again, I couldn't hear his response, but his tone had taken on a soothing timbre.

"Fine. But I'm not eating dinner with her."

He said something quick at that and then there was a bustle and footsteps. I jumped away from the door so as not to be caught eavesdropping, but didn't move fast enough, or moved too fast, because when Edward appeared in the room he saw me scurrying in a way that could only indicate what I'd been doing.

He narrowed his eyes and gave me that smug, knowing smile. That smile that seemed to have a direct voltage line to my lower regions since every time he gave it, my pussy buzzed and clenched.

There was no point pretending I hadn't been caught. "Eddie, huh?" I teased.

"Sisters have a way of poking, don't they?"

"I wouldn't know. I'm an only child. *Eddie*." I prided myself on my ability to poke as well.

"Oh, no. That's not for you to use."

I took a challenging step toward him. "Isn't it?"

"No. It's not." He said it so finally, I didn't dare refute.

He moved then to the wine fridge at the other end of the room and began sifting through bottles.

I stared at his back, clutching and unclutching my

hands while I tried not to be hurt that he'd dismissed my attempt to be more familiar, hurt that he hadn't actually greeted me. Hadn't said hello or even looked at me in a way that said he'd seen me.

So much for pleasing the man.

"A Malbec all right?" He was already unscrewing the cork, so I didn't think my answer was really wanted.

"Fine," I said anyway. Feeling defeated, I searched for another way to gain footing. The private conversation in the hall seemed as good a place to step as any. "She doesn't like me."

"Who? Camilla?" He didn't look at me while he dealt with the wine glasses and the pouring. "I'm sure that's not true."

He was condescending to me again, and it made my blood boil. I shot daggers at his backside.

His perfectly shaped backside.

Seriously, his pants had to be sewn on the way they showed off that rock-hard ass.

Forcing myself to focus, I pushed once more. "I am definitely sure that's true, and don't say I'm wrong. We both know I'm not."

He paused his task and looked at me, truly looked at me, for the first time that night. After a beat he shrugged. "She doesn't care for Americans." He poured the second glass and held it out toward me.

He could very easily have dismissed her acrimony as a symbol of loyalty. It wasn't like I wasn't aware of the feud between her brother and my father. Why hadn't he just said that's what it was? Was there more to her hostility than that?

I considered other motives as I sauntered toward him, and remembered with an odd stab to my gut the first suspicions I'd had about his relationship with his sister.

"I think it might be a more particular lack of caring, for Americans who are dating her brother." I took the wine glass from his hand, shivering when I "accidentally" touched his finger, despite it not being an accident at all.

His brow furrowed sharply. "Are you suggesting my sister is jealous?"

"You're as rich as God and yet your sister—who is older than me, I might add—still lives with you. It could lead some people to suspect there's more to your relationship than it first seems." I was goading him was all, but the little boy's eyes flashed in my mind, eyes that looked so much like his uncle's. They were so similar, he could have passed for Edward's son.

The thought brought on another stab to my stomach. God, I was the one who was acting jealous.

Edward's expression grew hard and mean. "I'm more than a little disturbed by your implication that my sister and I have anything other than an appropriate sibling relationship. She lives with me because she was going through a difficult time and needed support. I am her only family, so, of course, I endeavor to look out for her and Freddie in any way I can, including offering them my home when they need their loved ones close. I'll ask you kindly to never again suggest anything as crass or depraved or irresponsibly cruel where Camilla is concerned."

I never liked being scolded. Who did? Particularly I hated anyone ever thinking they knew better about who I should or shouldn't be, how I should or shouldn't behave.

But there was something about this scolding that especially stung. It sunk into my pores and stayed with me, the way that menthol cream clings and burns for hours after it's applied.

I wanted to scrub it off of me. Wanted to wash myself from his brusque words and earn words that would soothe instead.

That wasn't like me, though, and I didn't know where to begin.

I sipped from my wine glass, holding the swish in my mouth until the black cherry notes showed themselves before I swallowed. "*Freddie*," I said suddenly, noticing the child's name's similarity to Camilla's nickname for her brother. "Is he named after you?"

As soon as it was out of my mouth, it hit me that this could be taken as a further attack on his bond with his sister. "I don't mean that like it sounds. I meant..." What did I mean by it? "I heard what you said. I'm trying to understand, not belittle."

I bit the inside of my lip while I waited for him to respond, every muscle tense, my breath held tight within me.

Edward swirled the contents of his glass around once. Twice. Three times.

Finally, he answered. "After me and his father, Frank."

There'd been very little to read online about Camilla's husband, only that he'd died in a fire before her son had been born.

I didn't know anything about that kind of loss, and, yet, I did. Somewhere, deep inside me, hidden in a shadow, there was a part of me that did know. A part of me that remembered the kinds of pain that drove a person to search for safety in anyone and anywhere they could find it. I'd found my solace in a questionable friendship and a game that stole every essence of emotion and humanity from my soul.

Perhaps Camilla had found her solace in much kinder forms—a protective brother and an adorable child.

"He's absolutely precious," I said, the very thought of his chubby-cheeked grin putting a smile on my own lips. "I'm sure he brings a lot of joy to your world. I apologize for insinuating anything else was going on." I was even a little bit sincere.

More than a little bit, maybe.

His hard stare showed no signs of forgiveness. To be fair, it showed nothing at all.

I fidgeted under the uncomfortable weight of his gaze. "It's just…" I fumbled with where to go, what to say. "I know very little about you. You've given me so little to go on. It's hard not to let my imagination get carried away."

"Well, try," he said brusquely. He closed his eyes and pinched his fingers along his forehead just above his eyebrows. Then, with a sigh, he dropped his hand and opened his eyes. "Tonight should help. That's what this whole evening is for after all. To get to know each other. To start, anyway."

It sounded like he was trying to convince me, but I wasn't certain he wasn't trying to convince himself.

Either way, he'd given me a hint of where to go from here, and I wasn't about to ignore the path.

I smiled brightly, some of my anxiety releasing just from the act of putting on confidence. "I'm glad to be here for that very reason. Glad to have an opportunity to get to know you better. And I'm glad Camilla isn't joining us for dinner, not because of her apparent ill feelings toward me, but so that we can have that time alone to get acquainted."

It was hard not to think of all the possible ways we could get acquainted.

For the purpose of The Game, of course.

But there was that supercilious expression again, that arrogant smirk returned to his lips. "Oh, we aren't dining alone tonight. Camilla may have bowed out, but Hagan and Genevieve will be here as well."

"What?" I couldn't manage to be subtle about my surprise.

Edward pulled his phone from his trouser pocket and jabbed at the screen with his thumb. "Yes, it seems Hagan picked up Genny about half past so they should be here any minute now. Didn't I mention that before?"

He *knew* he hadn't mentioned it.

He enjoys this, I seethed to myself. Loves seeing me rattled. Fucking gets off on it.

If I wasn't sure before, I was positive now. The goddamned twinkle in his eye gave him away. Not only was he having fun, but he was gloating as well.

"But...but...but..." I stammered. "We don't even have our story straight! What do they know about me? What am I supposed to say about *us*?"

"You'll figure it out. I have a feeling you're quite good at coming up with stories on your feet." He winked, and the contemptuousness of it, of all of it, made him so easy to hate.

Combined with the cocky pose he'd assumed, leaving his hand casually in his pocket after returning his phone, he was also the cruelest, sexiest thing I'd ever witnessed in my life.

My composure was definitely on thin ice.

Before I could collect myself, the front door handle turned and in walked a young man and woman, each so strikingly similar in appearance to their father, it was impossible to mistake them for anyone other than his children.

"Ah, here they are. Just in time. Dinner's about to be served." He set down his wine and crossed to his daughter who kissed him on the cheek.

"We wouldn't think of being late. Believe me, we've learned that lesson." She exchanged a look with her brother, as if they were sharing an inside joke.

Then her eyes fell on me, and I waited to see how she addressed me, hoping to take my lead from there.

Unexpectedly, her expression turned confused. "Oh, hello. Who's this?"

Jesus Christ, he hadn't told his kids I was going to be here for dinner either?!

At least it wasn't just me he liked to unsettle. I should have taken comfort in that. But at the moment, all I could focus on was the growing unease stirring in my belly.

Edward swept in next to me, putting an arm around my waist and wrapping his other hand in mine. I tried to ignore the bolt of electricity that surged through me at his touch, and focused on his mouth as he announced, "Hagan, Genny, Celia Werner and I met this summer. She's the reason I invited you over tonight. I thought you both should meet the woman who's agreed to be my wife."

"Your...*wife*?" Hagan's eyes were as wide as his sister's.

My own shock was startling, and I'd at least had a sense of what was coming. Talk about awkward.

It was definitely going to be a long night.

At this rate, I had a feeling it was going to be a really long marriage.

20

There was an uproar of questions from his kids that Edward easily put to silence. "We'll discuss everything over dinner," he said firmly. "It's seven now. I'm sure Gavin is waiting for us to be seated."

With his palm pressed at the small of my back, Edward led us down the hallway toward the formal dining room pointing out the floor plan as we walked. "The staircase, of course. There's the lift. Both go to the lower ground floor as well as all the way to the top. Behind the stairs is the water closet. To the left is the kitchen—the one we use on a daily basis. The catering kitchen is downstairs. Farther down the hall is the salon. And here we are."

He dropped his hand, but I could still feel it there, as though he'd branded it into my skin. It made me dizzy, even when he was no longer touching me. That was how powerful his affect was on me. It lingered. It permeated the membranes of my cells. Got into my bloodstream. Altered my DNA.

I surveyed the room we'd entered. The traditional design had been continued in here in the two crystal chandeliers that hung from the patterned tray ceiling and the elegant dark wood table with intricate apron details and lion claw feet. There was room for twelve fabric padded chairs with cabriole legs, five on each side and one at each head, but only four place settings had been laid out.

Edward moved to the setting at the far head. "You'll sit here to my left, darling. Genny, you can sit by your brother this evening."

My knees buckled at the term of endearment, even though I knew it was likely for show. I was grateful it was only a few steps to my seat. The butler who'd greeted me when I arrived pulled out my chair for me to sit. I assumed he was Gavin, but later was informed his name was Jeremy. Gavin was the personal chef. I'd planned for an intimate dinner, but the level of staff on hand made me feel a little underdressed.

Edward, though, had worn casual, I reminded myself. He apparently liked a formal routine with or without the formal attire.

The next several minutes were spent settling in. Jeremy filled our wine glasses then set out our first course, a blueberry poached pear salad with candied walnuts. He'd barely had time to walk away after setting down the last plate before the inquisition resumed.

"If you're getting married, where's the ring?" Genevieve's sour expression, along with her tone, said she wasn't ready to accept the news of our engagement.

Without being told so, I had a feeling I was expected to help change her mind.

Here goes nothing.

I put on a friendly smile, one I'd carefully practiced for

just such occasions. "We haven't picked one out yet."

"I have it," Edward said in contradiction. "I wanted Celia to be sure about us before she put it on." He gazed in my direction as he took my hand in his, the one with the missing ring, and squeezed.

Oh, he was smooth. Real smooth.

And a good liar. I was sure he didn't really have a ring since this was the first I was hearing about it.

Genny wasn't so easily wooed. "And you're sure now? Because we haven't even heard of you before tonight. You can't blame us for thinking this is rather sudden."

Though she included her brother in the use of her plural pronouns, Hagan's congenial expression suggested he wasn't as suspicious as she was.

Ugh. I hadn't been prepared to deal with the frank grilling of protective offspring.

"I understand," I said, trying to imagine the scenario from her viewpoint. "I can't speak to your father's reasons for not sharing our romantic involvement with you both, but I can assume he didn't want to say anything until I had given him a definite answer. And I have now. And, yes, I am sure."

She didn't seem convinced, but before I had to endure another hostile round of interrogation from her, Hagan intervened. "Lay off her, Gen. We haven't even heard yet how they met. It was in New York, yeah?"

I glanced at Edward to see if he might take this one. Frankly, I would have loved to hear what he would have said.

He turned in his seat, fixing his gaze on me. "Why don't you tell them that story, darling?"

He was a cruel man, casually using that *darling* in that British dialect of his like it wasn't a weapon of mass destruction.

The sweep of his thumb along my knuckle wasn't helping my train of thought. "Okay. Sure." I sounded flustered. This wasn't going to cut it.

I could do better. I had this.

Gently, I pulled my hand out from his, which cleared my head immensely. *As close to the truth as possible.* "I've known about your father for years, obviously. His reputation proceeds him, but also I'd heard about him because my own father is in the media business."

Genny perked at this. "What did you say your last name was again?"

"Werner." I waited for her to comment again. When she didn't, I went on. "So, anyway. I'm not personally in the media business. I run an interior design company, and your father asked me to meet with him to discuss redesigning his office."

"Your office here?" Hagan directed this question to his father.

"Mm." Edward nodded, his eyes never leaving me.

"Thank God," Genny said. "That office is in bad need of a redo. It's abrasive and overly masculine and not at all welcoming to the female gender."

Under different circumstances, I had a feeling Genevieve and I might have gotten along splendidly.

Hagan shrugged. "It's not that bad. I sort of like it."

"You would," Genny muttered. She brought her focus to me, her eyes softer than they'd been before. "Was Dad as terrible to work with as I imagine he is?"

"He is," I said smugly. Honestly. "Within five minutes, I'd decided he was an incredible self-centered ass." I peered back at my husband-to-be and was surprised to see I'd amused him.

I liked that. Liked amusing him.

Liked it too much.

"Now, now, confession here." Finally Edward was stepping in. "I didn't really care about her silly office design ideas."

"Dad!" Genny gasped.

He put up a hand to shush her. "I don't really need my office redesigned. It was an excuse. I'd seen Celia at a charity ball, from a distance, and there was no way I could go without seeing her again. Hiring her was an opportunity to spend more time with her."

The ball was a nice touch, and then I remembered I really had attended a charity ball in the weeks before meeting him. "The Building Futures event?"

He nodded slightly, as if not quite sure he wanted to give himself away.

"Oh. I didn't know." I hadn't seen *him* there.

"Her hair was in this soft twist and she was wearing a slinky red gown with a slit up one side and these sheer panels up here and here." He gestured to his neck and then the sides of his torso. "She was absolutely breathtaking."

He was absolutely breathtaking. As in I couldn't currently breathe. He'd definitely seen me. How had I not noticed him?

"So, as I said," he continued, his hand finding mine again. "I made up an excuse to hire her, and, after I convinced her that I wasn't the complete ass she thought I was—"

I interjected. "Oh, no, I still think you're a complete ass."

"—after I convinced her that I had some good qualities despite being an ass," he corrected, "she agreed to go out with me. We were inseparable after that."

"Then why didn't you tell us about her?" Genny demanded, and now that the question was specifically directed toward her father, I didn't have to be the one to answer.

"Like Celia said, I wanted to wait until she'd made up her mind about me." His face turned serious. "It was terribly difficult to part with her when my business was over and it was time to come home, but I didn't want to push her. I'd asked her to marry me, because I already knew I wanted to spend the rest of my life with her, but I was asking a lot, expecting her to give up everything she had in New York to come live with me in my house. To fit in with my family. I knew she needed time to think about it, and I also knew if I told you both, I'd only get my hopes up."

He brought my hand to his mouth and kissed the inside of my wrist. "I'm so very glad that you changed your mind."

Warmth rushed up my torso, expanding through my chest and into my ribs. It was all a story, yes. I knew that's what it was. That it was all a fabricated lie. That he hadn't really meant any of the wonderful things he'd said about me. About us.

But there was a camaraderie about the whole thing. A sense of having someone on the same side that I hadn't had since I used to play with Hudson. We'd done this together too—made up stories. Pretended our lives were tangled in ways that they weren't, and that had been fun and exciting and amusing.

This charade with Edward felt like that. Like we were working together for a common end, and we were, actually. For once the goal wasn't to destroy someone else in the process, and I was surprised to find that missing element didn't diminish the experience.

Except, I *was* setting out to destroy someone in the process. I was planning to destroy Edward. I couldn't let myself forget that.

Whether or not Genny was satisfied with our ruse, Hagan was, and he turned conversation to his intern position he was doing at Accelecom in his spare time and then to a project he was involved with at school. Before the end of the meal, I'd learned he was graduating from university in the spring and planned to go work with his dad full-time after that and that I was closer to his age than Edward's, but just barely.

Genevieve was also at university and seemed also to be following in her father's footsteps, much to his chagrin. He insisted it was a terrible pathway for a girl, and wouldn't she be happier getting married and being a socialite?

I barely refrained from kicking him under the table for his sexist attitude. I had a feeling it came from a place of love. My father had encouraged me in the same way when I'd been younger, because he wanted me taken care of, not because he didn't think I was capable. And as much as he ignored me or overlooked me, he had always supported my decision to open a business on my own. Hopefully Edward would come to that place with Genny as well, eventually.

When the meal was over, Edward invited both his children to join us in the salon for an after-dinner drink.

"I can't, Dad," Genny said. "I really have to get back

to studies. I have a full load this term, and there's lots of reading." She turned to her brother. "If you can't take me home, I can call for a ride."

"I'll send you in my car," Edward said, looking aghast at the mention of his daughter in an Uber.

Hagan shook his head. "You'll do neither. I can take you. I can't stay either. I'm meeting someone in a bit."

Edward checked his watch. "At this time of night?"

"It's still early, Dad." The way he looked away when he said it told me exactly what kind of meeting he was escaping for.

"Very well. Before you leave, though. I need you to sign that proposal. It's up on my desk. I'll show you."

Edward and Hagan disappeared up the stairs, leaving Genny and me alone. We walked together to the receiving room to wait in thick silence. I had no idea if I'd won her over or not, but if the tension between us was any indication, I was betting the answer was no.

As soon as we'd made it to the front room, my impression was validated. "I know who you are," she said accusingly. "I know why he's really marrying you."

My stomach dropped, but I kept my head high. Edward had never said his children had to be kept in the dark. Maybe it was even better if they knew.

Or maybe that just complicated matters.

I wasn't ready to make a decision about it, so I decided to put the ball back in her court. "And what reason is that?"

"Because you're a Werner. Everyone knows how badly my father wants in with your father's company. I'd never thought he would go to these sorts of means, though."

"You sound as if that bothers you."

She sighed, running a hand through her long brown hair. "I suppose it shouldn't. It's what he wants, it's what you want. You're both adults. I'm assuming it's mutually beneficial."

"But…?"

She met my eyes. "But he was completely heartbroken when my mother left him. In some ways, it destroyed him. He's not the man he was before their divorce, and I guess I thought…" She lowered her gaze to the floor. "I'd hoped that he'd find that again. I'd hoped he could be happy like that with someone new."

Her tone was sad, and sad tones had never had much effect on me.

And yet, I wanted to give her a different story. Because I liked her, maybe. Because I could relate to her, being the daughter of a successful man like she was. Men who didn't give their daughters enough credit or time or attention.

Or because I wanted another story to be true, one different than the one we were living.

Or maybe it was because I simply wanted to see if I could convince her of something else. For the challenge of it.

I couldn't explain my reasons, but the urge was strong to correct her, so I did. "You're right," I said. "You're right that this started purely as a business decision. Edward wanted access to my father's company and I wanted his money and that was all. But that's not the case anymore. It evolved. I've never met someone like Edward. He challenges me. He gives me something that I didn't think I would ever have. He makes me feel things I thought were impossible to feel. He makes me look at the future as a possibility instead of more of the same old thing."

I stopped, stunned by how effortlessly the story had fallen from my lips. As though it were more honest than I'd realized. Honest stories always came the easiest.

"Anyway," I said, remembering that I had an audience. "My decision to marry your father is based on that, not on any mutually beneficial deal. Of course I can't speak for him, but I think…" What did I think? "Just don't give up on him finding happiness because of how we found each other. Your father and I are full of surprises."

She studied me for long seconds before gifting me the first genuine smile I'd seen from her all night. "Thank you for that. I don't know what to think right now, and I don't know how I feel about you, but I'm rooting for him. I hope he surprises me."

I sort of hoped he did too.

No, I didn't. I didn't want to be surprised. I wanted to know exactly where this was going. I wanted it to follow my predictions. I wanted to play Edward the way I'd played so many others and then get out and walk away, untouched as always.

But after Edward and his son had returned, and after we'd said goodbye to the kids and sent them on their way, when we were alone again, just the two of us, the tension I felt strung out between us wasn't the kind of tension that came from the thrill of The Game. It was darker and more taut, yet not too taut. Like it could keep pulling or it could break entirely and the not knowing which would happen made my skin feel prickly and hot and made me feel like I wanted to cry.

With his back against the front door, Edward looked me over, his gaze sweeping up my body with slow intensity, as though he were seeing me for the first time that evening.

Goosebumps broke out along my arms and the space between my legs began to throb.

"Nice work in there tonight," he said, his voice low. "With them. It was impressive."

"Thank you." I could feel the blush run up my chest and cheeks. It was the first time I ever remembered him complimenting me, and I hated that I cared, but I did. I cared. I wanted him to compliment me again and again.

His eyes grew dark and hooded and the tension pulled tighter between us. "There's a lot going on here, I can tell," he said, and I practically sobbed from relief that he was addressing it. "So let's go upstairs and sort it out, shall we?"

I didn't hesitate for one second before giving him the only answer I could. "Yes, please."

21

"It seems strange to be discussing our prenup when I'm still not wearing a ring." If I sounded bitter, it was because I was. When Edward had suggested we go upstairs, I'd naively thought he meant his bedroom. I'd certainly been on that page. The energy around us was so fraught and charged, I'd assumed he was there with me.

Instead, "upstairs" had meant up one flight to his den and "sorting it out" seemed to be completely administrative.

The paperwork was necessary for the marriage, I supposed. It was also boring. I didn't want his money. I wanted to ruin him.

I wanted him to ruin me, too. In a completely different way.

I glanced at the document in front of me, then at the still bare ring finger of my left hand.

"You're awfully anxious about that, aren't you?" Edward asked from the other side of the oversized mahogany desk. The formal setup made the whole thing even more tedious.

"What can I say, I like jewelry." A subject I found much more intriguing. I'd even taken the liberty of doing some of my own preliminary engagement ring browsing while I'd been sequestered in my hotel. "I can give you some ideas of what I like and what looks—"

He cut me off brusquely. "I don't need them."

"Oh. Okay." Back to tedium then.

Pretending to care about the prenuptial agreement, I picked it up and skimmed it halfheartedly. I could feel his eyes on me, which made the idea of actually reading even more preposterous. His gaze was too distracting. *He* was too distracting.

"Do you have any questions?" he asked after I'd flipped through several pages.

I couldn't remember a word of what I'd just read. Frankly, I was still thinking about the upstairs I'd believed he'd eluded to. If this level was devoted to his den and home office, where was his bedroom? The next floor? The top?

Then I did have a question for him. A valid one, I thought, considering it mostly concerned my agenda, not his. "You'll want me to live here with you, I assume. How exactly will that work as far as sleeping arrangements? Your children seem to believe we're going to have a real marriage. I'm not sure what your sister thinks or what you want her to think, but I'm imagining you'll want the ruse to be kept with everyone else. It will be hard to keep up that pretense if we're in separate bedrooms."

His lids appeared to grow momentarily heavy, a gesture I'd begun to realize was his version of an eyeroll. "I meant questions about the prenup," he said curtly. "But, since you've asked, I don't see that pretense will be a problem. The master suite is on the next level. Along with the bedroom and two dressing rooms, there's also a flex space for a nursery or a morning room or what have you. It's a decent size and will adequately fit a king bed. We won't even have to share a bathroom.

"Since that floor is completely devoted to the master suite, there's been no reason for anyone to go up there except for me. The guest rooms, including Camilla and Fred's room, are all on the fourth floor, and everyone tends to access that using the lift. No one will have any cause to know what happens—or doesn't happen—in our rooms."

It was almost refreshing to have grown up as wealthy as I had and still be surprised by the extravagant lives of other billionaires. An *entire floor* dedicated to the master suite? *Two* dressing rooms?

That was...wow.

But more than being impressed, I was disappointed. I'd hoped beyond hope that we'd have to share a room.

I wasn't ready to give up on that aspiration. "The house staff will know there's two beds being slept in when they make them up every day. You might think you have a loyal staff, but we both know no one can ever be truly trusted."

"Indeed." His smile, though tight, was agreeable, and for the briefest second I thought I might be on the verge of victory.

He stood up and crossed to the minibar. "However, there's no reason to need them to keep silent in this matter. Plenty of couples sleep in separate beds. It doesn't mean anything about their relationship or, for that matter, their sex life."

Somehow I'd momentarily forgotten how old-fashioned he was. Like, nineteen-fifties old-fashioned.

As if to bolster this stereotype, he began pouring cognac into two tulip glasses without asking if I wanted any. "Marion had her own bedroom when we were together as well, and that was a 'real marriage,' by your definition."

"You slept apart? No wonder that ended," I muttered.

"Pardon?"

Not wanting to discuss his "real" marriage, I looked back at the prenup still in my hand. This time I managed to focus enough that a section caught my eye.

When he came back to the desk and stood over me, holding a glass out for me to take, I ignored the offer and raised a curious brow. "There's a clause here for children."

A clause stating how much I'd get if we had kids when we got divorced. Ten million for each one, which seemed awfully generous.

And suspicious.

We weren't even supposed to be having sex. Was that a ploy? Was he setting me up to have a child with him after all? Was he expecting me to do in vitro, because no way. An heir to the Werner fortune, though—that made more sense than the ridiculous reason Edward had put forth before.

The notion of adding a baby to the bargain should have made me angry, but instead, a warm bubble of hope began making its way up my chest.

Because it would make this game easier, was why. No other reason. Certainly not because I wanted kids with him. Or anyone, for that matter.

But if I could use that excuse to get him into bed...

He still stood next to me, one cognac held in my direction. "My lawyer said it was irresponsible not to include it. You and I will be the only two who know it's there merely for appearances."

And just like that, the bubble popped.

I practically growled in frustration.

"Take the drink, Celia."

I started to shake my head, but his stern frown made me change my mind.

Relenting, I took the glass and brought it up to my mouth for a sip. I wasn't generally a fan of brandy, but I hadn't tasted any with quite as complex of flavor as this. There were so many different notes, I couldn't discern them all. Jasmine. Vanilla. Cigar box. Something earthy. I liked it.

I took another sip. "Are you hoping to liquor me up?"

"Why would I want to do that?" He sounded innocent, but he was far from. Every move he made was purposeful. Every action had a goal.

Maybe this time his goal was to get me in his bed.

A girl could hope. But I'd learned hope works best with action.

"I don't know," I said seductively. "So I'll agree to something not in my best interest."

He chuckled, and, admittedly, I liked the sound. I liked that I amused him.

"It's a digestive, Celia. Don't make more of it than it is." He circled to the other side of his desk, but didn't sit. Studying me, he took a swig of his drink, his Adam's apple bobbing as the liquid ran down his throat. "How does the agreement look?"

I blinked, tearing my gaze from his far-too-sexy swallowing action and forced it back to the papers. After a second, I put down my glass so I could fold the document in half. "It looks good to me at first glance. I'd like to have a lawyer look it over as well before I sign, if you don't mind."

"Of course. I'll email you a copy." He took another swallow, his expression saying he knew I would have signed it right then and there if he'd asked.

Tell me to sign it, then. Tell me so we can move on to what's next. I was pretty sure my own expression gave away my thoughts as well.

"I didn't expect your signature tonight," he said, reading me. "We'll do it in front of a notary. Make it legal and all that. I merely thought you should have the opportunity to go over it beforehand."

"How kind." I almost managed a smile.

"Besides, you might not want to sign it once you hear the other terms of our arrangement."

"You really do know how to set a girl up for thinking the worst, Edward. I'm not sure if it's a skill of yours or a flaw."

"Can't it be both?"

I squinted my eyes at him coldly, irritated that once again it seemed he was playing with me.

This was ridiculous. I had to be better about my moves. I could play him just as easily. It was second nature.

Edward was about to learn from the woman who'd practically invented the game.

22

Retrieving my drink, I stood up and scanned the room. Officially, he'd told me, his office was down the hall, an equally large space with his computer and his file cabinets where he did most of his work when at home.

This room was more relaxed, more like a library. For schmoozing, I assumed. Everything was for show. Shelves lined the room containing books that appeared to have never been read. Collector's editions of classics. The Renaissance paintings on the wall looked familiar, and I guaranteed they were originals. The carpet was plush with a complicated design. The furniture both inviting and expensive.

Knowing he was watching my every move, I sauntered over to the sofa near the fire, which had been roaring before we'd entered the room. I set my glass down on the end table, and I bent down to unbuckle the strap on one of my heels. "Go ahead then. Fill me in on these elusive terms. But don't expect me not to be comfortable for it."

I kicked off that shoe and began working on the next, never taking my eyes off him.

His lips twitched as if fighting a smile, and when he began to cross the room, coming straight toward me, I wondered if it was really that easy.

But he walked past me, stopping in front of the end table. Picking up my drink, he opened a drawer, pulled out a coaster, and set my glass on top.

God, he was more anal than my grandmother had been, and I was pretty sure that woman loved her furnishings more than me.

After kicking off my other shoe, I pulled my feet up under me and exaggeratedly lifted my drink from the coaster as if to say, *I'd only set it down for a minute.*

Edward ignored my pointed gesture and sat in an armchair cater-cornered from me. "I am what some might call a traditionalist," he said, as soon as he was settled. "I'm the man of the house, and, as such, I believe my wife's duty is to be by my side, first and foremost. It's her duty to submit to my authority at all times. Her primary focus is on my needs, and, in return, I will look after her needs. Certainly you are welcome to entertain yourself with hobbies and trivial pursuits, but I will not allow a wife of mine to have a career of her own."

"Wow." I blinked a few times. I was having trouble digesting all he'd said. No wonder he'd thought I needed the cognac. "That's so patriarchal. I hate to tell you this, but that way of thinking is considered out of vogue these days."

"I've never cared about popular opinion. Nevertheless, I'm aware that it would be an adjustment for you."

"An 'adjustment'?" It was an understatement if I'd

ever heard one. "You're asking me to give up my business." I wasn't about to tell him I'd already shut it down. Right now it was a bargaining chip.

"I'm asking you to give up your business for a better opportunity. I assure you the position of my wife comes with more prestige and higher pay."

I had to fight not to gape. "No one can ever say you don't have a big ego."

"I have a realistic sense of self."

He was such a narcissist, it was unreal.

"And the rest of what you said—you expect me to submit to your authority. What exactly does that mean? Because I know you're not talking about the bedroom." But I was sure he'd expect that in the bedroom too, if I ever got him to agree to taking me there.

"It means I'm the one in charge," he said, as though it were obvious. "I expect that you will want to argue with me about a myriad of subjects, and that's your prerogative, as long as you understand never to disagree or disobey me in public and that I will always have the final say. And, while you are free to speak your mind in the privacy of our home, I can't assure you that there won't be consequences."

I choked back a laugh. Was he serious? "Consequences? I'm dying to know how you plan to inflict consequences on a grown woman."

"As I will be the sole source of your income, I'm sure you'll see there are plenty of opportunities for punishment."

Everything he said was more flabbergasting than the last, almost as if he were trying to push my limits, but I refused to let him see me react. It helped that I didn't know how to feel about so much of it. It was disgusting what he expected of his wife. It was alarming.

It was also useful. Exposing his values alone would be enough to get him attacked by the Twitter Social Justice Warriors.

And beyond that...it was fascinating. I was utterly rapt with the idea. Surrendering total control to another human being—by choice, not manipulation—what would that be like? What *could* that be like?

It couldn't be at all.

There were flaws with his consequences, for one. "You're forgetting that I come to this marriage with my own money."

He crossed one leg over the other, propped his elbow on the arm of the chair and worried his chin with a single finger. "Ah, yes. But as your husband I will insist on over-seeing your spending, whatever the source."

No one had a say in what I did, what I spent. My parents had barely supervised my spending when I was a child. And he wanted me to let him tell me what I could and could not buy?

I took a long swallow of my drink.

He seemed to understand I was near a limit. "You'll find that I'm more than generous beyond these boundaries," he explained, trying to cushion the blow. "I will provide you a monthly allowance of one hundred thousand pounds, which will above and beyond pay for the kind of lifestyle you are accustomed to living. Any expenses over that will require my approval."

So he wasn't a monster. Not entirely.

But mostly.

I tried to fight the inclination to challenge him. Had to remember the goal. If it weren't for The Game, I would have left the room when the conversation started. I wouldn't even be in the room to begin with. There was a point to this, and I had to keep that in mind. Going along with his stupid rules and "expectations" now would make ruining him all the more victorious.

Except, he was maddening. And even with the silent pep talk, I couldn't resist pushing back. "Can you remind me again what it is that *I* get out of this marriage?"

"You get to be my wife," he said, as though there could be nothing clearer in the world.

I clenched my fist at my side, my fingernails digging into my palm.

After a breath, I said, with as much courtesy as I could muster, "As you've explained it, being your wife doesn't sound like much of a reward."

"I believe there are a lot of women who would beg to differ."

"But you're not asking a lot of women. You're asking *this* woman, and this woman wants to know what she gets out of it." There was no doubt I sounded snarly, but what the fuck did he expect?

"Fair enough." While I'd thought my bitterness might earn me a reproval, Edward seemed instead to be impressed. "As my wife, you'll have money, power, and a reputation that you can't earn on your own with your current credentials. You'll have respect from important people who, at the moment, don't even know you exist. Most importantly, you'll finally be able to move out of the shadow of your past, as I believe you want so very much to do."

A chill ran down the back of my neck. There was no

way he knew about my past, about the things I'd done to people. The games I'd played.

He was bluffing. He had to be.

I played dumb. "The shadow of my past...? I don't have a shadow on my past."

"I apologize," he said, his gaze digging into me. "The shadow of your father, I should have said." My chest loosened as the breath I'd been holding released. "Wouldn't you like to be known as more than just Celia Werner, daughter of Warren?"

"And you're offering me Celia Fasbender, wife of Edward. Forgive me if I don't see the difference."

"You became a daughter by the luck of the draw. You become a wife by being chosen. My decision to marry you signals to the world that I believe you are worthy of the title. Believe me when I say my approval carries a lot of weight."

It was the first time since he'd proposed his ridiculous plan that I considered that he actually did have something to offer me. I'd grown up believing an important man would want to marry me. Specifically, I'd believed that man would be Hudson Pierce, and when that option was taken away from me, I'd lost a sense of my identity. Even now I wondered what Hudson would think of me marrying Edward, if he'd regret letting me get away. If he'd finally see me as worthy.

Stupid, right? Weren't we past the age when women's lives were valued in relation to a man's?

I knew that, and yet I also didn't. It wasn't something I'd ever been able to explain to anyone, mostly because I couldn't begin to explain it to myself.

Now here, this asshole got it.

It annoyed me. It annoyed me that there was a part of me that still felt that way. It annoyed me that he knew that. It annoyed me most that, even if I acknowledged he was right, I would still never feel validated by this marriage because, even if no one else knew, *I* knew that none of it was real.

"That's so arrogant," I said, turning my irritation toward him. "And patriarchal. And intangible. Especially when you aren't truly offering me the position of wife."

"What do you mean?" He dropped his hand from his chin, and leaned ever so slightly forward, as though he really cared about my answer.

"I mean…" I had to pause to think about what I meant. Think about how to explain it. The last thing I wanted was for him to think I wanted something like love from him or that I was infatuated with him, which I most certainly was not. "What if I want a baby? I know you said you didn't want any more, but what if I do?"

He cleared his throat, seemingly surprised. "Might I remind you that I said we won't be having sex."

Right, right, that was another thing I planned to address before the night was over. "But I'm certain that you're going to be having sex elsewhere. And if you are, then I should be allowed the same."

He was going to say I wasn't allowed, and that would be a perfect opportunity to demand it from him. He certainly couldn't expect me to live as a celibate.

Except he didn't say that. "Whatever you do, you will be perceived as a faithful wife by everyone around us."

"That's not a no."

"It's not." But his jaw twitched, and I felt somewhat mollified that the idea of me sleeping with someone else might bother him.

Only, now I couldn't use that as a reason to goad him into sex with me.

I went back to my last line of interrogation. "Then, let's say I had a discreet affair and got pregnant?"

"You won't," he said with finality. "Not if you expect to stay living under my roof."

"So you'd make me get an abortion?"

"I'd make you get a *divorce*. And you can be sure that ten million mentioned in the prenup requires a paternity test."

I blinked, astounded by his inflexibility. "You really hate children."

"I won't raise another man's child."

And now I had another angle. "What if *your* mistress got pregnant?"

"They wouldn't."

I tried not to flinch at his reference to plural women. "Of course they wouldn't, because what you say goes, even with biology. Maybe you haven't yet heard that the only reliable method of birth control is abstinence."

"It's not quite the same comparison, though, is it? I could sire a child and no one would ever be the wiser. You, however, couldn't hide a pregnancy. In other words, what happens in this area with me and my mistresses, is really not any of your concern."

This, out of every unreasonable thing he'd said so far, this was the one that not only pinched at my ideals of equality, but also stung.

I didn't have any idea why I cared. I didn't like children. I didn't like him. It shouldn't have mattered what he did. Why was I pushing this when none of it mattered in the grand scheme?

We stared at each other, as though we were at a stalemate.

After several beats of silence, he sat back in his chair. "If you're set on having a child, I think you should consider backing out of this right now."

"I'm not," I answered too quickly. "I'm still young, though. That could change." It wouldn't, but that was beside the point.

And, though he'd closed the door on that protest, I wasn't ready to stop pushing back. "What if I don't think the monthly salary is suitable?"

"It *is* suitable."

"I might not agree."

A knowing smirk played on his lips. "You're just trying to test me. See if I'll budge on anything, and I won't."

We'd see about that. "What if I want to take a trip without you? Go and visit my friends back home."

"Then you'd approach me with the idea, and we'd discuss it."

I spelled out his subtext for him. "And you'd get the final say."

"Yes."

We were going in circles. I changed course. "I want two vacations a year without you. I walk out of this room if we can't agree on that."

"Sure." He'd given in too easily. It couldn't be that simple.

It wasn't. "I encourage you to take vacations, in fact," he went on. "Time for yourself is always a good idea. You decide when and where, and if it doesn't conflict with my schedule or my notions of where a wife should travel or who she should visit, you can take your little trips."

"Maybe I should rephrase—I want two vacations a year *guaranteed*."

"And you'll get two vacations. On my terms."

God, he was impossible. I could just imagine him in a boardroom. No wonder my father hated him. "You were right to assume these conditions would be a hard sell."

"And I'm not even finished." There was that grin again. The one that made my knees knock and my panties damp.

I threw back the rest of my drink and held it out toward him. "You might want to refill my glass before you go on."

He made no move to get up. "I think you've had enough already. I appreciate wanting to soften the punch, but I'd prefer you had a clear mind for this discussion."

It rankled me that he thought my alcoholic intake was his business.

And, also, it didn't. Also it felt natural. It felt nice, even. To have someone care enough about me as a person that he'd think my behavior even mattered.

I set the empty glass on the coaster he'd provided, and stared at the fire as I considered. "Is that an example of what it would be like? Bossing me around about when and how much I drink or what I wear or how I do my hair."

"Mm." The sound rumbled in his throat, and I willed myself not to shiver.

I turned my gaze toward him, finding his eyes already on me, as they so often were. *This is how he'll always be.*

This is how he'll always watch me.

This time I did shiver. "I'd have to stop calling myself a feminist."

"That's not what's making you hesitate."

I laughed out loud, glad for an excuse to break the increasing tension. "Oh, really? Then what is?"

"You're ashamed of how much you like it."

The blood drained from my face. I could feel it dropping through my body as fast as my stomach. He had no right. It was one thing to order me around, but he had no right to guess what I was feeling. No right, even if he wasn't wrong.

"Don't fuss because I've called you out. There's no need for that. There's a benefit in both of us being on the same page." As disapproving as his tone was, his scowl was playful, reinforcing my suspicion that he relished my discomfort.

I had nothing to say in response. I didn't want to give him an opportunity to see anything else about me.

He let the silence stretch out for a beat, then asked, "Shall I go on with my expectations now?"

"Sure," I said stiffly.

"We won't have a big wedding. A small ceremony in the salon should be sufficient. There's no need to wait. Sometime before the end of the year will do. We can arrange a date with my secretary. We'll want to be sure my schedule is clear so we can work in a honeymoon."

A small ceremony was fine. This wasn't a real wedding, after all, and I had never been fond of pomp and circumstance. But as sure as I was that he was simply goading me with all his demands, his last sentence was so infuriating,

I couldn't let it pass by without remark. "And why exactly would we go on a honeymoon?"

"Again, appearances."

Of course. *Appearances.*

"We'll go to my island in the Caribbean. It's beautiful there. You'll like it."

"I like sunny places." An isolated island in the Caribbean could be a good opportunity for seduction. "Anything else?" I didn't bother to hide my impatience, more than ready for this whole list of stipulations to be done with.

But Edward had more. "Your father…"

Ugh. My father. He didn't have to finish his sentence. "Yes, he is the reason for this marriage after all. I can't promise you anything from my father. He's his own person, and I have very little pull where he's concerned."

It was petty how much I enjoyed not being able to give him reassurances, even though, by lack of doing so, I was potentially ruining the entire arrangement.

Or maybe he'd change his mind and see he needed an heir for this to work out after all.

"I don't expect you to make any commitments on his behalf." He dropped his hand from his chin, punctuating what he intended to say next. "I do, however, expect you to make every effort to endear him to me. Show him that you believe in me and my motivations. Help him build con-fidence in me so that, when the time comes, he'll see me as the natural person to take over as the head of Werner Media."

I still contended that Edward had serious misconceptions about my influence.

But if all he wanted was for me to play nice, to play

like he was a good guy in front of my father, I could do that. It would be hard to deceive him in such a way, not hard like I couldn't do it, but hard because I was eager for the day that I could tell him what all of this had really been about. I couldn't wait to see Dad's face when he realized I'd destroyed his enemy.

That *was* what I couldn't wait for, wasn't it?

"Fine. Sure," I said, not wanting to think about it too hard anymore. "I'll do what I can."

"Excellent." Edward finished off his drink and stood to take both his and my glass back to the bar. I'd thought he had wanted to tidy up and was going to leave them there, but the asshole refilled his glass, leaving mine empty.

Yes, destroying him *was* what I wanted. Maybe I'd even be able to let my parents in on what I was about from the beginning.

"What have you told your parents about us?"

Except I'd forgotten for a second that Edward planned to dictate every aspect of my life. Best to keep them in the dark after all.

"Not a lot," I answered honestly. "I told them I was coming to London for a client whom I was also interested in romantically. I didn't tell them your name. I wanted to build you up anonymously before my father realized who you are."

Edward, having returned with his drink, perched on the arm of his chair. "Good. That's very good."

There was genuine admiration in his eyes, and, like a fool, that was all it took to revive the flutters in my belly.

I was keen for more praise. "After this is all decided, I'll tell them I'm engaged so they'll get used to the idea that I'm really with this mysterious guy. But I'll dodge questions about who you are until after we're married."

The other option was to not even tell my parents I was engaged until after it was a done deal, but I'd decided that wouldn't be the best way to win their support for this man I supposedly loved. I'd thought this all through already, and this was the much better plan.

I held my chin up waiting for Edward to agree.

He didn't.

"No," he said with a frown. "That won't work. I want them here for the ceremony. I need Warren Werner to watch as you vow to be mine."

Mine. That word sent a shot of heat through my bloodstream.

It's not real, I reminded myself. I wasn't really going to be his, and why would anyone really want that anyway after hearing all his expectations?

My annoyance was more with myself than with him, but his proposal was pretty dumb. "Uh, keep dreaming there, buddy. There's a whole host of reasons why that's not going to work."

"And they are?"

I swung my feet to the floor and leaned forward. "First, my mother would never let me get by with a small ceremony. As it is, I'm going to have to play along with her about wedding preparations until we tie the knot. Even then she might insist we do a redo just so she can go big. Secondly, if my parents were here before—if my *father* is here before we're married, he will definitely try to put a stop to it."

"Not if he believes you really love me."

"Even then." Surely he had to realize how much my

father hated him.

Edward tilted his head, his expression skeptical. "He'd prevent you from marrying your soulmate? The man you've waited for all your life? I seriously doubt any father can deny his only daughter's happiness, even if it's tied up in his business rival."

"Yes, but..." But Edward *wasn't* my soulmate. He wasn't the man I'd waited for all my life.

"You have to sell it that way," he said, reading my doubts which I was sure were all over my face. "And I trust that you can."

I'd been about to say it was impossible, but his trust in me made me hesitate. Could I really do this? Could I convince my father that Edward made me happy, that I wanted to spend my life with him?

It would be the hardest con I'd ever played. And I did like a challenge.

Still... "I don't know. I don't see how I'll get them here for it. I can put off telling them who you are for a while, but as soon as I tell them the wedding is soon and not a year or more away, they'll start demanding more information and once I say it's you, I'm not sure I'll even be able to keep my father on the phone to discuss it."

Unless...

"Then don't tell them you're getting married until you're face to face."

Edward voiced the very idea I'd just been considering. It had merit.

"Here's a thought," he said. "Tell them you're engaged, and you're in love and very happy, and that rather than tell them anything about your intended, you'd prefer for them to meet me in person. Then invite them to come to London. For your birthday, perhaps, if you need an occasion."

I nodded, seeing where he was going. "Then when they're here, 'Surprise! We're getting married right now.'"

"Exactly."

I sat back and pondered the idea from all angles. They'd be upset, of course, but in person really was the best way to convince them of something so big. "My birthday is November ninth," I said, doing the math. "Two months from now."

"I know."

For fuck's sake, Celia, do not get all giddy because he knows when your birthday is.

His gaze drifted up in thought. "I actually just had a project drop from my calendar in November. I think that will work perfectly. I'll check with Charlotte on Monday."

"Okay." I had to take a deep breath to keep the room from spinning. We had a date. This was happening. This was really happening. "Okay," I said again, steadying myself with the two syllables.

Edward's brows perked up. "Okay? To everything?"

I opened my mouth to answer, and then stopped myself. This was my chance to make my own appeals.

"Yes, okay to everything, but while we're negotiating..." I met his eyes and my heart skipped a beat at the intensity of our connection.

Damn, I really wished I had that second drink.

"Are we? Negotiating?" He was so smooth. So unaffected.

"While you're *demanding,*" I said, standing up. I tossed

my hair hoping it looked as sultry as it felt. "It seems only fair that I have a chance to make my own requests."

"Just so long as you understand that they are only requests."

The amusement was back in his expression.

I sauntered over to him, stopping directly in front of where he was perched. "Right. Because you have the final say on everything. But only once this arrangement starts, and, until there's a ring on this finger," I wiggled the appropriate digit, "I haven't agreed to anything yet."

Sitting like this, on the arm of the chair, his back straight, we were practically the same height. It occurred to me that this was the closest we'd ever been to having equal footing, and somehow that made me both heady and encouraged.

I reached out to rub the collar of his shirt between my thumb and forefinger, my breath stuttering under the thick weight of apprehension, my mouth watering from how close I was to touching his skin. This close, I could smell the liquor on his breath and the musky scent of his cologne and the fainter scent underneath of pure man.

"Tell me your requests." Was it my imagination or did his voice suddenly seem darker? Less steady?

"There's only one." I leaned in until my lips were near his ear. "I want to add sex to the deal."

He made a sound low in his throat, half like a laugh, half like a moan. "What, now?"

He turned his face toward mine, and now our mouths were only inches away from touching. I could feel the warmth of his exhale on my skin, sending a trail of goosebumps down my arms.

"Now, sure." Fuck, I was wet already. "But I meant in the marriage, too."

His lips danced around mine. "You don't know what you're asking for. You want to be humiliated, degraded, and hurt?"

Yes.

Because that was the goal of The Game.

But, also, *YES!*

Because, in that moment, there was nothing more I could imagine wanting than to be all those things, to be humiliated and degraded and hurt, by him. I wanted it so much I ached. Ached in places I hadn't known could feel.

I reached my neck forward, pushing my mouth toward his.

Just when I thought the kiss was inevitable, he leaned back. "You couldn't handle it."

I was frustrated, but he was still here. Still engaged in the conversation. I hadn't lost him completely yet. "How do you know I'm not into what you're into?"

He brought a finger up and traced the tip along my jaw-line. "If you were into what I'm into, you would settle for what I give and not try to demand more."

Somewhere in the back of my head, I understood what he was saying, that he wanted submission here, too. That he was the one who did the seducing.

But I was too desperate for him, and too scared that he wouldn't do the seducing if I pulled back. "I don't think it's fair to come to that conclusion while we're still in the negotiation stage."

I lifted my hand to cup his cheek, to hold his face still.

He caught my wrist before I reached my destination and brought it down to hold between us. "You still haven't figured it out, have you? This isn't a negotiation stage. There's no bargaining here, Celia. Not with me. There's what I want or there's nothing at all. I don't negotiate."

I studied his face while he spoke, so I didn't see what his other hand was doing until I felt the ring being slid down my finger, slipped past my knuckle, until it was snug at the base.

Surprised, I glanced down to see what I was wearing. Once I saw it, I couldn't look away. It was vintage and white gold and square—a ring I would never have chosen for myself. Nevertheless, it was exquisite. The center stone had to be at least three carats and was surrounded by a double cushion-shaped frame lined with shimmering round accent diamonds. Intricate milgrain details ran along the band. There were so many stones that, no matter which way I turned my hand, they caught the light.

I'd never been given anything as beautiful in my life.

"It's stunning," I said, barely able to speak over the knot in my throat. Where had it even come from? I'd thought he was being a dick when he said he already had something. He must have had it in his pocket all night long.

"It's stunning on your finger." He sounded almost as awed as I felt.

It made me feel beautiful, both his words and the ring itself and suddenly I wanted to do something for him, give him something that made him feel as good as this small object made me feel.

"Will you wear a band as well? I'd like to pick it out, if you'll let me."

He searched my face for several heavy seconds, his

eyes flicking more than once to my lips, and I was sure, absolutely sure he was going to kiss me.

I held my breath, waiting.

But he didn't kiss me. Instead, he stood and pushed past me, heading toward his desk. "It came in a set. I have wedding bands for both of us already."

I was still recovering from that rejection when he picked up the cradle on the antique phone I'd thought had been just decoration. "Ms. Werner is ready to go back to her hotel," he barked. "Bring the car around. She'll be down momentarily."

The message was clear. There'd be no kisses, no negotiating, no sex. Edward's word was law.

"I guess I'll be going," I said, as though I had a choice in the matter, fighting like hell to hold back tears. "Thank you for the wonderful evening."

I took off down the stairs, not waiting for him to offer to escort me or even say good night. If I stood around even a minute, I was afraid he'd see into me like he always did. Afraid he'd see truths about me I didn't even know myself.

It wasn't like I was leaving with nothing. We were officially engaged. I had a ring. He'd established the rules of this dark little game of ours. A game I was more committed to playing than ever.

I just couldn't say anymore if I wanted to play to destroy him or to win him.

23

"Look up, and don't blink," Jodie, my makeup artist, directed.

Don't blink was an easy enough instruction
to follow. My problem was fidgeting. I would never admit
it out loud, especially not to Edward, but I was nervous.
How had two months gone by so quickly?

That was a stupid question. I knew exactly how they'd
flown by—I'd been kept extremely busy, that was how.
The day after he'd slid the engagement ring on my finger,
Edward had thrown me into wedding planning, much to
my chagrin. I would have much preferred to hire a profes-
sional. The budget I'd been allowed for the event could
certainly have paid for one of the best and still had plenty
left over.

When I'd run the idea past Edward, though, he'd
been vehemently opposed. *"Your parents know you,"*
he'd said. *"The ceremony may be small, but they will
expect to see your touch in the details. If it's generic and
cold, they won't believe your heart is really in this
marriage."*

Well, because my heart really wasn't in the marriage.

"Besides," he'd countered when I'd continued my argument. *"You might find you enjoy it."*

I'd laughed in his face then. But the last laugh was his, because, although I'd been pissed to be tasked with the project, I *had* grown to enjoy it. It hadn't really been like planning a wedding—an event I had absolutely zero interest in taking part of—because the guest list for our ceremony was so small. It had been more like organizing a fancy party with flowers and live music and a designer dress and gourmet dessert trays. With a sizable budget and free rein to do whatever I wanted in the salon and dining room, I'd found the process similar to interior designing. The beauty was in the particulars, as Edward had suggested, and I'd gone all out making it feel like it was *mine*.

I was pleased with what I'd come up with, in the end. Proud. Excited, even. Definitely nervous to see it all go off without a hitch.

Between the planning and meetings with lawyers to both review and then sign the prenup, I'd barely had time for anything else, including seducing my husband to be. His schedule had been part of the problem. He had indeed been able to get the time off for a honeymoon, but he'd had to cram a lot of long days into the weeks beforehand. I'd convinced myself it was fine. My scheme required sexing to happen after vows were exchanged, not before.

That reasoning didn't seem to translate to my libido.

I'd spent eight long weeks drowning in want. While I'd stayed at the hotel the whole time, I'd made sure to connect with Edward whenever possible. His desire to be apprised of everything wedding related had made that easy enough, and as annoyed as I'd been with this specific demand, I'd taken advantage of it, using it as an excuse to meet for dinner or drinks. I'd inundate him with details and took every opportunity to brush past him and sit too close and accidentally touch.

But, as much as I'd flirted and prolonged these encounters, I'd left each night more aroused than when I'd arrived. He was good at that, I'd learned. Good at provoking me. Good at pushing the tension. Good at winding me up tighter and tighter and tighter until I didn't think I could stand another second without the crush of his lips against mine. Good at leaving me with the female equivalent of blue balls.

Tonight, though, everything would change. Tonight, we'd be married and instead of sleeping in a room halfway across the city, I'd be in a bed next door to him. This morning I'd checked out of my hotel and had my belongings delivered to my room in the master suite, and now, getting ready for the big event in *his* house—in *his* personal space—I already felt closer to my goal.

If I was honest with myself, that was what had me the most nervous. Not my parents' impending arrival, not the show we'd put on in this farce of a wedding, not the menu or the decor or anything to do with the actual ceremony, but what happened after. What happened tonight, when we were finally alone in the suite. That's what had me twitching and sweating. That's what had the butterflies swarming in my stomach like I was climbing the big hill of a roller coaster.

Jodie put her mascara wand down on the counter and turned back to me. "Okay, look right at me so I can see if your eyes are even."

I did as she asked, fighting the urge to glance at my reflection in the mirror behind her instead.

"You look fab, girl. Now, all we have left is your lips

and then we can get those curlers out of—"

A noise downstairs caused me to put up my hand to shush her.

"Did you hear that?" I strained my ears to see what else I could hear. Two floors up, most noise from the ground floor came up muffled or not at all, but I'd left all the doors of the suite open specifically hoping I'd hear the doorbell.

Jodie shook her head, her expression baffled.

"Did it sound like the doorbell? I swear it was the doorbell." I jumped up and ran to the window and peered down at the front step. "Shit! It's my parents! They're early!"

"Actually, uh, we're running a tad late." Jodie smiled guiltily, even though it wasn't entirely her fault we'd gotten behind schedule. A delay in the floral delivery had prevented me from getting started with my hair and makeup at the time I'd originally planned.

It didn't matter whether we were behind or on time—I had to greet my parents. I still had hot rollers in my hair, and I wasn't even dressed, but they still didn't know anything about what was happening today or who my fiancé was, and there was no way I was letting Edward get to them first.

I grabbed my dressing robe and tied it quickly around me. "I'm sorry. I have to go down there. I'll be back up as soon as I can."

Unless my father dragged me out of the house kicking and screaming. I hadn't totally ruled that out as a possibility.

Taking them two at a time, I rushed down the stairs, pausing on the next floor down to be sure Edward was still locked away in his office where he'd been sequestered until the ceremony. The doors were only slightly ajar, but I glimpsed a partial view of his backside and blew out a sigh of relief, and not just because of how damned good his ass looked in his suit pants.

While he'd agreed to every other one of my suggestions, my parents' arrival had been the one thing the two of us had argued about in the planning process. He'd wanted to be there when I told them who I was marrying. I insisted he wasn't. His presence would only stir my father up before I had a chance to offer any explanation, and even if I managed to get him to stay for the wedding after that, it would greatly reduce the chances of him ever liking Edward.

And there was no good benefit of Edward being there. As far as I could tell, his reasons for wanting to be were sadistic and mean. He wanted to see my father's face when I announced my engagement to his rival, that was all. It was only when I called him out that he backed down, lucky for me, because as he'd promised the night of our "negotiations," he really did have the last word on everything. Even then, I hadn't trusted him not to try to undermine the decision when the time came. Hence why I was eager to get downstairs.

When I got to the ground floor, Jeremy was just exiting the receiving room. "Ah, ma'am. I was just coming to inform you of your parents' arrival."

"I heard the doorbell, thank you." I started to move past him then stopped. "Jeremy, would you mind making sure that Edward doesn't come down here?"

I knew it was hardly fair, asking him to try to influence anything his boss did or didn't do, and his expression told me that he wasn't at all comfortable with the idea.

"Because it's our wedding day, and all," I said, hoping he'd buy the excuse. "The groom isn't supposed to see the bride until the ceremony." It wasn't like we'd purposefully been trying to honor the tradition. With both of us having separate agendas for the day, it had just worked out that way. It was now seven in the evening, and we'd only bumped into each other in the hall once, much earlier in the day.

"I'll do what I can," Jeremy reluctantly acquiesced. It wasn't a guarantee, but I'd take what I could get.

With that issue managed, I slipped into the receiving room. "Mom! Dad! You made it!" They'd actually arrived in London the day before, but this was the first time I'd seen them. Between their jet lag and the last minute preparations, it had seemed easiest for everyone involved to wait until tonight.

"There's the birthday girl," my father said, kissing my cheek as I embraced him. "You're not dressed yet? Are we early?"

"No, it's me. I'm behind."

My hands were both still around my father when my mother exclaimed, "Oh, Celia! That ring!"

I pulled out of his arms to show off the jewel I'd become quite attached to. After she oohed and aahed over it to her satisfaction, I moved to hug her. "You look fabulous, Mom. Is this dress new?" I knew it wasn't. She'd worn the metallic sequin gown for a charity event the previous year, but I figured they both needed as much buttering up as possible.

"This old thing?" she said, her cheeks getting red. "I was afraid I'd overdressed. You did say the party was formal?"

"I did," I said, cringing inwardly at her reference to a party. That was the lie I'd told in order to get them here and dressed appropriately. "I mean, it is. Formal. You both look great."

Okay, perhaps my nervousness extended to telling my parents the truth, too. Because right now my heart felt like it was about to pound out of my chest and my throat felt like I'd swallowed a quart full of sand.

Best to rip the Band-Aid off fast.

"Hey, um, let's sit down for a moment and talk." With my hand on each of their backs, I gestured them gently toward one of the sofas.

"I don't need to sit," my father said.

"Right," my mother agreed. "We're both eager to meet this man of yours. And don't you need to finish getting ready?"

"Yes, yes, I do. And you'll meet, uh, *my man* soon enough. Actually, that's kind of what I want to talk to you about. So could you please, for me, just sit down for a minute?"

"Sure, honey. Sure." My mother exchanged a glance with Dad, a glance that said *oh, no, the engagement's been called off.*

Of course they'd immediately think the worst. Maybe that would be to my benefit. They'd be so happy to find out I hadn't ruined things after all that they wouldn't care who I was marrying.

Yeah, right.

I waited until they were both settled on the sofa then I pulled an ottoman over so I could sit directly in front of them. As soon as I was seated, though, I started to panic. Should I have a drink for this? *They* should probably have a drink for this.

I shot back to my feet. "Can I get you something to drink? Some brandy? Scotch?"

"None for me," my mother said, giving her husband a look that said he'd better say the same thing.

I'd never realized how well the two communicated without words. It was something to aspire to in a relationship, really. If I ever had a real one of those in the future.

With no chance of liquor easing the sting of my confession, I sank back down on the ottoman and took a deep breath. "As I've told both of you already, I am...um, in love with Edward."

Way to sell it, Celia.

I could do better. I had to do better.

"I'm *completely* in love with Edward. Eddie." Eddie sounded like a good pet name, right?

"Edward...Eddie. Is that the name of your fellow?" My father didn't wait for me to answer before diving into his next question. "Is this his house we're at? This is a really expensive house, Madge. Did you notice it's across from Regent's Park?"

My mother nodded, her eyes wide and glimmering. "You didn't tell us this Edward was so well-to-do."

At least Edward's wealth impressed them.

It also gave me something to latch onto as I tried again to emphasize my "feelings" for my husband-to-be. "I guess that's because I don't even notice his money, Mom. That's how much I love him. How much I love Eddie. He's turned my entire world upside down. But in a good way! I can't even remember what life was like before him. He's... just..." What the fuck did women say about the men they loved? I'd gotten in the middle of enough relationships that I should know this.

The truth. Stick to as much of the truth as possible.

"I was numb before Edward. Since I've met him, I've felt things that I haven't felt in ages. He makes me excited. He makes me crazy. He makes me calm, too, strangely enough. Even when he has my stomach fluttering like I swallowed a bunch of bees, I feel anchored."

It was the first time I'd been honest with them about Edward.

It was the first time I'd been honest with myself, too.

My mother reached out to pat my knee. "Well, honey, that's what love is. I'm so happy you've found it, and with such an impressive man. What does he do again? Did you ever tell me?"

"Uh...he owns his own company. I'll tell you more in a minute, but first—"

The front door swung open, cutting me off mid-sentence. "Hello!" Genevieve said, smiling brightly. "Oh. I thought I was late. But you aren't even dressed yet. Is everything all right?"

I wanted to say, *No, everything is not all right,* especially when Hagan came in right behind her, but she'd likely already gotten that from looking at me. All the blood had drained from my face the second she'd walked in the door. I'd been so worried about Edward walking in and ruining my whole confession, I hadn't even considered the possibility his children could do the same thing.

This was fine. If I dealt with it swiftly and carefully, this didn't have to be a big deal at all.

I stood up, and my parents followed suit. "Everything's fine. I'm behind, is all, but I wanted to talk to my parents for a minute before the whole evening started." *Hint, hint, I want to talk to them alone.*

"Ah! These are your parents!" Hagan had no skills at reading subtext, apparently, and instead of rushing along he was now extending a hand out in greeting.

"Mom, Dad, this is Hagan and Genevieve, Edward's children." I turned to the siblings. "Madge and Warren Werner." It was a quick introduction, but adequate, and maybe now they'd get the clue?

Hagan didn't move. "Fantastic to meet you. Are you excited for the big event?" Obviously neither of Edward's kids knew the whole night was a surprise to my parents.

"For the wedding? Or for tonight's—"

I cut my mother off. "I don't want to be rude, but I really need to finish talking to my parents, and I'm sure Camilla could use some help with Freddie while she finishes getting ready."

Genevieve wasn't so obtuse. "Hagan, come on. Dad's probably pacing a hole in the carpet upstairs. Let's go check on him."

Thank the Lord they were leaving.

I'd just gotten my parents sat back down when Genny reappeared. "Whoops. Didn't shut the door. Wouldn't want Dad to see you before it's time."

I held a frazzled smile until the doors were closed, and she was definitely gone.

"What did she mean about her dad not seeing you?" Of course my mother hadn't missed that.

"Nothing. It's nothing." I shook my head profusely, refusing to figure out a better explanation. I needed to just get through this. She'd figure it out soon enough. "Where was I?"

"Those kids of his are adults," my mother said, not caring where I'd been before. "How old is their father?"

"He's a decade older than me, Mom. He had his kids young. Not a big deal." Seriously, if she was going to get worked up about our age difference, I didn't stand a chance with the other information.

"He's established, Madge," my father said. "That's what matters." He turned back to me. "You were telling us about Edward's business, I believe."

That hadn't actually been what I'd been telling them. "Right. But first—"

"Yes, but first…" My mother nodded encouragingly. "That's what you were saying."

"But first, I want to really be sure you understand how happy I am and how much I want to be with Edward."

My mother brought her hand to her heart like an actress in a melodrama. "Honey, you're making me nervous. What's wrong?"

"Are you knocked up?" My father's tone said he might have to kill my fiancé if I was, an almost comical reaction since I was already getting married. To be fair, he'd had the same reaction the one time I had been pregnant. At least he was consistent.

I laughed nervously. "No, no. I'm not pregnant." *That would require us to have had sex first.* "And nothing's wrong. But there are a couple of things you should know. Um." I blinked, the words stuck in my throat. Why was this so hard?

"Just spit it out, Celia." My father never had patience for drawn-out conversations.

"Okay. Right. Okay." I leaned over to take my mother's hand. "Now, don't be mad, Mom, but this isn't really a birthday party."

"Are you saying...?" She trailed off so I couldn't be sure she'd guessed accurately.

"I'm saying, surprise! I'm getting married!" I'd been joking when I'd originally proposed breaking the news like that, but, in the moment, that was the way it came out.

"Tonight? You're getting married *tonight*?" My mother was as taken aback by this announcement as I'd thought she would be. She carried on for another ten minutes this way. I was anxious about getting my hair done in time, so I was watching the clock.

My father, on the other hand, was pleased as punch that he wouldn't have to pay for a wedding, the bastard. It wasn't like he couldn't afford it.

"Mom, please," I said finally, wishing I could stop the seconds from ticking by. "I'm getting married tonight because that's the kind of wedding I wanted. Please, please accept that and don't ruin this day for me."

That clammed her up for all of one heartbeat. Then she was crying and hugging me—awkwardly since we were both still sitting—and telling me how happy she was for me and to just be included on my special day.

It was a knife right through the heart. If only I could tell her the truth.

My father fidgeted in his seat, obviously ready to be done with all the emoting. "Well, do we get to meet this Edward before the ceremony or is that going to be a surprise as well?"

I broke away from my mother's embrace and braced myself. "Actually, Dad. You've already met him."

And for all the times I'd considered him a dense old man, my father proved then and there that he was more quick-witted than I gave him credit for. "Oh, no. No, no, no." He stood up and started walking around the room, as if looking for a clue to confirm his suspicions. "An older British man with lots of money named Edward? A man who had been your client? I told you when you asked me about him not to work with him. I forbade you!"

"You didn't actually forbid me," I mumbled.

"It was implied! No way. There is no way in my lifetime that my daughter is marrying that man. No fucking way."

I rose to my feet and lifted my arms defensively, as if the posture could stop his anger. "Hold on. Can we talk about this calmly, please?"

"There is absolutely nothing to talk about." He snapped his fingers at my mother. "Madge, get up. We're leaving. Where did that servant put our coats?"

"Dad, don't leave!" If I hadn't been worried about messing up my makeup, I'd have tried to make myself cry. I knew how to do that.

It wouldn't have been that hard at that particular moment, actually.

My mother hadn't moved from the couch. "What's going on? I don't understand. Who is she marrying?"

My father's face went redder than it already was. "She's not marrying anyone! She's coming with us. Go upstairs and get dressed, Celia. We're leaving."

What was with all the men in my life thinking it was okay to order women around?

At least with Edward I'd gotten to choose it. My father just assumed that since he'd donated half my DNA that it was his right.

Well, fuck that. I wasn't having it. "I'm not going anywhere. I'm getting married."

"To whom?!" My mother was clearly exasperated.

Edward's voice boomed out in answer. "To me."

24

In all the commotion, I hadn't noticed the hall doors open or Edward walk in, but there was no way anyone could miss the authoritative way he spoke those two words. He commanded all attention, all three of us turning toward him the way daisies turned toward the sun.

"Edward," my father said tersely.

"Edward," I sighed at the same time. Mentally, I reserved the right to get angry later about his intrusion, but for now, in this exact point in time, I was glad he was there. I was relieved to have someone carry this burden with me.

Which was dumb, wasn't it? Because I didn't actually care about my parents' approval. That was *his* goal.

But maybe it wasn't about Edward, in the moment. This was about my father thinking he had a say in my life. This was about my father ignoring what he believed to be my happiness because of a stupid business rivalry.

This was about standing up for me.

And if Edward was going to be on my side, I was grateful for that. I was more than grateful.

As though driven by a force outside of myself, I floated over and sidled into him. He put a possessive arm around my waist, and extended his other hand toward my mother, who had finally managed to make it to her feet.

"I'm Edward Fasbender," he said graciously then kissed the back of her hand. "While I'd hope to best be known as the man who anchors your daughter, I believe your husband prefers to think of me as his main competitor."

Even as it was clear she recognized his name, my mother swooned, and who wouldn't? Edward was one smooth son of a bitch.

A son of a bitch who'd evidently been listening to—watching, even?—our entire conversation.

I reserved the right to be angry about that later too.

"I'm so very glad to meet you, considering what you mean to our daughter," my mother gushed. Legitimately gushed.

My father fumed, his fists curling and uncurling at his side. "Madge, let go of that man's hand. He's a conniving devil."

"It's not catching, Warren." Edward dropped my mother's hand, seemingly humored by the entire situation.

His amusement incited my father further. He pointed an accusing finger in Edward's direction. "You are truly incredible, Fasbender. After everything you've done, blocking my company's advances in the European market at every turn, going out of your way to sabotage the relationships I've worked my entire life to build..." He was so worked up thinking about Edward's supposed deficiencies, that he couldn't continue listing them.

Instead, he turned his finger toward me. "Don't you realize he's using you? He's not in love with you. He's just looking for another way to ruin me. He probably expects you to hand over company secrets. If you do this, Celia, if you go through with this, we're done. You're on your own."

It should have been validating. I knew my father wouldn't react well, and I'd been right. I'd been right about the depth of his hatred for Edward. It was the entire reason I wanted to play this game in the first place, because I knew how happy it would make my father to see Edward destroyed.

But I didn't feel anything like validation. I only felt empty and numb, a feeling I hadn't felt much of since I'd met Edward.

"Warren, that isn't at all true," Edward said calmly, in stark contrast to my father's ranting. "I do sincerely love your daughter. We both knew our pairing was not ideal because of who I am, because of who you are. Believe me when I say we fought our feelings knowing you'd never approve. But the heart wants what the heart wants."

He was lying out of his ass, and still I couldn't help the pinch in my chest at his declaration.

He dropped his hand from my waist, and left me for the mini bar. "I understand, though, that these are all just words. You have no reason to believe anything I say, nor should you. I certainly wouldn't be persuaded by romantic pronouncements if the shoe were on the other foot. I might add that there is a prenup in place protecting your daughter's assets, which should be reassuring, but still not exactly what you need to place your trust in this relationship."

He poured a brandy as he talked, and then crossed to my father, the drink held out in offering. "In light of all that, of the relationship you and I have had in the past, might I present this to you another way. You fear that I might have forged a relationship with your daughter merely for the benefit of my company. I propose that you have as much to gain from that scenario as I would. Perhaps this could be a union that removes the obstacles that have stood between us rather than building them up further."

For the first time since my father realized I was engaged to Edward, his demeanor cooled. His face, though still red, had lost some of its beet color. He actually appeared to be listening.

He still hadn't taken the glass offered to him, though, and now Edward nodded to it. "Take the drink, Warren. You watched me pour it. Clearly it isn't poisoned."

With a scowl, my father snatched the drink from his hand and took a long swallow before asking, "Are you suggesting an alliance of sorts?"

"In the future, yes. It's a possibility. Tonight, I believe our attention would best be spent on giving Celia the wedding she deserves, with both her parents in attendance."

My breath stuttered as it filled my lungs. It was a clever tactic, on Edward's part, making this whole night about a business advantage. On the other hand, he was an asshole for entreating my father this way. For tempting him with the very gold he hoped to get for himself through our nuptials. Especially without telling me about it first.

It was worse when I looked at it from my father's side. The fact that this was what potentially changed his mind, and not my own appeals, made me livid.

I half hoped he'd balk at the vague proposition.

He took another swallow of the brandy. "I'm not unreasonable. I can agree to set this aside for the time being with the potential of discussing it further in the future."

I wasn't the only one, apparently, who saw the sting in my father's response.

"Warren!" my mother exclaimed. She rushed to him so that she could lower her voice, but I could still hear her clearly. "You cannot use your daughter's happiness to negotiate business."

"I'm not," he insisted. "Celia already said this man makes her happy. Right, Ceeley, sweetie?" He didn't wait for me to answer before adding, "She's always been her mother's daughter. Why wouldn't she fall for someone so similar to her old man?"

I rolled my eyes. As if my father were anything like Edward.

Or, I hadn't seen a similarity until tonight. Now, as far as I was concerned, they were both devils. I had half a mind to walk out the door right then and fuck both of them over.

At the very least, I couldn't stand to be in the room with either of them anymore.

Without a word, I spun around and charged for the hall doors.

"Celia, where are you going?" my mother called after me.

I stopped and forced myself to put on a smile before turning back toward them. "I have to finish getting ready since it looks like I'm getting married in half an hour." I didn't wait for anyone's response—I definitely didn't wait for anyone's permission—before fleeing from the room.

So I'd get married. Sure. Fine. I'd go ahead with my plans to ruin Edward, but instead of doing it to make my father happy, I'd crush his hopes of a business alliance at the same time.

I wasn't doing this for him anymore.

I was doing it for me.

25

I was fifteen minutes late getting ready, but I wasn't too concerned about it. There were only six people in attendance for the actual ceremony besides the officiant and the bride and groom, and even though there was a party planned with more guests invited, we'd left ample time between to make up for a delayed start.

I probably could have made it on time, despite the interruption to deal with my parents, but I'd learned in the last two months how firmly Edward was attached to punctuality, and, call me a bitch, I wasn't in the mood to capitulate to him.

By the time I walked down the stairs at eight-fifteen, I suspected he was fuming. I was mildly surprised he hadn't come looking for me. I was even more surprised that he wasn't waiting in the hall to lecture me.

While Edward wasn't waiting, my father was. I wasn't any more interested in speaking to him at the moment than I was my husband-to-be, and when I discovered he was hoping to "walk me down the aisle," it was almost with pleasure that I explained to him that there wasn't an actual aisle for him to walk me down.

I wasn't entirely cruel, though. I allowed him to escort me down the hall into the salon, which, honestly, was essentially the same thing.

I'd seen the salon before I'd started getting ready so I knew what I was walking into, but the transformation of the interior still struck me as I entered. Practically a small ballroom, the space was easily a thousand square feet with gorgeous marble floors and a grand fireplace. Huge windows with heavy luxurious drapery wrapped around the outside of the room, alternating with wooden panels that showcased wall-mounted lights that matched the beautiful candle-style chandelier in the center of the ceiling. It was generously furnished with three large sofas, five decorative chairs, four side tables, a dining table, a piano, and several oversized floor vases, but I'd had half of the pieces removed for the event and the rest reconfigured leaving a generous section of the area open for the ceremony.

While romantic decor had never been my style, I did have a fondness for a good floral arrangement, and so when trying to be sure my touch was seen, I'd filled the room with flowers. Two columns with enormous red and white bouquets flanked the fireplace while eight smaller floral pillars were spread around the salon. Garlands sprinkled with red and white roses had been hung on all the lighting and along the window valances. The hearth had a spectacular arrangement of greenery and blooms, and the table, that would later hold decadent dessert trays and champagne, had a gorgeous centerpiece.

The heady fragrance of all these flowers was what hit me as I walked into the salon with my father. It was a soothing aroma, and as upset as I'd been prior, a blanket of calm fell on my shoulders, settling my nerves.

Until I saw Edward, anyway.

He'd had his back to me talking to the officiant, and I hadn't seen him immediately. My attention had first gone to my mother who was sitting on a sofa holding Fred. Camilla and Genny sat with her while Hagan stood off to the side, lost in his phone. No one had noticed us until my father cleared his throat, and then everyone stood and all eyes landed on me, Edward's last of all. He'd waited to finish whatever he was saying before turning, as though refusing to let anyone interrupt him, but then he did, and his gaze slammed into mine with violent force, making my knees shake and my stomach flip.

He pinned me with that gaze, not letting me move until he'd taken all of me in. And I stood there, unable to even breathe, while he did, waiting to see the verdict on his expression. I'd been anxious for this particular moment for weeks—anxious and eager—because the wedding dress I'd shown him, the wedding dress he'd approved when I'd met with him in planning, was not the one I was wearing. It was the same design—a trumpet style floor-length gown with a slit up one leg and a diamond embellished lace overlay that draped off the shoulder and down my arms.

Except, instead of being white, the dress I wore was red.

It had been an outright act of defiance. I'd assumed he'd disapprove, and he did, it was evident in the way the corners of his mouth turned down and the almost indiscernible twitch of his left eyelid. But along with his disapproval was a heated gaze of appreciation. It seared through me. Ignited my skin with its intensity. Lit the space between my legs until my pussy felt like it was a raging fire.

Whether his appreciation was for the way I looked or

the act of wearing it, I couldn't be sure. What I did know was I liked that look. I wanted him to look at me like that all the time.

To be fair, I was pretty sure I gave him the same sort of look.

He. Looked. Incredible.

I'd been too distracted to pay much attention when he'd stormed in on me with my parents earlier, and he'd only been partially dressed then, wearing his trousers and dress shirt and nothing else.

Now, with the addition of the slim fit jacket, the double-breasted waistcoat, and the red ascot tie, he was almost too handsome to look at directly. Damn, did this man know how to wear a tux.

I wondered if he knew how to take it off as well. Or if I'd ever find out.

"Well, here she is," he said, his eyes never leaving mine as he crossed the room to me. "I was beginning to wonder if you were a runaway bride, but now it's apparent why you took so long. You look stunning, darling."

The words were for everyone else, playing the part of an amorous groom. I wasn't stupid enough to believe anything else. He'd even gotten the chance to reprimand me for my tardiness, letting everyone know the late start was not on him. The words were definitely for the others.

But the gaze...

The gaze had been for no one but me.

He kissed me on the cheek, another gesture for appearances, and took my hand in his. "Shall we get started, then?"

The ceremony began with no other hitches. The officiant wore a stole and clerical garb, which made my mother happy, even though he wasn't a minister but rather a registered local authority. Good money had been paid to get him to come to the house as well as to approve the location since legally binding weddings in England usually only took place in churches or registry buildings. I'd chosen a minimalist script with only the barebones required to be legitimate. That made the whole thing, not only simple, but fast-paced.

After the officiant greeted everyone, we stated our declaratory words and then went directly to the vows, or the contracting words. Edward said his first, repeating the words he was given.

Then it was my turn. Which is when I learned that my groom had made a switcheroo of his own, because, while the vows I'd agreed to were traditional, they hadn't included the old-fashioned promise for the wife to "obey."

Now they did.

I hesitated when I heard the presider say it, not because I didn't intend to repeat it, but because the sneaky addition was a reminder of who exactly it was I was marrying, and I needed a moment to let it sink in.

Edward's brow rose as I paused, and I could practically hear his thoughts. *I told you my word is law. I told you not to argue with me in public.*

"To love, cherish, and *obey*," I said, feeling even more vindicated in my dress choice. Yes, he'd set submission as an expectation for his wife, but I'd worn red, and there was nothing he could do about it.

Obviously, there were ways to get around him.

Next came the exchange of rings. I hadn't yet seen the bands that Edward had said went with the one already on my finger, so when he pulled them from his jacket inside pocket and placed them in the palm of the officiant, I leaned in to examine them. My band had diamonds all around it in a delicate ornate setting. Edward's was a beautiful thick platinum with milgrain detailing and a high-polished edge.

They were both exquisite, but it wasn't the rings themselves that caught my breath in my lungs—it was what the presider said about them. "Rings are made of precious metal, but that same metal is also made precious by wearing them. These rings are even more precious as they have been worn before, celebrating the love and union of Edward's parents, Stefan and Amelie Fasbender."

"These were your parents' wedding rings?" I was too shocked to stop myself from saying the thought out loud. We were getting married with the rings that belonged to his *parents*? He'd put his mother's engagement ring on *me*? We didn't have a real relationship. Even if he hated his parents, why would he want to use their wedding set for this? He could certainly afford new ones.

It didn't make any sense.

I'd interrupted, and Edward gave me a stern look. I wasn't getting any answers now. It would have to wait.

"Sorry," I mumbled, turning my attention back to the officiant.

"These rings mark the beginning of your long journey together. They are a seal of the vows you have just taken. May they guard your love as they guarded the love of those who first wore them."

I couldn't wrap my mind around it even as Edward slipped the sparkling band on my finger.

When I picked up the larger band, I held it more delicately than I would have if it had been from a random ring set, and when I said the words that bound us together, "With this ring, I thee wed," a shiver passed through me, as though I could feel the presence of the woman who'd given it to her beloved before me.

After that, we were done. We were married.

The officiant pronounced us legally wed and congratulated us, and while our small gathering of family applauded, Edward put his arm around my waist and pulled me into him.

I'd somehow forgotten about this part.

We hadn't discussed it, and it wasn't written in the official script, but weddings typically ended with a kiss, and this one wasn't any different.

It wasn't the same kind of kiss that we'd shared before. That kiss had been hungry and wild and out of control and a little bit angry. But even while Edward's mouth met mine with purposeful composure, it was still dominating. Still possessive as his tongue slid against mine. Still made me dizzy and swept me off my feet with its intensity, and when he started to pull away, and I chased after him with my lips, he didn't deny me, pressing his lips once more to mine, drawing a small sigh from the back of my throat.

God, the man could kiss.

And I liked it.

And I'd promised to obey.

Boy, was I in trouble.

26

Someone opened a bottle of champagne, and a glass was put in my hand, but we barely had time for a toast before people were arriving. First it was the extra staff we'd hired for the evening. Then the pianist and the photographer.

At nine o'clock sharp, the guests began to appear.

There hadn't been many invited, fifty or so in total, mainly people high up in Edward's company and other important people he worked with. He called them friends, but I doubted the man had any of those.

Since I had only been in London a short time, and since my business had been temporarily shut down, I didn't have any "friends" to invite. There were some old acquaintances from school that had been close enough that they might have flown the distance, if I'd asked. But it was a loveless marriage and guests were only coming to the dessert and drinks portion of the night, so what was the point?

Having only my parents there for myself turned out to be a blessing. It made the rest of the evening easier to deal with. Edward expected me to be on his arm, ready to introduce to this person and that person, and then to stand there quietly smiling while he and the person talked about things that had absolutely nothing to do with me, and the photographer snapped candid pics.

It should have been more irritating than it was, to be arm candy. To be decoration. But, it gave me an excuse not to have to talk more to my parents. I didn't want to have to lie more about my relationship with Edward, and I didn't want to have to listen to my father daydream about the new relationship *he* hoped to have with Edward.

Beyond the excuse it gave me, accompanying my new husband around the room was almost fun. I'd only gone along with his stupid, old-fashioned ideas about the role of a wife because I didn't plan to be his wife for long. But playing the demure part wasn't as terrible as I'd imagined. I liked listening to the things he had to say. I liked other women looking at me with envy. I liked the men knowing they couldn't flirt with me or talk to me or even look at me without Edward being involved.

It made me feel like I somehow belonged to him. Made it feel like the ring on my finger actually meant something between us. Made me wish it *did* mean something.

We were an hour into the festivities when I finally got a second alone with him.

"You play the hostess very well," he said, his expression untypically warm, and I swear my heart tripped a beat.

It was ridiculous how the littlest compliment from him made me ridiculously giddy.

It also made me brave enough to ask the question that had been burning a hole inside me since the middle of the ceremony. "I didn't know our rings had belonged to your parents. Why…?"

I'd meant to put more after that why, but once I got there, I didn't know exactly how to phrase it without sounding ungrateful. *Why didn't you get new ones? Why would you want to use a family heirloom on me?*

The warmth he'd shown a moment before disappeared instantly. "They weren't using them anymore. Better on our fingers than in a drawer somewhere."

He was scanning the room, and I guessed he was looking for someone he hadn't talked to yet in order to get away from this conversation, which should have been a sign to end it right there.

It only made me want to push him more.

"But why wouldn't you save them for your children? Why didn't you use them when you married your first wife. Or…did you?" The thought made me suddenly ill. "Are you reusing them on me?"

He scowled at me like I was a ridiculous child. "Of course not." It was obvious he didn't want to say more, but after fretting for a few seconds, he went on. "They weren't in my possession when I married Marion. By the time I hunted them down again, she'd already grown attached to the set we'd gotten married with."

He'd had to hunt them down. When his parents had died, he'd been destitute. I'd learned that from my research. The rings must have been sold to help pay outstanding bills. They were probably difficult to find.

Then they had to mean something to him.

People didn't just hunt down old family items unless they meant something.

Edward waved at someone across the room and started

towing me toward them.

Still, I took the time of the approach to ask again. "If they were so important, why did you put them on *my* finger?"

"Because I did," he snapped angrily.

And then we were in front of the guest we'd been walking toward and Edward's features were schooled again and the subject was closed.

It was something I could ask about later when we were alone. But considering it was the first time I'd ever seen him lose his composure, I had a feeling I'd never get the real answer from him.

Or it was simpler than that and the answer was he didn't know.

I was still mulling this over, half-listening to him tell a story to his Chief Strategy Officer when I heard my father exclaim, "Ah, Ron's almost here!"

I obviously didn't hear him right, but apprehension flooded through me at the mention of the name.

With my hand still wrapped around Edward's bicep, I craned my neck in my father's direction. He was standing next to my mother typing into his phone, which didn't explain why I'd thought I heard him say my uncle's name. Because there was no way Ron could actually be coming here.

Could he?

Edward patted my hand, a subtle reminder that my focus should be on him, but then the doorbell rang and giving him my attention became impossible. I had to find out what my father had actually said, and who was here.

I politely excused myself then quickly pulled away

from my husband. I'd pay for that later, I suspected, but I figured he was so intent on me not challenging him in public that there was no way he'd challenge me right now either.

"What's going on?" I asked when I reached my father's side.

"Ron's here," he said as he tucked his phone back in his pocket. "Wanted to make sure he was at the right place before he got out of the cab, so he texted, but I bet that doorbell was him."

My throat went dry and my stomach dropped to my ankles. "*Uncle* Ron?"

"Of course Uncle Ron. Who else would I mean?" His eyes were pinned on the doors to the salon, expectantly.

"He's in London?" My voice had miraculously sounded steady.

"He's been in Frankfurt," my mom piped in. "We told him we'd be here for your birthday party, and he said he'd try to pop over. We didn't say anything because he wasn't sure he could make it. Isn't it wonderful that he did? He'll be disappointed to have missed your wedding, but he'll be so glad he got to see you on your special day."

Before my mother had finished talking, my father exclaimed, "There he is!" He waved excitedly.

I felt outside of myself, like I was somewhere else watching what was happening instead of being an active participant. My body turned toward the man approaching. I saw him, saw the familiar balding head and smarmy expression. My face even put on a smile, but I didn't feel present in any of the actions.

Then he was standing next to me, reaching out to give me a hug, and I let him, as though it were nothing for him to touch me. As though I were powerless to stop him. As though my insides weren't twisting and churning with horror.

He was still embracing me, his hands a little too low on my backside as he said something congratulatory a little too close to my ear when a third hand, a warmer, heavier hand—*Edward's* hand—pressed possessively between my shoulder blades, and I suddenly came back into myself.

At Edward's appearance, Ron let me go, his gaze lingering when his body no longer did.

"Darling, I believe we haven't been introduced," my husband said, pulling me tightly into his side.

It was only an accidental rescue. As selfish as Edward was, he'd likely only come over because he saw another man touching his wife—a man that he didn't know, no less.

But as inadvertent as it may have been, I clung to him like a lifeline.

"This is my brother, Ron Werner," my father announced excitedly, eager to be the one who made the introduction between them. "I don't know if you recognize him, Ron, but this son of a bitch who married our girl is Edward fucking Fasbender."

"Fasbender?" Ron mused. "From Accelecom, right? How did this pairing happen? Did you set up some sort of arrangement and not tell me, Warren? Brilliant."

I felt like I was going to throw up.

"Well, we're still in discussions," my father began.

But Edward spoke over him. "Certainly not," he said crossly, yet not loud enough to draw the attention of others. "My wife isn't some pawn to use to conduct business. She's a person with thoughts and feelings and free agency, and she chose to marry me, and you'd do well to remember that. Both of you. As for any dealings that might occur between Werner Media and Accelecom, we absolutely will not be discussing them tonight. If getting something out of my company is the only value you see in 'our girl,' I assure you that we won't be having any future discussions either."

If the photographer had taken a picture of us in that moment, I was sure that it would have captured four Werners with their jaws agape.

Correction—three Werners. I was a Fasbender now.

"If you'll excuse us," Edward went on, ignoring the shocked expressions of his audience, "my wife and I have other guests to attend to." With his hand securely at the small of my back, he steered me away from my family.

Instead of taking me to "other guests" as he'd said, he directed me to the champagne table. There, he poured a glass of bubbly and handed it to me.

"Drink this," he ordered softly.

I did. I drank it all down, wishing it were something a lot harder. Like cognac or Scotch or rubbing alcohol.

By the time I'd finished, I'd gotten my head back. I wasn't even sure exactly what had happened, but I was grateful and humiliated and ashamed and...confused.

Where had all that come from? After Edward had persuaded my father to allow me to marry with the promise of a potential business alliance, he now was the defender of my honor? What the fuck had changed?

Whatever it was, I wasn't sure I trusted his motives. I sure as hell didn't trust him.

"What was that about?" he asked. Strange since I thought *I* was the one who should be asking *him* that.

"What was what about?"

"You. Your uncle. What's going on there?"

Twenty-four years, and he was the first one to ask.

I didn't know how to feel about that. However I felt, I certainly wasn't going to start talking about it now. "I don't know what you mean."

"Cut the bullshit. You were white as a ghost. You were shaking when I touched you."

"I just...I didn't know..." I shook my head, looking for an excuse but my mind was blank.

After all the years of excuses, all the lies, I couldn't think of a goddamned thing, and that, on top of Edward being the one to really see me, on top of everything else that had happened that day, was the final straw.

I was pissed.

"You know what? *You* cut the bullshit," I said, turning on him. "This doesn't involve you. Why do you care?"

Edward reached out and drew his thumb softly against my lower lip, sending a parade of goosebumps down my arms. "It *does* involve me. Everything to do with you involves me. And I care because, my darling, I'm your husband. And not two hours ago, I vowed to protect and care for you. Or have you already forgotten?"

Tears pricked at my eyes, but I refused to let them fall. I refused to feel. Not for this. Not for him.

And I refused to believe he actually meant to honor his vows or this marriage or me any more than I meant to.

And I absolutely refused to believe he might actually care because, if there was one good thing to have come out of Ron's showing up, it was that he reminded me the lesson I'd learned a long time ago—when rich older men say they care, it only goes badly when they try to show you how much.

27

The after-party invites had stated the evening would be over by eleven, but, as happens, guests lingered until almost midnight. Not being night people, my parents had left earlier taking my uncle with them, thank God. I'd originally felt a tad guilty for my plan of bringing them all the way to London on the pretense of spending time with me and then, not only springing a surprise wedding on them, but also deserting them the next day for a honeymoon. Now, knowing they had Ron in town, the guilt was gone.

Emotionally and physically exhausted, I headed up to my bedroom ahead of Edward. I could hear him below as I climbed the last stairs, giving instructions to Jeremy, who I'd learned was more of a house manager than a butler. After spending the majority of the night on his arm, it felt strange to be away from him, like I was missing something. In contrast, I was very aware of the new band on my finger, pressing heavily into the webbing of my hand.

All in all, the evening had turned out acceptable. The

goal had been accomplished. I was married to Edward, and my parents were still speaking to me. It may have taken a few bumps to get there, but that was the way with projects that had any worth.

It *would* be worth it, wouldn't it?

I wasn't sure anymore.

At the moment, I could barely remember why I wanted to do this in the first place. Play The Game. Ruin Edward. The reward was the destruction. The reward was the numbness.

Did that reward always feel this abstract in the process?

Looking back over the last dozen years, I couldn't remember feeling...well, this much. Couldn't remember a time that I'd been more than blissfully empty. Right now I felt full. Full of rage and hopelessness and shame and loneliness and a bunch of other emotions I was too unfamiliar with to identify, and I just wanted them all to disappear. Go back to wherever they'd been hiding.

Maybe I was just tired. Tomorrow I'd feel better. Tomorrow I'd feel nothing.

Holding onto that hope, I found the energy to kick off my shoes, tug down my zipper, and shimmy out of the tight-fitting dress. I left it on the floor and trudged into my en suite to wash the makeup off my face. On the counter, I found the white lingerie set I'd left earlier. I'd bought them intending to seduce my husband on our wedding night, but now the mood was long gone.

Actually, no it wasn't.

Actually the mood was still very present. It was underneath all those other burdensome emotions, laying low but steady. A constant, throbbing undercurrent of need.

And, when I thought about it, I realized the other things I was feeling stemmed from this pulse, tributaries off a raging river of arousal. As if that sexual tension that had wound and wound and wound over the last few months had twined so tight that the strain had triggered other sensations. I probably wouldn't be so mad if it weren't for my fucking libido. I wouldn't be so melancholy. I wouldn't be so unbalanced.

And after all the shit Edward had pulled today—meddling with my parents, using me as bait for my father's business, expecting me to be his attachment while he mingled with friends, rescuing me from Uncle Ron and making me have nice thoughts about him—after all that shit, didn't I deserve to be relieved of this ache?

Fuck yes. I *did* deserve it.

My energy renewed by my resolve, I abandoned the face washing and freshened my makeup instead. Even after the long day, I still looked good. The soft curls had held. My eyes were sultry and expressive. All I needed was another coat of mascara and lipstick, and I looked brand new.

I stripped from my bridal undergarments and put on the sheer lace bralette and panties and the matching gossamer robe then spritzed some perfume and returned to the bedroom. Just as I slipped my foot into one of the red heels I'd worn for the ceremony, I heard Edward opening the door of his room.

Perfect timing.

The suite was laid out so that each of us could get to our rooms from the hallway, but there was also a door that connected us. I'd examined it earlier and discovered it wasn't locked, which meant I, of course, stuck my head in to check the space out. The design was more contemporary than the rest of the house, the colors all in shades of gold and brown, warmer than I'd expected from the man who slept there. The furniture was distinct and substantial without being too heavy. The chocolate brocade cloth headboard ran to the ceiling behind the bed, which was high off the floor, the centerpiece of the space, with two dark wood side tables on either side. In the far corner, a leather loveseat and high-back wing chair curved around a fireplace. I'd considered intruding further—poking around through his dresser, checking out the sturdiness of the mattress, leafing through the stack of books on the nightstand—but I'd already been behind schedule and couldn't spare the time.

Now I paused with my grip on the handle, knowing I should knock first. Knowing Edward would *want* me to knock first.

But I didn't want to knock.

I didn't want to ask permission to enter. I wanted to stride in boldly with confidence and cool composure. I wanted to command the situation.

So fuck knocking. Enough kowtowing to the man. I'd seduced plenty of men in my lifetime. I was good at it even. I was going to walk in there and slay.

I threw my shoulders back and then charged into his room. He was standing next to the upholstered bench at the bottom of the bed, where he'd lain his jacket, and, without it, I could see how well his dress shirt hugged his biceps and the way the waistcoat emphasized his trim torso. His profile was toward me, and, when I entered, he only swiveled his head to glance in my direction before returning to his task of unbuttoning his vest.

"*Now* you wear white," he said, his tone half bored.

He was being cheeky, and I almost laughed out loud at his attempt at impertinence. He'd loved the red dress, and, even if he wanted to verbally deny it, I knew the truth, and I was sure he knew I knew it.

Undeterred, I stepped further into the room, moving into his sightlines. "I don't expect to be wearing it for long," I purred.

His jaw ticked, but his face remained otherwise stoic, his gaze refusing to truly look at me. "We've discussed this."

"We never came to a resolution."

"It seemed resolved to me."

I resisted rolling my eyes. "Give a little, Edward." I sat seductively on the bench, my legs stretched out in front of me. "Give a little, and you'll be happy with how much I give in return. You want the picture-perfect wife? *Make* me a picture-perfect wife."

He finished unbuttoning his waistcoat and threw it on the bench beside me, still unwilling to give me his full attention. "I transferred your monthly allowance to your account this morning. Make yourself a picture-perfect wife."

"Money can't buy satisfaction," I replied tightly.

"Can't it?" He raised one brow in question and looked directly at me.

Once he did, he couldn't help but look at *all* of me. His eyes scanned down the length of me, and not only did I watch as he did, I could feel them as they took in each square inch of my body. Could feel them as they passed down my throat, as they slid over the curve of my breasts, as they lingered on the dusky peaks of my nipples, as they continued lower. By the time he'd made it down my legs to the stiletto heel of my studded Alexander Wang's, his pupils were dark and large.

He was interested. He was *so* interested.

And despite being interested, he strolled away from me, removing his watch as he did, and then placing it on his bedside table.

God, he was so difficult.

Seduction alone obviously wasn't going to work with him. I'd have to try another one of my best tactics—manipulation.

I stood up and followed behind him. "Listen, this makes sense. If you want this to look like a real marriage, then we should consummate it. At this point, I could walk away with an annulment. I could say whatever I wanted to about my reasons. *Publicly.* 'He couldn't get it up.' 'He wasn't able to satisfy me in the bedroom.' You're seen as an alpha in the business world. I'm sure a little impotence wouldn't be *that* concerning to your reputation. It might be harder to woo your mistresses, though, if they're worrying about your need for a Viagra prescription."

He turned then to look at me, amusement on his face.

I'd seen that expression before. Usually, I liked amusing him. Right now I wasn't sure that it was exactly what I was going for, but at least I had his focus. Maybe this approach was working.

I pushed further. "Or maybe your problem isn't getting hard, but…" I wiggled my pinky finger, suggesting he had a little dick.

He didn't have a little dick. I'd seen the outline of that big boy from across the room at The Open Door. I'd felt it against my belly when he'd kissed me in the bathroom at the Mandarin Oriental. It was a cock he should be proud of.

It was a cock I was dying to feel in the flesh.

"That's very funny," he said. "A clever way to try to get what you want. Someone ought to do something about your stubborn relentlessness."

"Maybe that someone should be you."

Again, his gaze traveled down to the tips of my breasts, which had tightened into hard nubs. "I don't respond well to being challenged, Celia," he said firmly, even though his eyes said differently.

If I could have breathed fire, I would have. "Forgive me for not having yet had a chance to read the Edward Fasbender handbook," I growled. "Have you read mine yet? If you had, you'd know that *I like sex*." I enunciated the last words to drive home the point.

He began to work on the knot of his tie, his forehead furrowed. "Perhaps I didn't make it clear that I don't expect faithfulness. Discreet indiscretions are completely permissible. Do you need help arranging a boy toy?"

This time I did roll my eyes. "I can get my own fuck boy, thank you very much. I don't want one. I want the convenience of fucking my husband!"

"The *convenience* is what brought you here tonight, then?"

I threw up my hands, exasperated. "Goddammit, Edward, *you* brought me here, okay? Is that what you want me to say? Well, there it is. I admit it. I'm attracted to you. I'm going out of my mind with how much I want you. I'm dizzy and aching and restless, and I swear if you don't touch me soon, I'm going to burn up out of need, and you'll have to explain to everyone that your new wife has left you widowed because she expired from a fatal case of lust. And maybe you think that's stupid and lame or desperate that I can be so into you when you're such an insane asshole, and maybe I am all of those things, but at least I'm owning it. I'm stupid *and* I need you to kiss me. I'm desperate *and* I need you inside me. So please quit being an obstinate jerk and give me something, I'm begging you. Please, please, please!"

I hadn't planned the outburst. The words just fell out, honest and raw, and, now having said it, I felt more exposed than if I were standing in front of him completely naked. There was wisdom to telling lies that lay next to the truth, but there was also prudence in sticking to a strategy that kept the cards close to the vest. This confession was the opposite of that. This confession was weakness and vulnerability and a big fat fucking risk.

It was also the first thing I'd said since I'd walked in the room—no, since I'd agreed to this plan, since I'd met him, even—that had earned me the gleam of pride I saw now in his features. And, though he hadn't said a single word in response yet, I could feel a change in the energy around him. An aura of invitation rather than rejection.

What had I just learned? Did he simply want to hear me say I wanted him? Was honesty one of his kinks? Or was it the begging that turned him on?

Or was I reading too much into nothing?

Each breath passed in shallow hopeful bursts as I waited apprehensively for him to say something. Say *any*thing.

He finished with his tie and threw it onto the nightstand, his eyes locked on mine. Then he turned his wrist up to undo the cufflink. "I'm the boss when I fuck," he said resolutely. "You should know that before we start."

I almost got down on my knees in relief. In gratitude.

Me. On my knees. Because a subject had told me he

was going to boss me around while he fucked me. *I* was always the boss when I fucked. I never gave up that control. What the fuck was wrong with me?

Whatever it was, I didn't want to fix it. I wanted this, wanted what he was giving. My pulse was racing with the wanting, but I played it cool. "And that's different from all the rest of the time...how?"

He tossed the cufflink on the table and began on the next one. "I haven't given you enough credit. It seems you do learn."

"Such an asshole," I mumbled, biting back a grin.

Before I even blinked, he'd pulled me to him, his hand wrapped tightly in my hair. "What was that?"

I swallowed, sure he could feel my heart beating through my chest. "You heard me."

He yanked on my hair, and I gasped at the bite of pain. "And that's why you want me. *Because* I'm an asshole."

It wasn't exactly what I'd said, and I didn't know if it was a question or if he thought he was simply repeating what I'd already said, reminding me. I was too busy staring at his mouth to think too long about it. I licked my lips in anticipation for the kiss I hoped was coming.

He jerked again, harder this time, pulling my gaze up to his. "When I ask you a question, I expect you to answer."

"Yes, Edward," I said, automatically, wanting to make him happy. "And yes. That's why I want you. *Because* you're an asshole." The stupid, lame, desperate thing was that I meant this too. I'd said before that I wanted him *even though* he was the shithead jerk that he was, but it was also *because*.

Admitting it made my already hot skin go up another

half a degree. And then another half when the admission earned me his drop dead sexy smirk.

Oh, God that smirk.

And would he just fucking kiss me already? I was convinced he was testing me to see if I could really handle letting him have the control. Honestly, I wasn't sure I could. His lips were hovering above mine, taunting me with their nearness. It would be so easy to press up on my tiptoes and close the distance between us.

But I didn't. I held back and waited for him to call the shots, even though it was killing me.

After another beat, he released his grip on my hair. "Take off your knickers. Lay down on the bed, bend your knees, and spread your legs."

Eager to comply, I scooted out of my panties. I considered taking off my robe and shoes as well, but he hadn't asked me to, and I wanted to show him I could follow directions since that seemed important to him. So I got up on the bed, letting the flimsy material of my robe drape around me, and I scooted back just far enough for my heels to perch on the edge. Then I spread my legs, like he'd asked, and felt a sudden rush of warmth from the scorching heat of his gaze.

"Now, play with yourself. Get yourself ready," he said, dropping his second cufflink on the table. "I won't be happy if you're dry when I go in." His tone was indifferent despite the look in his eyes. Despite the thick bulge of contrary evidence pressing at the crotch of his trousers.

I didn't tell him I was already wet. I'd given him enough honesty. He didn't need to see any more of my cards, though I was pretty sure the truth was obvious because, when my fingers worked their way down to my pussy in compliance, my lips were drenched.

Taking some of the moistness with my tips, I dragged my fingers up my slit to the swollen bud of heat above. With only a couple of swirls, my orgasm began to build, which was good since I needed the release, and I had a pretty strong feeling that he wasn't concerned about helping out. His expectation that I take care of all the foreplay by myself was a good indicator.

Or, maybe it wasn't all by myself, because, while it was my hand doing all the physical work, the way he looked at me while I played with myself was pretty damn hot. It was intense and appreciative, even as he meticulously rolled up first one sleeve and then the other to the elbow.

It also made me feel vulnerable, as vulnerable as when I'd confessed to wanting him as badly as I did, and, strangely, instead of shutting down my desire, the vulnerability only racheted it up a notch.

Fuck, I was going to come. Just from this. Just from his gaze.

"That's what you call getting ready for me? That pathetic attempt to get off? How disappointing." Edward's voice was harsh and taunting, and, as much as I liked pleasing him, it seemed I really did enjoy his cruelty as well, because those words were all the nudge I needed to send me over the edge.

It was a gentle climax, rolling quietly through my body. A soft whimper escaped my throat and my back arched, bending with the pleasure. It definitely felt good, but, after the weeks and weeks of tension, I wished it had been more. Though I'd faked several on more than one occasion, I wasn't a multiple O kind of girl. So this subtle serene orgasm was going to have to do.

But then Edward was there, still dressed, leaning over my torso, a hand braced at the base of my throat, the other pushing two long fingers inside me while his thumb rubbed roughly at my clit.

"I suppose I have to do this myself, don't I? Since you can't seem to get it right on your own." He hovered just above me, his breath hot on my skin while he expertly massaged my G-spot with each stroke of his fingers.

And somehow—impossibly—another orgasm racked through me with surprising speed and intensity.

"Yes, yes," I panted as my body shook with the release.

"Pitiable," Edward said, increasing the pressure on my clit. "You can do better than that. I thought you wanted this. I thought you wanted my cock."

"I do, I do!"

"Prove it, then. Show me how good your cunt will treat my cock. As of now, you don't deserve it." He added a third finger, and now he was truly fucking me with his hand, each thrust penetrating deep.

It was more than I could take, another orgasm already brewing low in my belly like a tumultuous storm, and I felt the impulse to push him away. Yet at the same time, my hips bucked up to meet each piercing stab, and the breathy words escaping from my lips were, "More! Please! More!"

Then it was upon me, a hurricane of a climax, whirling through me with violent fury. Black holes spread across my vision while tears leaked from my eyes.

"Ah, fuuuucccck!" I barely recognized the guttural moan coming from my mouth as mine. My fingers curled desperately into the bedspread at my sides. Sweat poured down my face, and my entire body went stiff, shaking uncontrollably while my pussy pulsed and clenched.

In the back of my head, I was vaguely aware of Edward still there, talking to me with urging words that I was too brainless to understand. One hand still sat heavily across my nape like a collar, but his other hand disappeared and a second later I heard the familiar unzipping sound of a zipper.

I was still vibrating when the head of his cock brushed across my entrance. "I'm not stopping to look for a condom, and I don't trust you with my cum, even if you say you're on birth control, so I'll be pulling out."

Without any other warning, he shoved inside of me on a low grunt.

And, holy shit, he was big.

I'd known he was big, but the visual evidence was much different than the tactile evidence. His girth filled me completely, pressed firmly against my walls. Each stroke in and out massaged places inside of me that had never been touched, and oh my God, I was definitely going to come again.

My heels flew off as my legs and arms went instinctively around him, both to bring him closer and to keep him from going anywhere. Oh, and also to hold on for my own dear life, because he rode me rough with deep, rapid jabs.

Even at his ferocious tempo, he barely broke a sweat. I was breathless and wild underneath him while he seemed almost unaffected.

His eyes, though. His eyes gave him away. I'd closed mine briefly first, and then I'd opened them to find him studying me intently with his heavily lidded blues. I had no idea what he saw in me, but what I saw made my stomach fly into my chest. There was a softness there I'd never seen in him before. A tenderness completely out of character.

Had that look always been there? Hidden by a grave exterior, did that look live beneath in the same way a nuclear core of emotion dwelt concealed inside of me?

I didn't know, but I hoped so. I liked that look. I wanted to hold onto it. I clung to it with my gaze, and brought my hands from his shoulders up to cradle his face.

He flinched at the touch, and growled. His hand moved to tangle in my hair, and he pulled viciously, as he had earlier. The message was clear—he'd fuck me, but he didn't want it to be intimate.

But he'd started it first, with that softness in his eyes, and I wasn't going to be outdone. I refused to remove my hands, even as his thrusts grew more brutal, and he shifted his pelvis to torment and brush against my sensitive clit.

It was a battle, his resolve against mine. His determination to stay cruel and hard versus my insistence to see more of the kindness peeking out from underneath.

And when his mouth crashed down against mine, and his lips kissed hungrily at mine, I claimed victory as mine. Because that kiss—*that kiss*, with its persistent strokes of his tongue and greedy nips of his teeth—that kiss was generous and warm and affectionate. That kiss was kindling, and, as I clutched my fingers in his hair and devoured what he gave, another powerful orgasm surged through me.

"No, you don't push me out," he said, as I clamped down around his cock, a ruthless smile on the lips that had just been locked with mine. "You let me in when I want in." He pushed harder, forcing his way through the clenching walls of my pussy.

When he was deeply seated, his cock buried inside me to the root, he leaned his forehead against mine, and in my hazy post-orgasm state, I may have heard wrong, but I swear he whispered, "It wasn't supposed to be like this. You weren't supposed to be like this."

And, for the briefest of moments, I considered abandoning The Game. Considered trying to be an honest wife. Considered trying to win his heart. To win his love.

Then he changed entirely.

Without disconnecting from me, he stood up to his full height, and pulled me closer to the edge of the bed, lifting my hips to meet his. Here, he pounded angrily into me, as though he were mad at me. As though he wanted to annihilate my pussy as punishment.

If that truly was what he wanted, to destroy me, I wasn't going to fight him. I was weak and boneless, and that could have been a decent excuse for letting him handle me in that manner, but it wouldn't have been honest. I let him because I wanted it, wanted his malice as much as I wanted any of him.

And even while I still had him, I wanted him. Wanted more of him. Wanted *all* of him.

After a few minutes of his ruthless driving, he pulled out and with his hand wrapped around his glistening cock, he jerked furiously toward his climax.

Wanting all of him as I did, I sat up and reached for him. I wanted that glorious cock. I wanted to touch it and tug it, and if he wasn't going to release inside my cunt, I wanted his cum on my belly, on my hands. In my mouth.

But he stepped back, away from me, and, a second later, he came, spilling milky white liquid over his hand. And if I for one instant thought he hadn't done it purposefully, that he hadn't done it specifically to deny me, his spiteful expression set me straight.

Like I'd said—he was an asshole.

Well, I could be an asshole too. As though I hadn't just come a miraculous four times—a mind-blowing four times—I pouted. "I thought I wasn't supposed to be able to walk afterward."

"Normally, that would be true. Consider this a wedding gift. I hope you enjoyed it because it won't happen again." He pulled up his pants, leaving them unzipped, the crown of his cock peeking out.

"Good. I'm ready for whatever it is you prefer." It was a lie. One thing this experience had taught me was I was not at all prepared for Edward Fasbender.

He smiled condescendingly. "I meant we won't be having sex again at all." Before I could argue, he went on. "I'm going to take a shower. I'll say good night now since you'll be gone by the time I'm done."

It was a hard and clear dismissal.

Fuming, I stared daggers into his backside as he disappeared into his en suite. Then I sat for long minutes, listening to the sound of the water turn on and the change in its spray when the firm body of the man who'd just fucked me stepped into it. Exhaustion had returned, and, though the sex had been vanilla, my thighs ached when I stood, and my pussy felt raw and sore.

I snatched my panties and my heels off the floor and retreated into my own room.

The fighting was over for the night. Each of us could claim at least one victory, but this wasn't over. There would be more battles in the future. We were married now.

And this marriage was war.

28

I awoke in the morning ready for our next skirmish.

Edward had risen earlier than me, though, so I was alone when Jeremy took my breakfast order. Camilla showed up just as I'd been served, but as soon as she saw me, she declared she and Freddie would be taking their meal in her suite and marched right back out.

Good for them. It wasn't like I wanted a side of noisy toddler and bitchy sister-in-law with my yogurt parfait.

Afterward, there was only time to finish packing my suitcase before we were to leave for our "honeymoon." Edward spent the entire forty-minute ride to Heathrow conducting last-minute business over the phone, which might have felt like a disappointing opportunity lost to needle him if we weren't about to be alone together for ten hours on a plane.

"I always forget how fast boarding is when flying by private carrier," I said as we climbed the steps of Edward's Gulfstream G650.

He'd barely spoken two words to me all morning, and I suspected he wanted to forget yesterday—more specifically, last night—had ever happened, but now he turned to me in surprise. "Your father doesn't have his own jet?"

I shook my head, knowing this admission would only further inflate his ego. It was probably good to give him a win every now and then, especially when it was such a trivial win. "He thinks they're too much hassle. He prefers to fly first-class commercial."

"'*Too much hassle.*' What a lazy bastard." His chin rose smugly as he took one of the front most seats.

I gave my coat to the attendant to hang up then surveyed the plane. There was a seat available facing Edward as well as one across the aisle. There were at least six other places to sit including a sofa and comfy chairs around a dining table.

Naturally, I took the seat across from him. "I've flown private several times, though." I didn't want him to think I was unsophisticated, and it was the truth. Hudson's parents had their own jet that we'd all used to take joint family vacations, back when the Pierces and Werners still got along. Then, later, Hudson had purchased his own plane that we'd used to travel the world.

This plane was admittedly more luxurious. More pretentious, too.

Edward scowled at me. "There are plenty of places to sit. Don't feel obligated to take the seat closest to me."

I couldn't decide if the rejection stung or if it was a sign I was getting under his skin. "Don't be silly. You expect your wife always at your side. Here I am."

"Well. I may not be here long. It's a long flight. I might take a nap." He smiled at the pretty brunette attendant as

she handed him the copy of *The Times* he'd requested before we boarded.

Too friendly of a smile, if anyone asked me.

"Oh, good," I said, refusing to let my feathers be ruffled. "I was thinking I'd do the same. There's only one bed
it seems, so we'll have to share." I gave him my own too
friendly grin.

"That won't be necessary. The sofa folds into a second
bed, though I don't think we'll need to use that if we take
turns in the bedroom. In fact, why don't you take yours
now?" He smirked, then his features softened as his eyes
traveled behind us.

"I'm not sleepy, yet. Thank you." I followed the line of
his gaze and found it latched on the attendant's backside
as she shut the cabin door. "Ah, I see. You'd prefer some
alone time with one of your whores."

"I wouldn't call Carlotta a whore. There's never been
money exchanged in our...*friendship*."

I suddenly wondered if the cabin had a knife sharp
enough for human mutilation. Surely it did. Now to decide
if it would best be used on Carlotta or my husband.

The witch approached us then. "We're ready for take-
off, sir."

I didn't miss how Edward's eyes lit up at the word *sir*.
"Tell the pilot we're ready as well, then. That will be all,
Carlotta, dear." His tone was thick and sultry and irritating.

I remembered then that words made excellent daggers.
"There is one more thing, actually, *Carla, dear.*" I'd totally said her name wrong on purpose. "I'm not sure if Edward has told you or not, but we were married yesterday.
Whatever ways you may have served my husband on these
flights in the past will no longer be necessary, as I am his

wife and can attend to his *needs* myself."

He'd said I had to respect him in public. He'd never said anything about respecting his women.

"Yes, Mrs. Fasbender," the tramp said curtly before taking her seat for lift off.

Edward began unfolding his newspaper, seemingly unruffled. "I must say, Celia, jealousy doesn't look good on you."

But I'd seen the hint of admiration in his features before he'd schooled them, a hint that said he very much liked the look on me, despite himself.

He hid behind his paper then, and I let him read unbothered while we took flight. I was a nervous flier, a fact I'd never admit, and the climb in the beginning always made me particularly anxious. I couldn't deal with Edward while I needed all my bandwidth to keep settled.

Once we were at cruising altitude, though, I could breathe easier, and I turned my attention back to the man across from me. I'd worn a sundress in preparation for the heat at our destination—okay, and because he'd once suggested he liked me in sundresses. Edward, though, had dressed for the cool temperature of London in a cowl neck blue-gray sweater and dark slacks. It was a casual look for him, but somehow he still appeared regal and distinguished. A magnificent savage beast.

It was hard to look at him now without remembering every detail of the night before. The way his touch had consumed me. The way his cock had moved inside me. The way his mouth had tasted. The way he'd let his guard down and shown me a sliver of what he hid inside.

They were sensory memories, and they made me feel hot and restless and desperate to have him again.

Which, apparently wasn't going to happen on the flight to the Caribbean, and even so, I wanted him. Wanted anything he'd give me in the meantime.

"Any news worth sharing?" I asked, hoping to draw him out.

He didn't even move the paper to look at me. "Nope."

I sighed.

"There's no story about Edward Fasbender's wedding? I thought you were too important not to get a mention." That ought to rile him up.

"No, we were mentioned. I didn't consider that news worth sharing since you already knew."

My eyes widened in surprise. "Really? What did it say?"

"You're welcome to read the paper when I'm finished," he said, clearly uninterested in conversation.

Ass.

"When do we arrive again?"

"We should land about four p.m. island time. It's a ten-hour flight. If you're bored already, I highly suggest you find something to do." He bent the corner of his paper down so I could see his face. "Something that doesn't involve me."

"I'm not bored, you jerk. It was a reasonable question." I quieted for a few minutes, staring out the window at the pool of clouds below us.

All right, I *was* bored.

"You know, you haven't told me anything about where we're going. Do we land in Nassau and then take a boat? Are there other people on the island? Will the flight crew be staying with us?" More importantly, would Carlotta also be there?

He shut his paper and folded it once to sit on his lap. "The crew will refuel and return to London tomorrow. There are other people in my company who use the plane to conduct business. The crew will return again in two weeks to pick us up.

"As for the island, it's five hundred and fifty acres located about fourteen miles off the coast of Exuma and has its own airstrip. The entire island belongs exclusively to me, but there are staff members who live there year round. They'll pick us up when we land and take care of all our needs while we're there."

"Any of those staff members part of your tribe of whores?" The possibility hadn't even occurred to me until just then. "Oops. I mean *friends*, not whores."

"Actually..."

My stomach dropped, and it had nothing to do with turbulence.

He chuckled. "No," he said taking pity on me. "They're a family, and while many of them are female, they're all either married, children, or old enough to be my grandmother."

"That's awfully ageist." I wasn't fooling anyone—I was relieved.

"Azariah is a lovely woman who I'm sure you'll get along with quite well. Even retired, she's feisty and bullheaded." He sounded proud, and that made my chest warm, both because I'd rarely heard him speak about another person with such reverence and because he'd equated the woman to me.

"I like her already." I thought about what else he'd

said. "You hired a family? How did that work?"

"It sort of fell into place. I wanted to find a Caribbean vacation spot as a birthday present for myself when I turned thirty. So I spent several days in the Bahamas looking for the property I wanted to purchase and became quite fond of the woman that worked at the hotel I was staying in, on New Providence.

"Not *that* kind of fond," he corrected, probably noting the look on my face. "She was a cook. I fell in love with her food. After I found the island, I asked Joette if she'd come back to London with me to be our personal chef. She declined, saying all her family was in Nassau. She went on to say she was the sole caretaker of her mother, and explained what a burden that had been since her husband had died the year before and she now had to both look after Azariah and work a full-time job. The hotel had also recently laid off a bunch of employees for the off-season including two of her sons. She still had a daughter working there with her, but their hours had been cut."

He paused a moment, remembering. "I knew what it was like to have to unexpectedly care for a family member and to not have the income to do so, and I suppose that's what gave me the idea to ask her if she and the children working with her would like to work for me, taking care of the island. She was delighted, and, in the end, all five of her children moved over with her, as well as their spouses."

"And her mother," I added assumingly. "That's an awfully generous offer. Especially coming from you. I never took you as a philanthropist."

"I'm not," he said sharply, as though the compliment had offended him. I suspected that it wasn't so much that he felt insulted as it was that he didn't like anyone knowing he had a kind bone in his body. "There is more than enough work for all of them, and it's a comfort to me to know that Amelie is being taken care of while I'm away."

"Amelie?" The name was familiar. "You named the island after your mother?"

"Yes. After my mother. Now, if you don't mind…" He took up his paper again and opened it up, putting the barrier back in between us.

I didn't mind. He'd revealed something, and not just that he wasn't completely heartless. Something that I'd been curious about.

He'd revealed that he truly did have fond feelings for his mother, fond enough to name a paradise island in her memory.

I closed my eyes and leaned back against the headrest, a smile on my lips, and fell asleep twisting Amelie's rings around my finger.

29

We landed late afternoon to an eighty-degree temperature and a balmy breeze that smelled like fresh seawater. I'd watched from the plane as we descended, realizing how small the stingray-shaped island looked from the sky. Even down on the ground, it was small, less than a square mile of land. It was nice that Edward had permanent residents to care for Amelie, but, man, didn't they get stir-crazy?

It would be a fantastic vacation spot, though, with its long stretches of white sand and the crystal clear, turquoise waters on all sides. Very romantic, and not much room for Edward to escape. Perfect for my seduction plans.

The airstrip was on the side of the island opposite to where the main living quarters were located. Mateo and Louvens, Joette's two oldest sons, met our plane with two jeeps—one for me and Edward and the other for the small flight crew. I was happy to find we wouldn't be riding with Carlotta, and even more delighted to discover that Louvens was taking the crew directly to the guest houses, almost a quarter of a mile away from the main house. They also had their own kitchens there, which meant I wouldn't have to see the woman again until we went home in two weeks.

It took only five minutes to drive along the perimeter of the island to the house, a stunning two-story Mediterranean style structure with exquisite columns, arches, balconies, and iron detailing as well as a cobblestone courtyard in front of it. I learned from Mateo on the drive over that it had been rebuilt when Edward bought the island, replacing an imposing castle that had stood there before. He'd left the almost two-mile network of paths that stretched south and west, though, making the island easy to get around by foot. The road didn't go as far, only extending along half of the perimeter.

The inside of the house was as spectacular as the outside, encompassing over ten thousand square feet of space. The ceilings were high, and the floorplan was original and open, connecting the living spaces without doors in between them. The gorgeous arches and columns from the exterior were repeated in here, but the highlight was the pocket glass sliders that ran between the family room and the covered lanai.

No, that wasn't the highlight. The real highlight was the backyard with its outdoor kitchen, hot tub, and a pool that spread across the length of the back of the house. There was only a handful of yards of patio beyond the pool before running into the smoothly raked beach and the cerulean waters of the Caribbean.

It was truly paradise.

My only complaint was the layout of the bedrooms. Unlike the setup at the London house, the two master suites were on opposite sides of the main floor here, with all the shared living spaces in between. They were nearly identical in structure, each with its own en suite, walk-in closet, and sitting room with glass pocket sliders that opened up to the backyard like the family room.

Like both the London house and the Accelecom office, the decor of the Amelie house was traditional, but the style was looser. Edward's bedroom was done in a striking red and gold, and, while I would definitely have taken it further if I had the chance, it wasn't a bad design.

My room, on the other hand, left a lot to be desired.

The hardwood floor was covered with a gray shag that matched the bedding. The walls were a boring yellowish brown, the curtains were a plain white, and the furniture was too modern for the rest of the house. Architecturally, it was charming, but all the interest in the room had been dulled down.

"It was decorated to Marion's specifications," Edward told me later when I complained.

We'd been on the island almost three hours and were eating dinner in the formal dining room at the front of the house. I'd suggested dining in the smaller, radial dinette that overlooked the backyard, but he'd said it wasn't big enough.

It wasn't big enough, I discovered, because, while we weren't joined by the flight crew, we were joined by several of the staff members that lived permanently on the island. It had come as a surprise when, after Joette and Tom, her oldest daughter, finished cooking the food, they carried it out to the table to be served family style and then sat down with us along with Mateo and his wife Sanyjah, Louvens, and Tom's husband, Peter. Jeremy would never have dined with us in England. Edward had a strictly formal relationship with his staff there. Here, he was relaxed and familiar and almost friendly.

"You won't mind if I redecorate it then," I said, hoping his friendlier mood extended to me as well.

"Eh," he finished swallowing the bite of rock lobster he'd just put in his mouth and washed it down with a swallow of chablis. "We really aren't going to be here that long. Can't you live with it for now?"

"Of course I can." I knew the rules and didn't want to argue in front of others.

But there was a difference between arguing and discussing. "I didn't mean right now anyway. I'm sure we'll be back here in the future though. I could take the measurements while we're here and work on it from London. I'd spend my own money, naturally."

His smile was forced. "We can discuss it more later."

We couldn't discuss it later, though, because dinner went long with Mateo and Louvens entertaining us with tales of island life since the last time Edward had been there. Then there were the updates on the family members that hadn't attended dinner and the children—apparently there were fourteen kids under the age of eighteen. Shockingly, Edward knew the name of every one of them and asked about each of them by name.

So much for the notion that he hated children.

Then after dinner, he disappeared into his library to share a drink with the men, and though I'd meant to stay awake planning to attack him with my feminine wiles, the travel and the time change caught up to me, and I fell asleep in an armchair in my sitting room.

We have two weeks, I told myself as sleep closed in on me. I'd have my chance to be alone with him later.

30

A week later, I still hadn't managed any one-on-one time with my husband.

He was avoiding me.

Mornings he left early for a run around the island. When I asked to go with him, he allowed it, but he didn't alter his pace and there was no way I could keep up with his long stride. Breakfasts he took by himself in his sitting room, and no matter how hard I tried to get him to let me join him, he always refused.

The rest of the day he spent working in the library. If I happened to come by for a book or some paper to write on or even if I decided to lounge on the patio outside the floor-to-ceiling windows of the room, he'd move into his study and lock the door only opening it for Joette when she brought him his lunch.

With nothing else to do, I passed my time walking on the beach, swimming in the pool, and reading while loung-ing on the lanai. There wasn't much else to do. The internet on the island was spotty at best, and I couldn't even download anything to my ereader. Thank goodness Edward had a pretty extensive collection of books in the library or I would have died of boredom. After only a few days into our honeymoon, I'd finished four full-length novels and gotten a pretty decent tan. I was the picture-perfect trophy wife, exactly what my husband had wanted.

Dinners continued to be spent as a group, though the family members that joined us weren't always the same. I soon met Erris and Dreya, Joette's youngest son and daughter, as well as both of their wives, Marge and Eliana. The kids never came to the house, and neither did Azariah, but I had a feeling Edward snuck away to visit them all during the day when I wasn't aware because of some of the things that were said over supper.

Evenings were always spent divided—the men in the library smoking cigars and drinking cognac and the women not allowed. It was old-fashioned and gross, and, though I had a standing invitation to join the ladies on the lanai, I usually retreated to my bedroom.

On day seven, I couldn't take it anymore. I'd come here to seduce my husband. Not only did I need Edward to have sex with me in order to carry out my plan, but I needed him to feel comfortable having *his* kind of sex. Mean and sadistic kind of sex. And it wasn't going to happen as long as we had guests encroaching on our time together.

Determined to kick everyone out, I stood outside the library and took a few deep breaths, trying to get up the nerve. He'd be mad that I made a scene, I was well aware. I could live with that. Maybe it would even lead to some kinky form of punishment.

One could dream.

"You must be furious at that one for spending so much time with them," Tom said, coming up behind me. She spoke in the typical Bahamian dialect, dropping sounds, so what she'd said sounded like *Ya mus be furious a dat one for spendin so much time wit dem.* It had taken me a day or two to get used to it, but now I barely had to ask anyone to repeat anything. "You should do something about it."

"I'm planning to. I was just about to go in there and tell everyone they had to go home." I didn't need anyone's permission to do it, but it was so nice to have someone sympathize with my situation that I couldn't help leaning on her for reassurance.

"Mmm," she said with a frown. "Are you sure that's such a good idea? Edward doesn't seem to take kindly to folks confronting him. Unless it's Azariah. She has that man wrapped around her finger."

I never thought I'd be as jealous of an eighty-five-year-old woman as I was of Azariah.

And now I was doubting myself. "What do you suggest I do? It's our honeymoon, for crying out loud."

"What you need to do is put on something really sexy like and flaunt around in front of those windows. He'll take notice and kick the boys to the curb."

It wasn't a bad idea. I'd tried to do exactly that several times already, putting on a revealing swimsuit and prancing in front of the windows. But, since Edward had holed himself off in his study, he'd never been around to see.

I hadn't considered trying it late at night. Now that I had...it was brilliant.

Thanking her, I excused myself and ran to my bedroom to change into my skimpiest bikini—I'd brought one for each day of our trip, all of them pretty risqué. Red seemed to be my power color as far as Edward was concerned, and the classic string variety was never a bad choice.

A few minutes later, I strode out onto the lanai from my sitting room wearing nothing but my red string bikini and a strappy pair of Louboutin wedge sandals.

"Look at you!" Tom said, while the other women cat-called.

"I was just thinking I'd take a swim," I said innocently, walking over to join them. They were sitting out of the sightline of the library, but I had to pass them to get there and it would have been rude not to at least talk to them first.

"You're not fooling anyone," Eliana said. "You're here to catch the attention of that beefcake husband of yours."

Everyone laughed—not *at* me in that awkward embarrassing way, but conspiratorially. The kind of laugh that was nice to get.

"Sit down and have a drink with us first," Joette said. "The men are in there drinking brandy, but we have the good stuff—Sky Juice." She held up a white-colored drink that looked like milk with ice. In other words, disgusting.

But the women were friendly, and it had been so long since I'd had companionship… "Sure. I'll take one."

"You can have mine. Just made it," Tom said. "I'll go whip up another for myself."

I sat down on a lounge chair and took a sip of the beverage, which turned out to be a concoction of sweetened condensed milk, gin, and coconut water. Generally, I didn't like sweet alcoholic drinks—and this one was particularly sweet—but, right now, with the sound of the ocean crashing on the nearby shore and the Caribbean breeze carrying the salty garden scent of the island, it seemed fitting.

I drank slowly, chatting with the women while I did. They were very different than the people I usually spent time with, very down-to-earth and unbothered. Back in New York, everyone seemed to always be rushing around doing Important Things and swallowing down Xanax with their Phentermine like they were the secrets to success. Even though I'd been gone from that world for several months now, my brain still operated at the same speed. Talking to the islanders made me slow down, made my thoughts pause. It was nice to have the change of pace.

While we didn't talk about much that was important, I did learn a few things, such as that Eliana was Dreya's second spouse. She'd been married to Louvens previously, but once they'd all moved to the island together, she'd fallen in love with his little sister, which seemed pretty scandalous for such a tight-knit group. The strangest part was that they all still lived here.

"Because of the children," Eliana said. "Louvens is a good father."

"And we'd never want to split up the family," Dreya agreed.

I also learned that the segregated after-dinner arrangement was new. Edward had apparently never employed it in the past.

"When Camilla is here, and when he was married to Marion, everyone usually hangs out together," Joette said.

"If we even stay after dinner," Tom added. "Most times we go straight home."

It was because of me. He was definitely avoiding me.

But it was a relief to know that he wasn't as archaic in his traditions as he'd made me believe.

The women seemed to realize it had to do with me, as well. "He's nervous around such a pretty bride," Dreya said.

"I doubt that's it," I protested.

"Maybe he's forgotten what to do in the bedroom," Joette giggled.

"No, he definitely hasn't forgotten." We'd only been together that one time, but he'd definitely known what he was doing.

At this rate, though, *I* was going to forget. "Well, ladies, I think it's time to do my thing." I swallowed back the last of my cocktail. I was just starting to feel the buzz—Tom made her drinks strong—and it was exactly the confidence I'd needed for my strutting.

"We'll get ready to go," Joette said. "I have a feeling we're about to be sent home."

I prayed she was right.

Throwing my shoulders back, I paraded along the line of the house, passing the rest of the family room windows, circling along the curve of the dinette, finally ending up at the library.

Here I paused to stretch, exaggeratedly, making sure all my best features were on display. I could feel eyes watching me, which could have been all in my head, because I refused to look. The outside lights were on, though, and the entire backyard was illuminated, so at least I knew I wasn't being swallowed up in the dark of night.

Assuming I had his attention, I sat down on one of the deck chairs and stretched a long leg out and removed first one sandal than the other. When they were off, I stood up again, turning toward the pool so that my backside faced the library windows. I adjusted my bikini bottoms, pulling them out of my butt crack where they'd bunched up when I sat, then strutted to the pool and jumped in.

It was only five minutes later that our guests were gone.

I was swimming laps, but I heard Mateo come out and call the ladies inside. A minute later the family room doors slid shut, the lights went off, and the whole middle section of the house was dark.

I finished my lap and, only then, did I look for Edward.

I found him immediately, standing at the library window, one hand holding a drink, the other shoved into his trouser pocket, his eyes pinned on me.

Even through the glass and the ten yards that separated us, I could feel his angry, rabid want. It was lasered in my direction like a death ray, ready to obliterate me at a moment's notice.

I was instantly wet, and not just because I was standing chest-deep in the swimming pool.

We stayed like that for what felt like forever, our stares intense, each of us waiting for the other to call chicken. When it was clear he wasn't going to make the next move, I decided that I would. I'd started this, after all. Might as well finish it.

Never taking my eyes off his, I stalked out of the pool. I'd forgotten to bring a towel—*whoops*—so I was wet and dripping as I moved toward him. As I passed the outdoor shower—a single pipe coming out of the ground with two heads—I decided I wasn't done taunting him. I turned on the water and waited for it to heat up before standing beneath it, letting the spray fall over my hair and down my back.

Still, I watched him. Watched him watching me as I reached behind me and pulled the strings of my top and let it fall on the ground in front of me. Next, I untied first one side of the bottoms, then the other, until I was standing naked under the rushing stream.

He'd never seen me completely naked, and if I'd ever thought he never had the interest, that thought was proven entirely false when Edward pulled his hand from his pocket and braced it against the window above him, as if he needed the support to stand.

I understood the feeling. My knees felt weak, too, even as I felt stronger than I had all week. Bolder than I had in months.

I'd gotten him. He'd come to me now. There was no way he could resist.

Relishing in the early satisfaction of victory, I closed my eyes and threw back my head, bringing my hands up to cup my aching breasts then sweep down to rub against the swollen lips between my thighs.

And I waited. Waited for the sound of a door sliding open. Waited for his footsteps across the cement patio.

When a couple of minutes had passed with no sound and no Edward, I opened my eyes again. The library was dark. No one stood watching me at the glass. I was alone outside.

I scanned the windows looking for him inside. A second later, a light turned on his bedroom. Then he was in his sitting room, and I held my breath, waiting for him to open his patio door and summon me inside.

But he only closed the curtains, cutting off my view to his bedroom. Cutting off my view to him.

And I knew without actually trying that, if I went to his patio door on my own, I'd discover that it was locked.

31

I woke up the next day with new determination. The previous night hadn't played out the way I'd wanted, that was certainly true. But it was the closest I'd been in a week to seeing Edward crack. My behavior had had an effect.

Obviously, that meant I should do more of the same.

I'd set my phone alarm extra early and dressed in short shorts and a sexy sports bra—not one of those ones that squished everything together, but a Brazilian design that resembled a bikini top with black mesh that showed off a whole lot of breast. I gathered my hair into a ponytail, put on my running shoes, and then, instead of asking Edward if I could join him on his morning run, I snuck outside and kept out of sight behind the trees at the end of the courtyard.

I had to wait around almost half an hour until he showed up, but when he did, I slipped out of my hiding spot and jogged up next to him. "Oh, hey. I was just taking my run too. I'll tag along."

He grunted, his eyes sweeping down my body, lingering on my cleavage, then, as I'd predicted, he took off at a sprint I couldn't keep up with.

It was all good. Keeping up wasn't the goal.

I'd only run with him twice since we'd been on the island, and I knew from that, and from watching him, that he went the same way every time, going east along the network of paths and then north until the trail ended. Then he took to the beach and followed the shoreline south until he returned to the house.

I also knew from my conversation with the women the night before that Erris and his wife Marge, were the official gardeners, and today, along with Louvens' help, they planned to cut back some plants that had been damaged in the last big storm on the southwest shores of the island— right along the last quarter of Edward's run.

So, instead of dragging behind Edward, I took my own course, veering west to the beach. I jogged along the coast until I spotted the three working in the brush. I waved at them enthusiastically, so enthusiastically that I "forgot" to watch where I was going and "tripped" over myself. I went down flat on my ass.

Yeah, I totally faked it. I was a pro at this shit.

The three gardners ran over to me immediately, making a big fuss with, "Are you all right?" and, "Do you think you can walk?"

I assured them I could, but Louvens and Erris helped me up anyway, and as soon as I put weight on my right ankle, I pretended to cry out in pain.

"I think I twisted my ankle," I said, grimacing.

"I'll help you back to the house," Louvens volunteered.

Perfection.

He'd already been the one of the three who couldn't take his eyes off my breasts. I mean, they looked good. It wasn't his fault. He was actually a decent guy, and not that I believed that a woman's clothing choice allowed men to do what they want with her, but, if I wore something provocative, I certainly expected people to look.

I'd assumed that when he offered to help, Louvens meant that I could lean on him as I hobbled back to the house.

Nope. He lifted me into his arms and proceeded to *carry* me. The man was so much cooler than I'd predicted. Stronger too.

And my timing was impeccable, because when we were just out of sight of the others, about halfway to our destination, Edward came running by, finishing up his course.

"What's going on? What happened?" He was breathless from exercise, genuine concern etched in his features.

"Mrs. Fasbender had a fall and twisted her ankle," Louvens said.

"Oh, Louvens," I said, pouring on the sweetness. "You should really call me Celia." His face happened to already be at chest level, but I pushed my shoulders back so my breasts would be even closer. As a reward for being so heroic, of course.

He really was an attractive guy, I noticed now. Very muscular. The kind of muscular that was earned by good old-fashioned hard work and outdoor sport rather than scheduled exercise.

Edward glowered, and I could see the debate in his eyes. Should he offer to carry me back himself? Should he let his single handyman do it, knowing his scantily dressed wife would flirt with him all the way there?

Edward was a different kind of fit, with a long lean runner's body and tight muscles from regular weight-lifting. He was definitely capable of hauling me himself, and, I suspected, that his deep sense of possessiveness would never allow him to let another man so close to me, no matter what he said about letting me sleep with other people.

Or maybe that was just how I wished he felt.

Because the devil only said, "That's very kind of you, Louvens. I would have made her tough it out herself. What's a little pain, after all?" He looked specifically at me when he said that. Then back to Louvens. "Good luck making it all the way back to the house."

He took off, resuming his earlier swift pace.

Fucking asshole.

"I can make it, Mrs—Celia. Don't worry." Louvens proved himself, barely breaking a sweat before he approached the back patio.

Edward, on the other hand, faltered. He belied his detached, cruel facade when I spotted him watching for me at the library window. Just as he had the night before, he kept his eyes pinned on me until I was safely back on the ground and Louvens had said goodbye. Only when he was walking away did Edward disappear back to his desk.

And then I had another idea.

"Who cares for the pool?" I asked Tom later that afternoon.

"Mateo. He does everything with the water. The boats, the pool, the fountains." She was putting away groceries from Eliana's earlier mainland run.

I leaned my hip against the kitchen island. "Boats?"

"Do you want Mateo to take you out?"

Not at the moment, but it would have been nice to at least been told of the option. *Thank you, Edward. Not.*

"No, no. Not today, thanks. But I think the chemical balance is off in the pool. It has a weird odor that it didn't have yesterday."

"I'll call him to come out," she said, pulling out a jar of Blow Pops and placing it on the counter.

"Thanks. Oh, and can I have one of those?" I pointed to the candy.

"Help yourself."

Awesome. I could use a prop.

When Mateo arrived a half an hour later, I walked out wearing designer sunglasses, high-heel sandals, and a strappy white bikini that was so skimpy it could barely be called clothing. The bottoms had the smallest strip of material possible to cover the crotch and the top was only a band along the bottom, two thin straps going up around the neck, and flesh-colored mesh over the breasts with a cutout daisy-shaped flower covering the nipples. To top it all off, I was sucking on a big red Blow Pop.

In other words, I was walking porn.

I pulled the Blow Pop from my mouth and squatted next to Mateo where he was stooped to check the pool's chemical levels. "What does the reader thingy say?" I asked.

I didn't really care about the answer, but he was facing the house, and, though I wasn't even sure Edward was currently in the library, I wanted to be seen talking to yet another man if he was.

"It's, uh." He glanced over at my breasts—because breasts—then quickly looked away, his cheeks reddening. "Well, the salinity looks good." He hit a button on the reader. "And the PH level looks okay too. But let me try the manual color tester just to be sure."

"Oh. Is the machine thing not always accurate?" I heard the slide of a glass door, but I forced myself not to look up. For all I knew, it could be Tom bringing out iced tea. She was really thoughtful like that.

But in case it wasn't Tom, I put the Blow Pop back in my mouth. My lips and tongue were already cherry red from the candy. I'd checked before I came out.

Mateo was more modest than Louvens, but always eager to share knowledge. "The digital tester is accurate as long as it's calibrated correctly. The color tester is more work, but a little more reliable. I just need to—"

"Is something wrong with the pool?" Edward's voice boomed from the lanai.

Bingo.

I looked up at my husband but let Mateo answer. "Nah. Just testing the chemicals," he said.

Edward came closer, stopping at the edge of the pool across from us. "I thought you tested it on Friday."

"I did, but Celia..." We were still crouched down, my cleavage still prominently on display so when Mateo glanced over to gesture at me, he once again caught an eye-full.

Quickly, he stood up, his cheeks going brighter than the last time. "Mrs. Fasbender, I mean, noticed a strange scent," he said to his boss.

Edward crossed his arms over his chest. "Oh, did she,

now." He was clearly displeased.

Slowly I rose to my full height and pulled the Blow Pop from my mouth. "It's probably just my nose. I think it's clogged or something. I must be getting a cold." I draped a hand on Mateo's shoulder. "I'm so sorry to make you come all the way over here for something so silly."

Edward's eyes narrowed.

Mateo glanced at my hand then to my husband then back at my hand. He swallowed. "It's not a problem. It's my job."

"You'd better come on inside and rest then, darling. Fight that cold before it settles in."

"I guess that's my cue to say goodbye," I said, too quietly for Edward to hear. Leaning in, I placed a sugary kiss on Mateo's cheek then sauntered around the pool toward the other side.

Edward watched me the whole way.

"Are you going to come tuck me in, my dear husband?" I asked when I was closer.

God, the look on his face. He wanted to hurt me.

It was fantastic.

I wished he would.

"The point is rest, not recreation," Edward said, specifically for Mateo. There hadn't been any "recreation" between us since we'd arrived on the island, and no reason for me to think it was happening now, no matter how much I wanted it.

"I don't think there's much of a difference when it comes to us," I said coldly and softly enough that no one heard but him. I was almost to him now. The patio was large enough that there was no need to get this close, but there had also been no need for Mateo to come over and measure the pool chemicals.

Edward said nothing until I brushed past him. Then he grabbed my arm, firmly, and yanked me toward him.

Yes, yes! He was effected. He was cracking. He was losing control, and any minute now he'd have to kiss me.

Would it be now?

I held my breath and waited, my heart thundering in my chest, my skin burning under his grip.

His gaze lowered to my lips, but he didn't lean in. "I thought you twisted your ankle."

"Oh." I lifted my leg and circled my foot around. "I guess it's better now." I held up the Blow Pop and gave it an exaggerated lick with my tongue. Since he hadn't made good use of my mouth, I reminded him what he was missing.

His eye ticked. "Careful, Celia. You're pushing me."

Good. That was the whole idea.

He let go of my arm with a flourish, almost like he was throwing it away. Throwing *me* away.

I shook myself and lifted my shoulders back proudly. Then I popped the sucker back in my mouth and went into the house, letting him watch me walk away.

32

I'd gone back to my suite when Edward ordered me there, took off my shoes and sunglasses, and plopped onto the bed, hoping he'd follow in after me, despite what he'd said.

I must have fallen asleep because, next thing I knew, I was having one of the baby dreams I sometimes had. It was different than usual, though. Instead of being hazy and still, it was vivid and full of motion. Normally I only *felt* like I was in it, but this time I could actually see myself.

There was a man, as always, and for the first time, *he* was holding the baby. But he was in front of me so I could only see his backside and the baby bundle over his shoulder, and I wanted to get to him—get to both of them—so I was walking toward them.

But it was one of those dreams, where the more I walked, the farther away he got.

So I started running. And running. And running. And running, never getting closer.

And suddenly the baby was gone, and the man was behind me, and instead of wanting to get *to* him, I wanted to get *away*. I ran faster and faster, as fast as I could go, but he was on my heels, chasing me. Reaching for me.

"*Careful, Celia,*" he said just as his fingers dug into my arm.

I woke with a start. It was dark out, which made sense since the sun had been near setting when I'd been at the pool with Mateo.

But it felt *too* dark. Like I'd slept too long.

I picked up my phone to check the time, the only thing it was good for on the island because I had zero service. *Seven-twenty.*

Dinner was always at seven sharp, and Tom always came to get me if I didn't show up on my own.

I must have missed her knock, and she hadn't wanted to disturb me.

I got up and started toward my closet to look for something suitable to wear to dinner since I was still in my bikini, then changed my mind. If Edward was cracking, this wasn't the time to back down on my game.

As soon as I walked out of my room, I could tell something was wrong, and it wasn't just the weird energy clinging from my bad dream. The whole house was dark. And quiet. There should have been raucous laughter and the scraping of utensils against plates.

I wandered through the kitchen on the way to the dining room. It was empty and clean where usually it was a mess until after Joette and Tom cleaned it up, which always happened after dinner.

There was no way a meal had been prepared in there.

The dining room was also empty, as I knew it had to be. I continued past it toward the library, where, at last, there was a light on.

As much as I hated myself for it, I was relieved when I saw Edward. I'd begun to fear everyone had gone somewhere without me.

He was sitting behind his desk, a pair of reading glasses propped on his nose. I hadn't seen him in eyewear before, besides sunglasses, and I had to catch my breath. Was there no look this man couldn't carry off? Not only carry off, but fucking excel at?

"Where is everybody?" I asked, stretching my hands over my head. I actually needed to stretch this time. It wasn't part of my plan to torment him, but, hey, it was a nice side effect.

Or it would have been if he would have looked up from his computer. "I told the staff not to come in tonight," he said plainly.

"Really?" Tom hadn't said anything about it when I'd talked to her earlier. "Any particular reason?" Maybe he wanted to dine alone with me.

God, I hope he wanted to dine *on* me.

"Yes, actually. I couldn't continue to bring guests into my house when *my wife*," he emphasized the last two words, "can't seem to keep from flaunting around in scanty swimwear, now could I?" He turned and bent his head to peer at me over his glasses. "Case in point."

His tone had an edge to it, suggesting he was angry and only barely able to restrain himself. Not just angry, but *really* angry.

There wasn't going to be any dining with me *or* on me.

He was such a sore loser, because that's what this was. A loser's move.

"So you just canceled dinner because you're mad at me?" If he was going to be angry, I was too, and I wasn't even going to try to hide it.

"You're welcome to prepare something for yourself. Joette left a couple of sandwiches in the fridge. I'm sorry—I already ate them."

Bullshit.

He was so transparent. So arrogant. So maddening.

I called him on it. "Bullshit."

"Excuse me?"

"You aren't sorry."

He took off his glasses, set them on his desk, then sat back and stared at me smugly. "You're right. I'm not."

His contemptuous response only fueled my anger. "And you didn't tell everyone to stay away because you're worried about your wife parading around inappropriately." I took a step toward him. "You did it because you can't stand how it makes you feel when other people look at me."

"Pfft."

"When other *men* look at me." I was purposefully taunting him, because fuck him.

He shot up from his chair and leaned one fist on the desk, the other hand curled with one sharp finger stabbing at the wood as he made his points. "I told you before we were married that I expected you to be a model wife." *Stab.* "That you were to be perceived as *faithful.*" *Stab.* "Parading around in next-to-nothing in front of my staff," *stab,* "And flirting with anyone that has a cock," *stab,*

"Will not be tolerated."

Fuck. He was really, *really* mad.

I really, really shouldn't keep provoking him.

Why was I never good at doing what I should?

"Won't be tolerated by *you*, you mean." I took another step toward him.

His eye twitched. Twice. "Damn right."

"I should be punished then, shouldn't I?" I asked in a put-on cutesy voice. "For being such a *bad* wife."

I was next to him now, at the side of his desk. So close I could feel the heat of his rage radiating off of him.

He said nothing, but I could see a vein in his neck pushing tautly against his skin.

"For being such a bad girl." I was wicked. I really, really was.

"Celia—" He warned.

I leaned against the desk at this angle, mimicking his position, my breasts thrust out in front of me. My ass high in the air. "You *want* to punish me, don't you? You want to *hurt* me. I can see it in your eyes. I bet you want to bend me over your knee right now and spank the living—"

And then he was behind me, one hand pushing me over the desk, the other furiously pulling my bikini bottoms down before his palm smacked against my skin, hard. Incredibly hard. And fast, six, seven, eight times.

Nine.

Ten.

Each slap got harder, more difficult to tolerate. I'd been spanked by a lover before, sure I had. But it had always been fun. Playful.

This *hurt*.

A lot.

My ass was on fire. Tears ran down my cheeks. I cursed and yelled and wriggled, trying to get away from the next blow, but his hold was too strong, and all I managed to do was wiggle the rest of the way out of my bikini bottoms.

His punishment went on. Fourteen? Fifteen?

I lost track.

"You want to be punished?" he asked between hits, his voice raw and threadbare.

Yes.

I didn't say it out loud. I couldn't. My throat was clenched, choking on my cries. And even if I could talk, I was too in my head for words, too busy trying to shut down the pain, trying to go numb. Trying to deny that I *liked* the pain. That while my ass ached and burned, my pussy was wet and throbbing and begging for more.

"You might regret getting what you asked for," he said then, as if he could read my mind. The slaps stopped, but his hand pressed against my middle back stayed fixed in place, and I could hear the sound of his belt buckle.

Oh my God, he's going to use his belt!

Could I take it? I didn't know. I wasn't sure. I already probably wouldn't be able to sit for a week.

But it wasn't the cool slap of leather that touched me next. It was the tip of his cock, lining up at my entrance. Driving in with one fierce thrust.

A sob broke through my throat, and more tears fell, this time tears of relief. *Yes, yes, yes.*

I chanted it over and over as he pummeled into me from

behind, silently at first, then out loud. "Yes. Yes. Yes!"

His hand moved from my back to my head. Seizing a fistful of hair, he pulled me upright and moved his other hand to the front of me, collaring my throat.

"You parade around here," he said, his cock ramming into me with vicious strokes, his pelvis hitting my burning ass with each thrust. "Tempting my staff, tempting *my* men with what belongs to me."

And that was the start of my orgasm. I could feel it like the beginning of a yawn, starting soft and tentative but heading quickly to a point of inevitability.

With one hand still wrapped around my neck, he grabbed onto one cup of my bikini top and snatched it down with one swift swipe. "These? These magnificent perfect tits?" He crushed my breast in his fist. "These belong to *me*. You hear me?"

"Yes, yes." I wasn't sure if I was answering him or if it was just the only syllable I could say at this point.

He squeezed harder around my breast. "I own *this*. I own your cunt. And you flaunt your body around like it belongs to you? How dare you? How *dare* you?"

I exploded.

Energy released inside me like a nuclear bomb, radiating through my limbs. Fireworks shot through my vision. My body shook violently, and my pussy locked down on Edward's cock, and I knew right then, knew without a doubt, that I was changed. That this man had found something in me and released it, and there was no way I would ever be the same.

I was still trembling through my climax when Edward pushed me forcefully back to the desk then abruptly pulled out of me. I was too weak to protest. Too weak to attempt to claim his cum, and it turned out I didn't have to because the next thing I knew he was letting out a guttural moan and drops of warm fluid were spilling along my lower back.

He'd claimed me. I was his.

And I was happy.

I sighed, a euphoric, satiated kind of sigh. I lay there, unable to move, unable to do anything but breathe. I heard the zip of Edward's pants. Heard him pacing behind me. Heard him curse as he kicked something hard and loud.

I stood up then, and turned toward him, my ass aching with the movement, just in time to catch my swimsuit bottoms when he threw them in my direction.

"Get out," he said with vile detest. "I can't look at you right now."

Apparently the guy wasn't great with after care.

I didn't move. "Edward...if you're worried that you went too far..." I cleared my throat, complete honesty hard for me. "If you think I didn't like it...don't worry. I did."

"I can't listen to your bullshit lies right now. Get the fuck out of here." He stormed past me toward the windows, refusing to look at me.

I pivoted, my gaze following his backside. "It's not bullshit! I mean it, I liked it. I *loved* it."

I wasn't lying either. Not even a little bit. It wasn't about my scheme to ruin him. The Game was the furthest thing from my mind.

"Please do it to me again," I went on. "Not right this second, maybe, but, you know. When my ass doesn't feel like it's just been shredded."

He continued to stare out into the night and let out a harsh laugh. "You just don't know when to stop, do you?"

"And you don't know when someone is laying it all out on the line. I'm being one-hundred percent genuine. I am *into* this. That was incredible. I want more of it. Please, please, please, bring it on."

A beat passed.

Then he shook his head. "It won't work, Celia. I know about you. I knew what kind of woman you were when I married you."

I felt that rush of panic I always had when he said cryptic things like that. That punch of dread that made me jump to conclusions and think that he knew something about my games when there was no way he could.

"I don't know what you mean," I said, breathing my way through the alarm.

He turned to face me, his expression stone. "I mean, my dear wife, that I know about your ruse. How you plan to get me to rough you up in the bedroom then go cry abuse to the authorities."

I felt the blood drain from my face.

"Or maybe that's not exactly the scheme, but something along those lines. Am I warm?"

He didn't know. He couldn't. He was fishing. He was making a guess.

I clung to my best line of defense. "I really don't know what you're talking about, Edward. That you would think me capable of—"

"Shut up." He sneered at me. "You're a pathetic liar."

Now I was mad. Because, sure, fine, I'd planned those things, but he couldn't *know* that, and I was abandoning that plot, and I was not lying about wanting more sex like that, and being called a liar the one time I wasn't lying was just fucked up.

"You're crazy, you know that?" I seethed. "You're making shit up. If that were really true, and if you really knew that before we got married, why would you even marry me?"

"Because I want those Werner media shares."

That hurt. More than the spanking, somehow. I knew we weren't married for love, but his greed hadn't been so evident before. I hadn't felt like such a prop.

Layered over the hurt was indignant anger. He'd only said he wanted to helm my father's company. Now he expected to get his shares? What the fuck was the guy smoking?

"You're not getting anything from my father. You aren't getting anything from me, either, for that matter."

"I'll have those shares," he said adamantly.

"Over my dead body."

I knew then what was coming. Somehow, I knew, even though I couldn't possibly know, couldn't possibly even guess, and this inky black foreboding crawled up through me, spreading up my spine and traveling through my limbs in exactly the same way my climax had stretched through me moments before.

And before the words came out of his lips, I already felt their impact, already felt the air slam out of my lungs, and my knees crumple, unable to hold my weight. Felt the snaking cry of terror lodge in my throat before the smirk settled on his mouth.

And in that way I was almost prepared—*almost*— when he said the words that would later haunt me in my nightmares and brought the dream I'd had earlier crashing to the forefront of my mind. "That is precisely why, my little bird, I intend to kill you."

Edward and Celia's story continues in
Slay Two: Ruin.

With her heart literally in his hands, Celia will have to try and bargain with a devil.

ALSO BY LAURELIN PAIGE

Visit www.laurelinpaige.com for a more detailed reading order.

The Dirty Universe

Dirty Filthy Rich Boys - READ FREE
Dirty Duet: Dirty Filthy Rich Men | Dirty Filthy Rich Love
Dirty Sexy Bastard - READ FREE
Dirty Games Duet: Dirty Sexy Player | Dirty Sexy Games
Dirty Sweet Duet: Sweet Liar | Sweet Fate
Dirty Filthy Fix
Dirty Wild Trilogy: Coming 2020

The Fixed Universe

Fixed Series: Fixed on You | Found in You | Forever with You
Hudson | Fixed Forever
Found Duet: Free Me | Find Me
Chandler
Falling Under You
Dirty Filthy Fix
Slay Saga: Slay One: Rivalry | Slay Two: Ruin
Slay Three: Revenge | Slay Four: Rising
The Open Door

First and Last Duet: First Touch | Last Kiss

Hollywood Standalones

One More Time
Close
Sex Symbol
Star Struck

Written with Sierra Simone

Porn Star | Hot Cop

Written with Kayti McGee under the name Laurelin McGee

Miss Match | Love Struck | MisTaken | Holiday for Hire

Let's stay in Touch!

I'm on **Facebook, Bookbub, Amazon,** and **Instagram**. Come find me. I totally support stalking.

Be sure to **join** my **reader** group, **The Sky Launch**, facebook.com/groups/HudsonPierce

Check out my website www.laurelinpaige.com to find out more about my books. While there, sign up for **my newsletter** where you'll receive a **free book every month** from bestselling authors, only available to my subscribers, as well as up-to-date information on my latest releases.

Only want to be notified when I have a new release? Text **Paige** to 21000, and I'll shoot you a text when I have a book come out.

About the Author

With millions of books sold worldwide, Laurelin Paige is a New York Times, Wall Street Journal and USA Today Bestselling Author. Her international success started with her very first series, the Fixed Trilogy, which, alone, has sold over 1 million copies, and earned her the coveted #1 spot on Amazon's bestseller list in the U.S., U.K., Canada, and Australia, simultaneously. This title also was named in People magazine as one of the top 10 most downloaded books of 2014. She's also been #1 over all books at the Apple Book Store with more than one title in more than one country. She's published both independently and with MacMillan's St. Martin's Press and Griffin imprints as well as many other publishers around the world including Harper Collins in Germany and Hachette/Little Brown in the U.K. With her edgy, trope-flipped stories of smart women and strong men, she's managed to secure herself among today's romance royalty.

Paige has a Bachelor's degree in Musical Theater and a Masters of Business Administration with a Marketing emphasis, and she credits her writing success to what she learned from both programs, though she's also an avid learner, constantly trying to challenge her mind with new and exciting ideas and concepts. While she loves psychological thrillers and witty philosophical books and entertainment, she is a sucker for a good romance and gets giddy anytime there's kissing, much to the embarrassment of her three daughters. Her husband doesn't seem to complain, however. When she isn't reading or writing sexy stories, she's probably singing, watching shows like Game of Thrones, Letterkenny and Discovery of Witches, or dreaming of Michael Fassbender. She's also a proud member of

Mensa International though she doesn't do anything with the organization except use it as material for her bio. She currently lives outside Austin, Texas and is represented by Rebecca Friedman.

Made in the USA
Middletown, DE
14 January 2022

58669395R00177